Text Me Baby One More Time

TEAGAN HUNTER

Teagan
xoxo

To Laurie.

Half the shit I decide to do is last minute, and you're always there to make it happen. You're da best. Thank you for wrangling this crazy kitten.

SHEPARD

Around these parts, I'm a king.

That's not me being cocky; I'm just being realistic.

No matter where I go, people stare. They look at me like a fucking celebrity or some shit. Pictures, my autograph—begged for. People go out of their way to gain my attention, even if only for a moment—especially women.

In fact, it's about to happen right now.

At 10:30 PM on a Wednesday night in the middle of Smart Shoppe, aisle three.

I see the thirst in her eyes the moment I turn the corner. Her back snaps up straight when she notices me, a hungry grin stretching across her red-painted lips. She tosses her perfectly curled, long locks over her shoulder as she forms her plan of attack.

She's hot as fuck, I'll give her that. She's not quite what I normally go for in a girl, but I'm not one to say no to pussy.

It doesn't hurt that she knows how to wear a pair of jeans like a second skin.

I bet her legs would look pretty damn great wrapped around me.

My lips—and dick—twitch at the thought.

She thinks that's her cue and begins her approach, taking long, exaggerated steps toward me, her hips swaying back and forth as she moves closer.

"Hi." Translation: *You're hot.* "I'm Brandi, with an I." *Stripper name.* "You're Shep Clark, right?"

I try not to snort at her *I'm so innocent* act. She knows exactly who I am—everyone does.

Just like I know she wants me to take her back to my apartment and fuck her until the sun comes up.

Though I've sworn off meaningless flings, I'm considering it. It's been over a month since I acquainted myself with anything other than my hand, and it's getting old—quick.

"I watch all your games—you're good."

"I know."

She takes a step closer and laughs. It's one of those playful, slightly husky laughs girls do that don't sound genuine.

Another step closer, our feet now touching.

Her fingers trail along the arm I have outstretched against the shelving. "I haven't seen you on the field lately, though." Her lips jut out in a frown. "What gives?"

I gnash my teeth together, jaw clenching tightly at the inquisition.

It's true, I'm taking some time off from the game—but not by choice, just so we're clear.

You get into one little bar fight, cause a measly couple thousand dollars' worth of damage, and suddenly you're "troubled" and "need a break".

It's bullshit.

"None of your business."

She either doesn't hear the bite in my tone or chooses to ignore it.

"It's a shame, so much talent being wasted. But…" Her eyes flick to mine, another grin dancing on her lips.

They're plump, kissable. I bet they'd look even better wrapped around my cock.

Based off the pulsing Shep Jr. does at the idea, I'd say he agrees.

She pushes onto her tiptoes, bringing her mouth to my ear. "Baseball isn't the only thing you're talented at, right?"

Fuck no, it isn't.

I slide an arm around her waist, pulling her tight little body against mine.

She purrs—literally fucking purrs like a cat—at the move. I want to shove her away for that alone, but honestly, my dick is lonely.

"How about we get out of here?"

She giggles. "I'd like that, baby."

Baby.

I stifle my groan at the pet name. I fucking *hate* pet names. To try to get myself in the mood a little more, I run my nose along her jaw, and she giggles.

I also hate giggling.

Good thing sex doesn't have to involve talking. It'll be a whole lot of moaning and orgasms, just like I like it.

"I know a—"

"Really, universe? *Really?*"

The words are muttered, but there's no denying who is standing behind me, her cart mere inches from ramming into the back of me, and I'm sure that's entirely on purpose.

My chest feels like it's about to explode. It always does when she's around.

It doesn't matter the situation, doesn't matter what insults she's hurling my way—anytime Denver Andrews is near me, my attention is solely hers.

Like now.

Stripper Brandi doesn't notice her, or the change in my demeanor. She continues to try to paw at me while I work to disentangle myself from her grasp, trying to escape because whatever this was going to be isn't going to happen. I've lost all interest in going home with her.

Especially now that I'm reminded there's so much more out there for me.

Like Denver.

The only good thing to come from my...*leave of absence* from baseball is coming back home. I knew Denver didn't move after graduation, knew she'd still be here...knew we'd eventually run into one another.

I was counting on it, actually.

I have a lot to make up for, especially to Denny. I planned to seek her out, get her to forgive me—I just didn't realize I'd be starting my *I'm sorry for sucking so much ass* apology tour tonight.

"Can you not have sex in the middle of the grocery store? It's disgusting."

I grin and spin toward the intruder, still holding on to Stripper Brandi for show.

"Is that jealousy I detect, Denver?"

"Your name is *Denver*? Like the state?"

Holy fuck. My standards are shit.

I drop my arm from around Stripper Brandi's waist and take a step away from the stupidity, unable to handle it any longer.

"Look, Brandi with an *I*, it's not gonna happen tonight."

Harsh? Possibly, but I've done this enough times to know getting straight to the point is the only way I'll be able to get a girl like Brandi to back off.

Her mouth falls open. She quickly slams it shut and rolls her shoulders back. "She can join. I don't mind."

"While that's a *lovely* offer, *Brenda*," Denver says, butchering her name on purpose, "that would be a hard pass from me. I'd rather peel my own toenails off than ever—and I mean *ever*—see Shep naked."

I smirk at the vivid imagery. "Now, now, Denny, we both know the lie detector would determine that's a lie."

"You wish it was a lie, *Slug*."

I grunt in distaste at the nickname, because she of all people knows how much I hate it, and I know what it means when she uses it.

"What are you even doing here, Andrews?"

"Grocery shopping. This is the grocery store, isn't it? That's what you're supposed to do here—*not* other people."

Stripper Brandi gasps at Denny's words, and I can't help but laugh.

She always did get right to the point. There was never any pussyfooting around with her, and it's something I've always loved about her, even when I was supposed to be hating her.

"You have a point there," I concede.

"She does?"

"She does," Denny tells my…well, whatever Brandi is. Potential hook-up? *Ex* potential hook-up?

"Listen, Strip"—I catch myself at the last moment—"*Brandi*, like I said, it's not going to work tonight."

Her lips fall into a pout. Suddenly they don't look as kissable as they once did.

And it's all fucking Denny's fault.

I glance over and can't help but compare her to the girl I had plans to use as a distraction tonight.

It's late, and we're at the grocery store, yet Stripper Brandi is dressed to impress, right down to the studded boots on her feet.

Denny…well, she's dressed all right, but it's clear she isn't trying to impress anyone with what she's wearing.

She's clad in bright teal yoga pants and a soft gray sweater hanging off one shoulder. Her dark hair is twisted into a messy knot, not an ounce of makeup is on her face, and with the way I can see her nipples straining against the thin cotton of her sweater, I'm fairly certain she isn't wearing a bra either…and I'm not going to argue with that.

It's simple, and she even looks a little homeless, yet I can't stop my eyes from lingering on her. It's not because of the homeless thing, either.

It's simply Denny. It's always been that way with her. No matter how much I want to, I can't hate her the way she hates me.

Honestly, I never hated her at all.

"Can I at least give you my number?" Brandi asks, pulling my attention back to her.

I won't use it, but… "Sure."

She holds her hand out, waiting for my phone, but I know a whole hell of a lot better than to hand my precious over. When it finally dawns on her that I'm not going to give it to her, she digs into the oversized purse dangling off her arm and pulls out a wad of receipts and a pen. She quickly jots down digits I don't plan to use and folds the scrap of paper, dragging this out longer than she needs to.

"I hope we can pick this back up…" Her eyes dart toward Denny. "Later tonight."

"It's after ten thirty—don't you have school tomorrow?" Denny taunts.

Stripper Brandi huffs then stretches onto her tiptoes to press a kiss to my cheek. "I'll be up."

As she disappears around the corner, Denny bursts into hysterical laughter.

"Please tell me she knows you're not going to call her." She stares after the girl, adding, "That is your MO after all."

I ignore the jab, because I deserve it. "I mean, she *did* think you were named after a state, so you tell me."

"God, Shep, you sure know how to pick 'em."

That's funny coming from Denver.

I picked her once a upon a time too.

We fall into a silence, and it's not one of those comfortable kinds you share with old friends. It's awkward as fuck, which isn't exactly surprising.

If we're not slinging insults at one another, we don't know how to act. You'd never guess from the way we interact that Denny and I share a long, painful history.

"Well, this tension-filled silence is my cue. Have a good night with your right hand, Slug."

And there it is.

This tension she's referring to is unfinished business. We both know it, and if I can get Denny to give me the time of day, I intend to finish it.

"I'll have you know I'm a switch-hitter. I was going to give Lefty some showtime tonight."

"Such a gentleman," she tosses over her shoulder as she pushes her cart down the aisle and away from me.

My shoulders sag in relief as she retreats—but only for a moment, because I know exactly what's coming next.

Misery. Anger.

Toward her. Toward myself.

Denver Andrews used to love me. Now she hates me.

I used to love her too…and I still do.

Two

DENVER

I'm a big believer in *everything happens for a reason*. I'm one of those weirdos who truly subscribes to the idea that everything is mapped out for us from day one, even when we can't see it for ourselves.

That said, why in the actual fuck the universe decided I should run into my ex...well, whatever he is...in the middle of Smart Shoppe while I'm dressed like *this* is beyond me.

I could slap myself for running to the store for the famous period trio—you know: sweets, salts, and stoppers—wearing this outfit.

Or non-outfit.

It's just whatever I found lying around on my way-too-messy apartment floor.

Of course the universe would screw me over and I'd run into my mortal enemy.

Okay, that might be a *little* harsh, but the last person I expected to see was *him*.

Shep Clark.

The Shep Clark.

The guy I moved across the country to be with.

The guy who broke my fragile heart.

The guy I hate.

That Shep Clark.

I had to endure four years of college with the man who unceremoniously ended things. He ruled the campus, and I could never truly escape him.

When he was drafted for the MLB, I was ecstatic. He was leaving, meaning I'd *finally* be able to put Shepard Clark behind me. Sure, I was a journalist in his alumni town and I'd probably have to run an article or two on him and his accomplishments, but I could deal with that.

To actually have to *see* him, though?

I'll take *No Fucking Thank You* for $200, Alex.

He may be a baseball legend to everyone else in this town, but I won't be falling at his feet anytime soon.

Not again.

I angrily march myself down the aisle, pushing my cart much faster than I need to. I just want to get out of here before I run into Shep again. I don't even pay attention to the chips I toss into the cart, something I'm certain I'll regret later.

I don't bother scoping out the ice cream selection for something new. I know I'll inevitably choose my trusty mint chocolate chip—*the green one, thank you*—and cookies and cream in the end.

I bustle over to the feminine products and grab the biggest pack I can find before making my way to the front.

It would be my luck that they've closed self-checkout, there's only one lane open, and the oldest lady on the entire planet is sliding groceries across the scanner in a painfully slow manner.

Eff you, universe.

I push my cart up behind the woman in front of me, who I'm fairly certain is the second oldest woman on Earth, then rest against the handle.

The cashier scans a box of cereal and I swear it takes a full thirty seconds to do so.

I'm going to die here.

My eyes drift toward the gossip magazines lining the shelves to my right. Normally, I ignore this trash, but I'm bored and since I'll probably be here for another fifteen minutes, why the hell not.

I reach for one featuring my favorite Chris then something catches my eye.

Is that...

Holy crap, it *is!*

Can I not escape him?!

Shep's mug shot is plastered across the front of the local newspaper—and my rival paper at that.

Local Star Arrested for Destruction of Property the headline reads.

Looks like King Shep went and did another dumbass thing—started a fight and racked up a pretty penny in damages to the inside of a fancy-schmancy club a few hours north of here.

He's lucky he's not being hit with assault charges too.

I sneer at the paper in front of me. The urge to rip every copy off the shelves just so I can burn them all is strong.

Shep doesn't deserve *any* kind of attention. He's a liar, the biggest asshole in the history of assholes.

I hate him with a fiery passion.

I scowl at the image of his face, resisting my desire to snatch and burn, and instead grab a candy bar sitting below the papers, open it, and shove at least half into my mouth.

"Wow, I'm impressed."

I groan when I hear his voice.

"Go away."

"Can't—it's the only lane open."

"What are you even doing here, Slug?"

I swear I can hear him grind his molars together at the nickname. *Good. Asshole.* His dentist must have a hell of a time rooting around in his mouth with how much he gnashes those teeth.

"Grocery shopping. This is the grocery store, isn't it? That's what you're supposed to do here," he deadpans, repeating my words back to me.

"I hate you."

"You only think you hate me, Den."

I roll my eyes even though he can't see me, and he chuckles because he knows I did it.

I'm certain he's standing back there with that famous smirk of his lining his lips. That's the thing about Shep—you can never tell if he's upset or not because he's always sporting that fake-ass smile of his.

But, if you look close enough, you can see his jaw tick.

That's his tell.

I nod my head toward the magazine racks. "I see you still don't have your shit together."

"And I see you're still as uptight as ever. You can take the girl out of that sheltered Montana life, but you can't get the stick out of her ass."

I whirl around at his words.

In true Shep fashion, the smirk is there—but that jaw? Tight, teeth gnashing painfully.

It appears I've ruffled the king's feathers.

"Seriously, Shepard, why are you here? I thought you were off playing in the big leagues."

His eyes shift toward the newspaper, lingering there for several beats before he pulls his attention back to mine.

"I'm...taking some time off."

I raise a brow, unconvinced. He'll have to try a little harder, *especially* with me. "From the MLB?"

"Yes, Denver, from the MLB."

"But this is your first year. Your stats are outstanding for a rookie. You can't miss the end of the season..."

He leans closer, his grin returning. "I'm aware of how my baseball career is going. Question is, how do *you* know?"

My cheeks heat and I hastily take a step back, tripping over my own feet and bumping into my cart, sending it rolling forward with a force I didn't intend.

"Ouch! My hip! You've hit me!"

My heart hammers in my chest as I turn toward the older woman in line in front of me.

There my cart sits, right against her hip. Sure, it probably didn't hit her *that* hard, but it did make contact.

"Oh gosh, I am *so* sorry, ma'am! I didn't mean to run into you. I tripped on my flip-flop and lost my balance. Please, ma'am, I apologize."

She huffs and turns away from me, dismissing my sincerity.

Shame radiates through me. I feel horrible, and it's all Shep's fault. If he wasn't all up in my personal space, I wouldn't have had to move. Then I wouldn't have tripped and run into the cart, pushing it into the woman.

Fine, fine—it's *my* fault for letting Shep get to me, but whatever. Semantics.

"Add my stuff to her order—I'll pay for everything," I instruct the cashier. It's the only way I can think of to make this up to her. My mom would whoop my ass if she'd seen what happened, and she'd demand I make it better...*now*. This is how I can do that.

The woman ahead of me mutters something I don't quite catch

before collecting the last of her bags and pushing her way out of the store.

That's it. Nothing else.

"Are you serious?" I mutter to no one as I watch her walk away without looking back. "I accidentally hit her with my cart, offer to pay for her groceries, and she doesn't even say thank you? This night cannot get any worse."

"Better knock on wood, miss," the cashier warns.

I ignore her and load my groceries onto the belt.

"I think I love tonight," Shep comments.

Before I think twice, I launch whatever's in my hand at him, and he barks out a laugh, catching it with ease.

Stupid freakin' baseball reflexes.

"Ah, this explains why you're extra grouchy tonight."

I take a look at the box I launched and, yep, just my luck—I've thrown my tampons at him.

Awesome.

"I wish they would have smacked you right in the eye—with the corner of the box, to be specific."

"Now that," he says, tossing the feminine products into the air and catching them without looking, "is rude as hell, Andrews."

"I hate you, Shepard Clark," I repeat with as much venom as I can muster.

Cue famous grin. "You only wish you did."

The worst part?

He's right.

"How? How is this my life tonight? First, I run out of tampons, then I run into the king of assholes. Next, I accidentally ram my cart into

17

an old lady, fork over sixty bucks I was *not* expecting to spend in order to remedy that situation, and now I have a flat tire. Great. Just great."

I toss my head back on a groan and stare up at the night sky.

"What in the hell is your problem, universe? Huh?"

No response.

I raise a hand and flip her the bird.

"Well, screw you too then!"

"I always did have you pegged as a little crazy. Glad I wasn't wrong."

Shep's footsteps echo across the otherwise quiet parking lot as he comes to stand next to me, staring down at my flat tire.

"King of assholes, huh?"

"It's fitting."

"You're not wrong."

I raise a brow, surprised he agreed so easily.

I peek at him out of the corner of my eye, watching as he stares down at the ground.

Shep is insanely attractive—even I can't deny that—but it was never his looks that drew me to him. That would have been impossible, anyway, since we only communicated via text message at first.

Tonight, he's dressed simply, his long legs clad in dark jeans. A white t-shirt covers his broad, muscled shoulders, and he's even wearing a black pair of those old man shoes that seem to be a thing these days.

His hair is perfectly messy, the black locks pushed around in an artful yet effortless way. His hazel eyes are shrouded in shadows, and not just because of the dark and dingy parking lot we're standing in.

There's something on Shep's mind, and I'm certain it has to do with that article.

A part of me wants to ask him about it because, being a journalist, I'm a naturally curious person. More so, though—as much as I hate to admit it—I want to ask him because of the Shep I used to know.

Thing is, he hasn't been that person in a long damn time.

"You have a spare?" he finally says.

"In the trunk."

"Want me to help you?"

His words surprise me so much all I can do is stare at him.

He lets out a bitter laugh. "Quit acting so fucking surprised, Den. I'm not a monster."

"Could have fooled me."

He snorts. "Okay, fine. I deserve that, but final offer—you want my help or not?"

It's on the tip of my tongue to say yes because I'm tired and bloated and I just want to go home and eat my now melting ice cream, but this is Shep I'm talking to here. I *cannot* let him in again, not even a little bit.

The pain that came with that mistake last time was enough to set my heart on fire for years.

I'll pass.

"No."

He stands there, not moving, eyes hard.

"I'm not some helpless little girl, Clark. I can change a tire by myself."

He looks around the lot one more time—for what, I don't know—before giving me a nod. "Suit yourself then. Good night, Denver."

"Night," I mutter as he turns on his heel and walks in the opposite direction.

Letting out a huff in a mixture of relief and irritation, I dig my keys from my purse and unlock the doors to my hatchback. I toss my bags into the passenger seat, roll up the sleeves of my sweater, and pop open my trunk.

I push aside all the miscellaneous crap I have back here, namely those reusable bags I *always* forget to take into the store, and pull up the compartment to grab my tire.

"What the *shit*, universe! Are you messing with me right now?"

There's a giant nail poking out of the spare.

Of course there is.

I hear tires approach, but I don't turn around.

I don't have to; I know it's him.

"Want a ride?"

I slam my trunk closed, not taking a single moment to second-guess myself before saying, "Yes."

Three

Unknown: MAYDAY, MAYDAY. We have a MAJOR problem.

Denver: ???

Denver: Who is this?

Unknown: Shepard Clark, a friend of AJ Sutton.

Denver: How did you get this number?

Unknown: AJ, obviously.

Denver: He just gave my number to some random creep? I'm going to murder him.

Denver: Go the hell away.

Unknown: I would but…this is important.

Unknown: You're Denver Andrews, right? Best friends with Allie Hanson?

Denver: …yes?

Denver: How do you know all that?

Unknown: I told you—AJ.

Unknown: He's my Allie.

Denver: So he's your best friend? Why don't you just say that?

Unknown: Because guys don't say shit like "best friends". We're all just buddies. You wouldn't understand.

Denver: Clearly.

Denver: What do you want?

Denver: Wait…how do you even know AJ? You live on the other side of the country.

Shepard: Stalked me that fast, huh? I'm impressed.

Denver: Shit up.

Shepard: I most certainly will not shit up.

Denver: I don't even know you and I already hate you.

Shepard: Somehow, I doubt that.

Shepard: To answer your question, I know AJ from baseball camp. We go to the same one every summer, have since we were little. We've bonded over the years.

Denver: Then why haven't I ever heard of you? I've known AJ for years too.

Shepard: Actually, you probably have.

Denver: I'd remember a stupid name like Shepard.

Shepard: Because you have SO much room to talk, DENVER.

Shepard: Seriously, really weird name you have there.

Denver: I'll let my parents know you

23

approve.

Denver: Still haven't heard of you.

Shepard: He ever mention anyone named Slug?

Denver: YOU'RE Slug? THE Slug?

Shepard: Ah, so you HAVE heard of me before.

Denver: Heard of you? You're all he talks about during baseball season. "Man, I wish Slug could have seen this…" "Dude, bro, Slug killed it in his game last night."

Denver: His crush on you is annoying.

Shepard: What can I say? I'm a legend.

Denver: I believe I've rolled my eyes at the mention of you no less than 100 times.

Shepard: You mean you were rolling your eyes in ecstasy, right?

Denver: Are you trying to make me puke?

Shepard: Whatever you need to tell yourself.

Denver: Why are you still messaging me? GO AWAY, SLUG.

Shepard: Because I have something important to tell you.

Denver: I'm starting to believe you don't.

Shepard: Because I'm being conversational? HOW DARE I USE MANNERS.

Denver: Out with it already!

Shepard: Fine. AJ is going

Denver: Going to?

Denver: What? The store? The mall? Hell? Cool story. I don't care.

Denver: I lied. I do care. WHAT THE HELL, SLUG! You CANNOT just leave me in suspense like that!

Denver: Seriously. It's been five minutes.

Denver: You're totally getting off on this, aren't you?

Denver: You're just staring at your screen watching and waiting for another panicked message from me.

Denver: Whatever. I'm done. I'm blocking you.

Shepard: WAIT! DON'T!

Shepard: My brother came in and interrupted me. I didn't mean to hit send yet or leave you hanging.

Shepard: You still there?

Shepard: Wait…are you doing what I just did to you? UNINTENTIONALLY, I might add.

Denver: Possibly.

Denver: Now tell me what you know.

Shepard: AJ's planning to propose to Allie at homecoming next month.

Denver: You're shitting me. We're in high school. HIGH SCHOOL. This isn't some TV show on the CW where they get married and spend the rest of their lives together despite a teen pregnancy and a crazy nanny and all kinds of other nonsense…that doesn't happen in real life!

Shepard: While that is oddly specific, I

agree, and that's what I told him (with less details, of course).

Shepard: He's insane. We're way too young for that shit, but he's all starry-eyed and in love.

Shepard: Please tell me Allie is going to let him down easy.

Denver: Honestly? She'd probably think it was romantic as hell and say yes.

Shepard: Our friends are morons.

Denver: Finally, something we can agree on.

Denver: I told Allie.

Shepard: But you kept my name out of it, right?

Denver: Yes. You're the asshole in this friendship, not me.

Shepard: So we're friends now, huh?

Denver: Gross. No. NEVER.

Denver: I meant acquaintanceship. We're

just two strangers working together to keep their moron friends from making a huge mistake. Besides, I hate you, remember?

Shepard: Guess that's the second thing we can agree on.

Shepard: What'd Allie say?

Denver: She said he's a moron, but he's HER moron…and she'll be saying yes.

Shepard: For fuck's sake… WHAT IS WRONG WITH THESE TWO?!

Denver: They're deranged.

Shepard: I'd say. I'd never propose to my girlfriend.

Denver: You have a girlfriend?

Shepard: Jealous?

Denver: No, just curious about who in their right mind would actually date you.

Shepard: Har-har-har.

Shepard: I have a "girlfriend".

Denver: Thanks. That really clears

things up for me.

Shepard: There's this girl who is a friend. Everyone assumes she's my girlfriend. We just kind of...roll with it.

Denver: But...why?

Shepard: Well, I'm trying to focus on baseball, so I don't need a girlfriend complicating my life. She's gay and doesn't need that complicating her last year of high school. It keeps a lot of people off our backs.

Denver: That's sad. But sweet.

Denver: I'm sorry, but did you just out your friend to me? Because that's not cool.

Shepard: She's sitting right next to me and said it was okay if I told you since you live across the country. She's deemed you "safe".

Shepard: But if you tell ANYONE, I'll kiss you.

Denver: Don't you mean KILL?

Shepard: I said what I meant. You "hate" me, so kissing you would be a worthy punishment.

Denver: Interesting logic.

Shepard: I'm a smart man.

Denver: I wouldn't go that far.

Shepard: Now that you know my secret, you gotta tell me one of yours.

Denver: I'll pass, thanks.

Shepard: I bet you're real fun at parties, Denver.

Denver: Um, what?

Shepard: Never mind. LAUGHING OUT LOUD.

Denver: I'm sorry…did you stalk my BookFace account? Are you making fun of me?

Shepard: Possibly.

Shepard: But also not. I find it a little cute that you don't know internet lingo.

Shepard: And weird since you're in high school and it's how half the girls talk.

Denver: I'm not…allowed to have a social media account. My parents don't know about it and I can only use it when I'm with Allie or at the comic shop. This phone I'm texting on? They don't know that exists either. I bought a pre-paid with my babysitting money. There. That's my secret.

Shepard: Please, please, please tell me you're using a flip phone.

Denver: I am.

Denver: You're laughing and I'm flipping you off right now.

Shepard: I kind of figured.

Shepard: I am curious though…comic shop?

Denver: Did I say that? I meant COFFEE shop.

Shepard: No, no, it's too late now. I know you're a closet nerd.

Denver: *shrugs* They have free WiFi.

Shepard: And the comics aren't bad, right?

Denver: I don't know what you're talking about.

Shepard: Whatever you need to tell yourself.

Shepard: We need a plan of attack, but I have practice, so I gotta run. Later, Denver.

Denver: Bye, Shepard.

Shepard: Can we talk for a second about how our friends' names are Allie & AJ? Like that Disney girl band that was popular several years back?

Denver: I have no idea who you're talking about, but this is hilarious.

Shepard: How do you not know? They were ALL over the place.

Denver: Um...

Shepard: I'm waiting.

Denver: You can't laugh.

Shepard: I feel like I need to be very honest with you, Denver, and I cannot promise I won't laugh.

Denver: We aren't allowed to watch TV outside of family time. My parents keep the TV in a locked cabinet. We can only watch it on movie night.

Shepard: For your own sanity, I hope you're joking.

Denver: I am not.

Shepard: I think I need a moment to let this sink in.

Shepard: HOW… WHAT… WHO… Holy shit.

Denver: You feel better?

Shepard: No.

Denver: I don't either.

Denver: I just Googled who you're talking about. That is quite funny.

Shepard: Just think—if they get married, they'll have to live with that for the rest of their lives.

Denver: Another reason we need to talk some sense into them.

Denver: Any luck convincing AJ he's a

moron?

Shepard: No. He's too stupid to realize it.

Denver: Allie is now wearing a rubber band around her ring finger…"to practice".

Shepard: These two disgust me.

Shepard: Don't they know love comes and goes?

Denver: You a cynic, Shepard?

Shepard: I'm a realist, Denver. I'll never settle down. There's too much out there for us to experience for that to happen.

Shepard: Besides, do you REALLY want to be with the same person forever?

Denver: You are asking the wrong person, buddy.

Shepard: Oh god. Please tell me you're not one of those weirdos who believes in soul mates and fate and all that true love bullshit.

Shepard: Valentine's Day is a commercial holiday. Santa Claus isn't real. And you can't die from mixing Coke and Pop Rocks.

Shepard: Just wanted to point all that out in case you believe in that bullshit too.

Denver: Cynic.

Shepard: Realist.

Denver: I believe everything happens for a reason, even if we don't know what it is at the time. I believe things are mapped out for us. It may seem like we're making all the decisions, but it's what has been intended all along. I DO think you can settle down with one person forever.

Shepard: Yet you're against AJ and Allie getting hitched?

Denver: I never said that. I said I was against them doing it in high school. I never said I didn't think they'd last forever.

Shepard: I give it until spring when they're deciding on which colleges to go to.

Shepard: College ALWAYS breaks people

up.

Denver: They could stand the test of time, Shepard. You never know.

Shepard: Shep. Just call me Shep.

Denver: Can I call you Slug?

Shepard: FUCK NO! I HATE that nickname.

Denver: Why?

Denver: It's kind of cute.

Shepard: You think slugs are cute?

Denver: Hmm…good point. No.

Denver: Why do you hate it?

Shepard: Because it symbolizes a whole bunch of bullshit.

Denver: You're talented when it comes to explaining things. Has anyone ever told you that?

Shepard: That was sarcasm, right?

Denver: DUH

Shepard: It's just… No. I'm not telling you this shit. It's mushy.

Denver: You tell me a secret and I'll tell you one of mine. Like last time.

Shepard: Fine. Here goes…

Shepard: My dad always called me Slugger. It was his thing and I hated it when he was around, but after he passed, I missed it all the time. Enter my stepdad, Jack. He was into the whole Slugger nickname too. I missed my dad so much that I loved it when Jack called me that, so I didn't mind. I kind of thought it was…

Shepard: Holy fuck, I can't believe I'm going to say this, but…I thought it was fate or some shit, like it was meant to be between him and my mom, Rose.

Shepard: Anyway, he called me Slugger, but then…then he and Zach shortened it to Slug because, and I'll be honest here, I kind of turned into a conceited prick for a bit when I was about 14/15. They said I was "slimy like a slug". My team picked up on the nickname. AJ picked up on it. It stuck. I became Slug.

Denver: I have a lot of comments.

Denver: 1. Your mom's name is Rose, and your dad's name is Jack? Like Titanic?

Shepard: Your parents let you watch Titanic?

Denver: I watched it at Allie's. She's obsessed with Leo.

Shepard: Yes, those are their names. They met at grief counseling. They're both widowed.

Denver: I'm sorry for both of their losses. And yours. As much as my parents drive me bonkers and I hate living under their rules, I can't imagine losing one of them.

Denver: 2. I promise to only ever call you Slug when I truly hate you. It'll be code so you'll know I'm pissed.

Shepard: I think you just called us friends again.

Denver: Shut up, Shep.

SHEPARD

Dog food.

All I was going to the store for was some damn dog food.

But here I am, hard as a fucking rock while driving down the county road with Denver Andrews as my passenger.

She spoons a mouthful of mint chocolate chip ice cream into her mouth and moans.

Again.

Is she trying to fucking kill me?

She hopped into my truck with her bags and immediately began rummaging around in my glovebox, not stopping until she found the lone random plastic spoon in there, and then she proceeded to pop open a pint of my favorite ice cream.

She *knows* it's my favorite too.

"I didn't expect you to drive a truck."

"Yeah?"

She shakes her head. "You don't seem like a truck guy."

"What kind of guy do I seem like, Den?"

"An asshole."

My body shakes with laughter at her deadpan answer.

"And what else?"

"Sports car. Definitely sports car. You have that *I have a small dick and need to make myself feel better about it with horsepower* sort of vibe."

I grin. "While it's oddly specific, I see what you mean. It's the jock angle, right? Most jocks are like that."

"What made you get a truck? It's kind of…hot."

"Well fucking well. Did you just call me *hot*, Denny?"

She shifts uncomfortably in her seat, rearranging herself until she's sitting up straighter. She shoves another mouthful of ice cream in then says, "No."

"Huh? I couldn't hear you through all your manners over there." I snatch the container of deliciousness out of her hands. "Give me that. I didn't say you could eat in here anyway."

She reaches for it, but I pull it from her grasp.

"It was going to melt, you dick. Give it back!"

"Nope." I pull the plastic spoon from the pint and lick it clean, not letting myself think too long about the fact that this is probably as close to kissing her as I'll ever get. "Mine now."

Denny groans, and I almost wish I hadn't stolen her ice cream because I'm definitely missing her moans.

She crosses her arms over her chest, her eyes falling to slits as she glares at me. "You cannot eat and drive."

I toss a wink at her. "Watch me."

"I hate you."

"You keep saying that, but the fact that you're in my truck proves differently."

She pulls on the locked door handle, testing to see if she can jump out, I'm sure. I mean, we *are* going slow enough for her to survive.

"It's called desperation, Shep."

"Bullshit. You could have easily called a cab or an Uber. It's called convenience."

"I'm sorry, you want me to call a car at *this* hour? And get murdered? Wow, I knew you hated me, but I didn't know you hated me that much."

I never hated you, I want to say.

I don't.

"You tried to murder me with a box of tampons earlier. Fair is fair."

"Oh my god. You can live without an eye, Shep."

"Not if you're a famous baseball player."

"Oh, famous, huh?" She laughs. "Someone's getting a little big for their britches."

"You *did* just see my face on the cover of a magazine, right?"

"It was a *local* gossip trash-zine, and it was your mug shot. Are you *really* proud of that?"

There are a lot of things in my life I'm not proud of—what I did to Denny being one of them—but the thing that really hit home for me? Almost losing everything I've worked so fucking hard for because I couldn't handle my emotions like a goddamn pre-teen.

After I nearly lost my career over my unresolved issues, I vowed to turn my shit around and get it together before I mess up so bad I can't charm my way out of it, turning over a new leaf and all that other sappy *look at the new me* shit.

I shovel the ice cream into my mouth to avoid answering her, taking the biggest bite I can while keeping the truck on the road.

We're quiet for a few miles, sitting in that same uncomfortable silence as before.

"What happened anyway, Shep?" she asks in a hushed tone.

It's an easy story to tell, really. I was in a club up north hanging with some pals and we started bragging about our best college conquests. Are we immature pigs? Probably, but it was fun and innocent.

Until someone brought up Denny.

I saw fucking red.

All over my hands. All over the floor.

I beat the shit out of the guy and broke a few things in the process. Luckily, he didn't press charges, but the club did for destruction of property.

My coach and PR team decided I needed some time off to "clean up my act". With this *and* what happened with my brother and his girl my senior year of college—another stupid fucking mistake of mine—I'm on thin ice.

"It's nothing," I tell her eventually.

"Shepard..." It comes out as a plea, and I want to spill all my secrets to her right here.

I don't.

"What are you doing? Why are you messing this up? It's all you've ever dreamed about."

I snort. "Messing it up—like I'm doing it on purpose or some shit."

"Aren't you?"

"No!"

She flinches as the word vibrates across the cab of the truck.

"No," I repeat quietly. "I'm not. It's just...I get..."

"Stupid?"

My lips twitch. "No. I get...emotional."

Her hand flies to her mouth as her lips drop apart in false shock. "Why, are you telling me you, Shepard Clark, king of assholes, have...*feelings*?" She pokes at me. "You telling me there's a heart in there somewhere?"

You know I have a fucking heart, Denny. You of all people know I do.

My skin burns from the touch, which is so fucking stupid considering it was just a poke, and I shift away from her as best I can before it's painfully obvious that my cock is straining against my jeans, begging to be touched.

I toss her an easygoing grin, hoping she doesn't look at my lap. "Under all the ice, sure."

"Layers and layers…and layers of ice," she quips. "So, you gonna tell me what really happened?"

"If I tell you my secret, will you tell me one of yours?" I bargain like old times.

"You don't deserve my secrets anymore, Shep." I glance over at her to see she's staring distantly out the windshield. "We both know that."

I don't disagree with her, because she isn't wrong.

I lost that privilege when I screwed up.

Add that to my *very* long list of mistakes.

"How's Zach doing? Your *Titanic* parents?"

I smile at the thought of my mom and how happy she is with Jack, but that old familiar sting of missing my father hits me and it hurts so fucking bad.

"Mom and Jack are good. Zach and I…well, I'm not really talking to Zach right now."

She laughs dryly. "Of course you're not talking to your brother. What'd you do, Shep?"

Annoyance tickles at me. "Why do you assume *I* did something wrong? Why can't it be his fault?"

"Because I know you better than that. You're the king of screwing things up."

"King of assholes, king of mistakes—no matter how you look at it, you're still calling me the ruler, Den."

"You're obnoxious."

"Yet here you are."

"Desperation, Shep. Desper-fucking-ation."

"Whatever you need to tell yourself, Denny."

"You can pull in right here."

"Huh." I pull the truck up to the window of the security checkpoint. "I didn't realize we lived so close to each other."

Her eyes widen. "You live here now?"

"Yeah, while I'm…taking some time off."

"Oh."

I can't tell if that's a bad *oh* or a good one.

With Denny? Probably bad.

She leans over the center console and waves to the old man sitting inside the hut.

His eyes narrow as he tries to get a look inside the cab.

"Roll your window down, dumbass," she hisses.

I comply because I'm truly afraid she's about to murder me.

"You know him?"

"Of course I do." She rolls her eyes. "What? Think he's going to attack me?"

"You never know these days…"

"I'm fairly certain he served in World War II. He wouldn't hurt a fly."

I glance over the old man again, noting the patriotic hat he's sporting. Fine, he seems harmless.

I roll the window down.

"Hey, Captain." Denny beams his way.

"Ah, Bucky, I didn't realize that was you. I was about to hit my panic button. I don't have these plates in the books."

My breath hitches.

Captain America and Bucky.

She's supposed to be *my* Bucky, not his.

It takes all the strength I can muster to not turn her way, to not let her know just how much it stings that she'd let someone else call her that.

"Just me, Cap. My tire went flat on my run to Smart Shoppe."

The wrinkled old man narrows his eyes at me. "You didn't hitch a ride with some stranger, did ya?"

"No. I know him." I whip my head her way, surprised she'd admit that out loud. "Unfortunately," she adds as I stare at her with a smirk.

Ah, there she is.

"Should I let him through?"

"You'd be my favorite man in my life if you did."

"If he gives you any trouble, Bucky…"

"Hit him where it hurts. I know, Cap."

The old man gives her a thumbs-up and me another glare before pressing the button to lift the gate.

"Cap and Bucky, huh?" I say as casually as I can while pulling forward.

She purses her lips but doesn't address my inquiry, instead directing me to the building she lives in. "Up ahead and to your left."

Fine. You win this round, Denny.

I follow her directions until she tells me to stop.

"This is me. See ya."

She grabs her bags and hops out of the truck before I can say anything else.

What the…

45

Oh hell no.

I shift into park and toss open my door.

"Denny! Wait up!"

She whirls toward me, wide-eyed and startled. "What the hell are you doing?"

"Walking you inside."

"Like hell you are. I'm not letting you know which apartment is mine. Besides, you can't just leave your truck in the middle of the parking lot."

"Watch me," I say, catching up to her. "You are *not* walking up there alone in the middle of the night."

"What did you think I was going to do if you weren't here? Have Cap walk me inside? There are like two dozen stairs in that building— I am *not* going to be responsible for the death of Captain America."

My lips pull into a grin, and I can see the fire in her eyes the moment they do.

I've missed that fire.

It's the same look she'd give me all throughout college anytime our paths would cross. It'd burn especially hot whenever I'd have another girl on my arm.

I always did like playing with fire.

"It's not happening, Shep," she says with a false finality.

"Like hell it isn't, Andrews. Better get moving or the rest of your ice cream is going to melt."

She stares down at her paper bags, mouth agape. "How did you know I have more ice cream?"

I lean toward her until our faces are inches apart and regret it immediately.

She smells like mint chocolate chip and I want to press my lips against hers to get a taste. Her green eyes—which remind me of that green mint color I love—are bright and clear as she stares up at my six-foot-two frame.

"Because I know you better than anyone else in this entire world, Denver."

My eyes drift to her lips again as they part on a gasp.

She inches closer.

Lips nearly touching now.

Eyes locked in an intense stare.

The urge to press my lips against hers swells, but I know I shouldn't. I'd be pushing things way too far.

Besides, I don't deserve her kisses.

Not anymore.

"Did."

I can hardly hear her over the drumming of blood pumping through my veins. Her tongue darts out and she wets her lips.

"You *did* know me, Shep, but a lot has changed in the last six years. I'm not the same starry-eyed girl who fell for all your lines. I won't fall into that trap again."

She stands tall and takes a step away from me.

The pounding in my ears begins to subside as she puts distance between us.

I miss the pounding.

"Thanks for the ride. Goodbye."

Goodbye, not good *night*—so permanent.

So certain.

So…not going to fucking happen.

I lost Denver once before. It's not going to happen again.

Five

DENVER

"No way!"

"I know! Can you believe it? After all these years, it's finally happening. I'm getting married!"

I stare down at the phone screen, laughing as my best friend, Allie, flashes me her huge diamond ring again.

Turns out I was right—Allie and AJ could stand the test of time. College did nothing to diminish their love for one other. All it did was feed it.

It's weird, though, that AJ would choose today of all days—the one after I spend a night with Shep—to propose.

Shep.

I try to shake away the memory of his jaw tightening when Cap called me Bucky. I remember the first time the old man called me that, how the simple nickname tugged at my heart. It didn't hurt like it usually did when I heard the name. Instead, it felt good…like it used to when Shep did it.

Last night when I saw the obvious hurt on his face when someone else called me his special name for me, I had to work extra hard not to react. In fact, that's what the whole evening with him was like: a fight not to react, not to fall back into old patterns.

Shep being Shep, he followed me into my dreams last night, and I spent most of the evening tossing and turning, trying to outrun his apologies and pleas, his excuses.

I finally pulled myself out of bed at four AM and devoured my other pint of ice cream, trying to chase the demons away with sweets.

It didn't work, and I'll be honest, I'm a little grateful for Allie's wakeup call. I don't know how much longer I could outrun him.

Plus, I could use the good news she's delivering.

"I can't believe this is *finally* happening," I say to my glowing friend through a yawn. "You two have only been together forever."

"I know!" She squeals with delight for the billionth time during our video chat. "AJ surprised me with breakfast in bed this morning."

"That I didn't burn!" I hear AJ yell.

Allie giggles at her fiancé then leans toward the camera to whisper, "That bacon was *totally* burnt." She laughs again. "Anyway, I couldn't wait until our next random coffee date to tell you, so I had to call ASAP!"

I smile at my best friend, the girl I've known since I was eight, my heart bursting with joy for her. She deserves this.

Allie followed AJ across the country so he could play baseball and attend college with his best friend.

Me? Well, I followed Allie.

Or at least that's the story we went with.

"Even though you woke me up ten minutes before my alarm was

set to go off, I'll forgive you." I wink. "I'm so happy for you, Allie."
I'll be alone forever. "Your dreams are coming true."

"They are. They really, really are. Now all we have to do is find
you a man you don't kick out of your bed in the morning!"

"Just let me set her up with one of my teammates!"

"Tell AJ I do *not* want to date one of his softball teammates. It's
softball, for grown-ass *men*."

Unfortunately for Allie's fiancé, his baseball skills didn't lead him
to the shining career Shep has ahead of him, so now he plays softball
with a bunch of old grumpy men. It's kind of hilarious.

"You could go on *one* date just to please him, you know. He's one
of your oldest friends."

"Yes, and you both know me well enough to know I don't date
jocks."

"That's not entirely true, Denny."

I narrow my eyes at her. "Watch it. Just because you're engaged
doesn't mean I won't hang up on you for bringing *him* up. Besides,
we're not exactly on a private phone call right now."

"Oh, please, like AJ would care."

"Allie…" I warn her.

"Fine, fine," she concedes. "I'll let it go…for now." She pushes
her curly blonde locks to the side. "Want to grab lunch today?"

"Can't." I sigh. "I have a huge project due tomorrow so I'm not
taking a lunch break today. Maybe Thursday? I wanna see that rock in
person!"

"It's a date."

"Hey, you're done dating! You're all mine now," AJ says, now
sounding closer than he did before.

Allie screams with delight and the phone shakes and goes black,
yet all sounds are still coming through.

"Oh my gosh, AJ! Stop it!"

50

He growls and says something I can't quite make out.

There's moaning.

Then there's a gagging noise. That one is coming from me.

I quickly press the red button to end the call, shaking my head at my best friend.

Allie and AJ are *finally* getting married.

And that means...

Oh, shit.

The sound of the doorbell chiming echoes off the walls, stopping all bad and horrible thoughts I was about to have about me being Allie's maid of honor and who AJ's best man will probably be.

I groan as I'm forced to pull myself from my cozy bed.

I can't tell if my displeasure is because I have to leave the warmth of my moose-printed quilt way before I wanted to, or if it's due to the thoughts trying to barrel through my mind.

Probably a little of both.

"What is with people being early this morning? First Allie, now Monty. Guess we're going to continue that torment from yesterday, huh, universe?"

I snatch my robe off the handle of my closet door and wrap it around myself just as the doorbell goes off again.

"Yeah, yeah, I'm coming, Monty!"

I shake my head at my twin sister. Of course she's early. It's Monty, the proverbial good girl. She'll never not be early.

For twins, we couldn't be more opposite, and I don't just mean in our looks.

Where Monty has long, beautiful red locks, I have choppy dark hair. She'd give Casper a run for his money in paleness, and I have a natural olive tone.

Monty is the epitome of a goody two-shoes. She doesn't cuss, she's never late, and she *always* follows the rules.

I'm…well, let's just say I'm a whole hell of a lot more free-spirited than she is. I only have one life, and I'm not living it by anyone else's rules.

I still wonder if the hospital switched one of us at birth, but despite all our differences, we're extremely close. When she moved out a few months ago to live with her super sexy boyfriend—who also happens to have a kiddo—we vowed to still have breakfast together at least twice a week.

Today is Wednesday, which means pancakes and peanut butter, and she's also here to give me a ride to work because my car is still at Smart Shoppe.

I hurry down the hall and through the living room, twisting the lock before padding back toward the kitchen without even glancing at my chronically punctual sister.

"You're early," I say as she pushes open the door. "No talkie. Need coffee. It's already been an eventful morning and I need caffeine."

"Expecting someone at this hour?"

I stop dead in my tracks, a shiver running up my spine at the deep voice.

What in the…

I whirl around, pulling my robe tighter against my body, trying to hide the fact that I'm wearing skimpy pajamas and *no* bra.

"What the hell are you doing here, Shep? And how do you know where I live?"

"It's weird—your morning security isn't nearly as worried about your safety as Captain America was. All it took was a grin and he let me right through the gate."

"How'd you know which door was mine?"

"That one was a little harder to figure out. I had a general idea because of last night, though I wasn't quite sure about the number."

52

He points to my door. "The big D hanging on the door kind of gave it away."

I grumble at the décor.

That giant D was Monty's idea.

Dammit, Monty.

"Good morning, Denver."

"Go to hell, Shep."

"I'll take that as you're happy to see me."

"Is that what that means to you?" I snort as I continue my quest for caffeine. Shep pushes the front door closed and follows me. "Your dates must be an interesting bunch if you find that welcoming."

"You're so cheery in the mornings. I forgot that about you."

I move around the kitchen, pulling the canister of coffee from the cabinet and dumping a few scoops into the basket. I don't mess around with those one-cup machines. Those are for sissies who quit at one cup.

Ha. One-cup coffee. Like that's a thing or something.

"What are you doing here, Shep?" I ask once I set the machine to begin brewing.

"I assume you've already spoken to Allie."

"I have."

"And?"

I raise a brow. "And I called that shit. I told you they'd last forever."

He grins, and in the bright morning light filtering through the windows, he looks nice…normal.

Not the asshole heartbreaker I know he really is.

I pluck a mug from the cabinet above the coffee machine and pour a healthy dose of joe in it before padding over to the fridge to grab my favorite vanilla caramel creamer. I dispense just enough to make my coffee a shade lighter, cap it, and return it to its spot.

"Just cream, no sugar."

I hate that he still remembers my coffee order, and I hate that he knows it despite never even being with me while ordering coffee.

Attentive bastard.

I rest my back against the counter and face him.

Shep's eyes fall to my hands, which are currently curled around the mug I'm holding. He squints, studying them. I think nothing of it until his full lips drop open and his hazel eyes find mine.

His brows slam together, but not in anger.

It's confusion that fill his expression.

Curious, I glance down.

Oh god.

My heart rate soars when I realize what cup I've grabbed from the cabinet: my alumni mug, the only one I have from my college days...the one that boasts we have the best baseball team around...the one with *23* on it to highlight our most valuable player in the college's history.

Shep's number.

I don't own a single sweatshirt or pair of sweatpants from my time spent at college, but the moment I saw this mug in the campus shop, I knew I had to have it.

Even though I hated his guts, it called to me.

So, I bought it, and I use it every single day.

I just wish today I'd have paid a little more attention to my routine.

"It was a gift," I lie. "I couldn't very well turn down a gift."

"Right," Shep mutters, his eyes back on the mug, mind whirling.

I lift the mug and he follows my movements, swallowing thickly the moment my lips graze the rim like it's his skin they're touching.

His stare doesn't leave the mug, not even as I lower it.

"It doesn't mean anything, Shep."

Finally, he snaps his attention back to my face.

"I said right, Denny."

He clears his throat and glances around my apartment. It's small but cozy and perfectly me.

I know the moment he spots my collection of comic-book-based movies because he grins and shakes his head.

When he's done surveying the small space, he turns back to me, still smiling.

How in the hell can he be so smiley this early in the morning?

"So, Allie and AJ."

"Yep, Allie and AJ," I repeat.

"You know what this means, don't you?"

I sigh, because I know exactly what this means. It means all those thoughts I was trying to avoid earlier.

"It means we're probably going to be spending a lot of time together over the next year or so, helping them plan and attending to our best man and maid of honor duties…unfortunately."

His grin grows. "Try again."

"Try what again?"

"That timeline."

"What about it? Most couples are engaged for about a year. They need the time to prepare, to make book venues, to…"

The words die on my lips.

That's *most* couples, but not Allie and AJ.

They're not most couples. They've been waiting for this for years now.

"Please tell me Allie isn't going to spring some crazy, impossible date on me."

"Fine. Allie most definitely is not going to spring some crazy, impossible date on you."

"That is *not* reassuring, Shepard."

He lifts a shoulder. "You told me to say it."

"I will toss this very hot coffee right in your face. Don't push me."

"You'd never hurt this handsome face of mine."

I lift a brow.

"Fine, maybe you would," he mutters. "Anyway, they're wanting an October wedding—their promise ring exchange anniversary, to be exact."

"October? But it's already September. That's…"

"Next month," he confirms.

"How do you already know all this?" I question.

"AJ has had this planned for months, Den. I knew it was happening."

"You couldn't have warned me about this last night?"

"And ruin the surprise? The romance in it?" He shakes his head. "Never."

I cock my head and meet him with curious eyes. "You believe in romance now?"

His jaw tightens for only a moment, but I see it before he pastes on a fake smile and says, "Me? Romance? Never. I told you, I'll never settle down."

It feels like a lifetime ago when Shep told me differently, and the elation I felt when he said so runs through my veins—only to be replaced by the ice put there by his betrayal.

My favorite mug nearly slips through my fingers as my brain strolls down memory lane.

I tighten my grip as it begins to slip and give myself a shake, pulling my mind back to reality.

I jolt away when I realize Shep's standing right next to me. I'm even more surprised to see he's pouring himself a cup of coffee.

"Oh, sure, help yourself."

"I will, since you're a terrible host and all."

"I'm sorry I didn't practice my manners on my *uninvited* guest. My bad."

"Damn right it is." He winks over the rim of the cup before taking a sip and resting his back against the counter, standing way too close to me for comfort.

Heat is radiating off him, and it feels so good licking at my skin. If I were brave, I'd step closer until I was pressed against him, until I could feel his skin on mine.

But I'm not brave, and I'm not stupid enough to let myself get sucked into Shep's web again.

Instead, being the smart girl I am, I set my mug on the counter and move away, distracting myself with getting the mix prepared for the pancakes I'm about to devour with Monty.

"Are you still going to be around in October?" I ask him, setting the skillet on the stove. "Or are you going to leave the duties of maid of honor *and* best man to me then try to take the credit?"

"I'll be around."

I sneak a peek at him, finding him staring down into his coffee mug with creased brows. How he drinks his coffee black is beyond me, though I did read an article once that said psychopaths drink black coffee…so I guess it makes sense.

"But that's…"

"The rest of the season. I'm aware of when the baseball season runs, Den."

"Are you in that much trouble?"

"Yes and no. I'm a valuable player and they know it, so it's more a matter of me getting my poster-boy image back on track. They want me to do a few charity gigs, personal interviews, and the like so I can get back in everyone's good graces."

My ears perk up at *personal interviews*.

My editor would kill to score an interview with Shep. He's notorious for avoiding them, which is odd because the guy loves the spotlight otherwise.

There's a promotion open at work and I know if I could get Shep to sit down for something and allow me to publish it, I would be first in line for the position. It's something I've been working toward, a salary I could really use, and a foot into so many doors for my future.

"Interviews?" I ask casually, crossing in front of him to reach into the cabinet on the other side of his head.

I stare at the shelf, waiting for his response.

When he doesn't give one, I glance around the open cabinet door.

His arms are crossed and he's looking at me in amusement.

"What?"

"Oh no, don't you *what* me with all that false innocence in your voice. You want something."

I shove my head back into the safety of the cabinet. "I don't know what you're talking about."

I pull down the pancake mix and chocolate chips I plan to add, but I don't move—not until Shep pushes on the door and closes it with a soft thud.

"You want an interview."

"I…" I lick my lips and brush a stray hair out of my face.

Oh god, my hair. I didn't think to check it before I opened the door because I was expecting my sister, not my ex.

I must look like a hot mess right now.

Fantastic.

I move around the kitchen, grabbing a mixing bowl, whisk, and the half gallon of milk from the fridge. I measure out the ingredients, dump way too many chocolate chips in, and whip it all together.

"Denny?" my unwanted guest pushes after several minutes of me ignoring him.

Damn. I thought for sure he'd leave if I waited long enough.

I drop the whisk and face him, squaring my shoulders and pulling my big girl panties up.

"Yes, Shep, I want an interview. There's a promotion coming up at work, and scoring an interview with the famous Shepard Clark would put me at the top of the list for it." I take a deep breath. "So, yes, I want an interview."

He takes another drink of his coffee, eyes never leaving mine as he studies me. He knows how hard it was for me to say that out loud to him, to say I...need him.

Unable to endure his stare for another moment, I turn away, pouring batter into the skillet and focusing on making breakfast.

"Okay."

"W-What?" I sputter.

He shrugs. "Okay. I'll do an interview."

I narrow my eyes at him. "What do you want?"

He lets out a hearty laugh, one that sounds almost a little...maniacal.

"What makes you think I want something?"

"Because I know you."

He gives me a pointed look. "As you so kindly pointed out last night, a lot can change in six years."

"Sure, but this isn't one of those things."

Another sip of coffee. Another smirk.

"You're right. It's not."

He finishes off the hot liquid in his hand, rinses his cup, and sets it in the sink before turning back to me.

"I have conditions."

I roll my eyes and cross my arms over my chest, jutting my hip out against the counter, bracing myself for the long list I'm certain he's about to regale me with. "Of course you do. Name them."

"I have a few charity events coming up. I need a date."

I stumble back at his request, stunned.

"I'm sorry, you want *me*"—I press my finger against my chest for emphasis—"to be *your*"—finger pointed at him now—"date? *Date*?"

"Yes. No hanky panky involved." He pauses then winks at me. "Unless you want it to be involved."

I shiver at the idea.

He believes it's in disgust and laughs, but I know it's because the idea slides inside of me and hits me right between my thighs.

Treacherous body.

He waves a hand. "It's strictly for show. It'll be a great opportunity for you to see me in other environments for the interview, too."

He's not wrong.

Damn him for not being wrong.

"Is that it? I just have to be your date to a charity gig or two?"

His eyes spark with a mischievous glint, and I know that's not all he wants.

"I need to do some damage control with my parents…and Zach. Especially with Zach."

I let out a dry laugh. *Of course.* "What did you do, Shep?"

"Something really fucking stupid that I need to fix. I need to show them I have my life together, show them I'm better than I was in the moments I can't take back and I'm growing up."

"Are you though?"

He grits his teeth together and hisses, "Yes."

I point the spatula at him. "I'll believe it when I see it."

He rolls his eyes in response.

"How does this involve me?"

"My parents and Zach have come to accept AJ as another member of the family over the years since he moved out here. They'll be at the wedding for sure, and I want you to be my date."

"No."

My response is instant. Final.

There is *no* way in hell I'll be attending a wedding with Shep.

Especially not with Shep.

A charity event? Sure. We'll be in a professional context the whole time. There's no way anything could go wrong there.

But a wedding? The most romantic setting of all? No way, no how.

Why would I do that? To remind myself of everything I don't have?

I flip the pancake, ignoring Shep.

Moments later he pushes off the counter and past me.

"Where are you going?" I say before I can bite my tongue. I've been hoping he'd leave since he got here, so why would I want him to stay now? And what is with my body betraying me today?

"I'm leaving."

"We're not done discussing this."

He stops and turns toward me. "But we are. You said no to one of my conditions—no deal."

"Shep, I can*not* go to Allie and AJ's wedding with you."

"Why not?" He appears calm and collected, but I know better as he stalks back toward the counter, his hazel gaze intense. "I'm not asking you to marry me, Den."

God, do I hate how much his words sting.

Hate how my heart begins to thump in my chest and my entire body sags with the overwhelming weight of his words.

I slide the pancake from the skillet and onto the waiting plate, pouring more batter in its place.

"It's not even a real date," he continues, speaking like he didn't just shatter my heart in two all over again. "Besides, we'll already be paired up the entire night as best man and maid of honor. What's the harm in being my date, especially when it gets you that interview and probably that promotion?"

He has a point…and I hate that he has a point.

I particularly hate that I'm actually considering saying yes. I could use that raise. I could use that foot in the door.

More than that, I deserve both.

What's the harm in one night anyway?

"I…"

I can't say it.

"Last chance, Denny," he says quietly.

I close my eyes and exhale a steadying breath, trying to summon up some courage.

I vowed I'd never get caught up with Shep again, not when I know how damaging it can be.

But that was six years ago.

I'm a whole different person now. What if Shep is too? What if he's not lying about changing?

And what if who we are now is better than who we were then?

"I'll do it."

He beams at me, the glow of victory spreading across his cheeks.

"Great. I'll see you next Friday night."

"For what?"

All too quickly, he reaches over the counter, plucks the pancake from the plate, and winks at me before taking a bite and heading toward the front door to leave…finally.

"Our first date," he calls over his shoulder.

I groan. "How many events are there going to be, Shepard?"

"Five."

"Five?!" I screech.

"Yep." He pulls open the door. "Pick you up at seven. Wear something sexy."

I chuck the spatula at his stupid grinning face and listen to him laugh the whole way down the hall.

What have I gotten myself into?

Six

Six years ago, September

Shepard: Are you at the nerd shop?

Denver: STOP CALLING IT A NERD SHOP!

Shepard: All I'm saying is my big brother is the biggest nerd I know and even he doesn't hang out at comic book stores.

Shepard: So, yeah, YOU'RE A NERD.

Denver: THEY HAVE FREE WIFI!

Shepard: Uh huh. Sure.

Denver: God I hate you.

Shepard: Liar. I think you're actually starting to look forward to my texts.

Denver: I'm really not.

Shepard: So many lies leaving that pretty mouth of yours.

Denver: Pretty, huh?

Shepard: What? I'm a teenager with eyes, hormones, and an always-half-hard dick. Yes, you're hot, Den.

Shepard: Don't make it weird.

Denver: I won't.

Denver: You're hot too, Shep.

Shepard: You just made it weird.

Denver: EYE ROLL EMOJI

Shepard: You know you can just use the emoji, right?

Denver: I don't know how!

Shepard: You, my technology-deprived friend, are sad.

Denver: I can still block you, ya know.

Shepard: Oh, did you finally figure that feature out? Look at you, getting all fancy with the technology! Gold star for Denny!

Denver: Allie showed me, you ass.

Shepard: I kind of figured.

Shepard: Wait...did she ask who you wanted to block?

Denver: It's Allie—she's nosy as all get-out, so yes.

Shepard: What'd you tell her?

Denver: What do you mean? The truth. Why would I lie?

Shepard: Did she say anything?

Shepard: About us...talking, I mean.

Denver: No.

Denver: Should she have?

Shepard: No. At least I don't think so.

Shepard: It just surprises me.

Denver: Well, she did say one thing but it's so stupid and it will never, EVER happen, so it's not worth repeating.

Shepard: I'm sitting on the edge of my fucking seat here, nerd.

Shepard: Tell me.

Denver: Apologize for calling me a nerd and I'll think about it.

Shepard: No. It's the truth.

Shepard: Wait, no—you're right. I'm so sorry for calling you a nerd, Den.

Shepard: Clearly, you're not a nerd. You're a geek.

Denver: Hate. You.

Shepard: Lies!

Shepard: Now tell me.

Denver: She said…and I'm quoting this so don't get mad at me for the name…"Wouldn't it be, like, so cute if you and Slug started dating? Then you two would be together forever like AJ and me. OH MY GOSH, DENNY! We could have a DOUBLE WEDDING!"

67

Denver: Then there was a lot of squealing and gagging happening.

Shepard: I'm going to assume the gagging was you trying not to puke at the thought of us getting married?

Denver: No. It was Allie because I choked the shit out of her to get her to shut up.

Shepard: DAMN! You're dark, Den.

Shepard: I like it.

Shepard: Maybe we SHOULD think about this double wedding thing…

Denver: Don't think I won't choke you too.

Shepard: Stop pretending to hate me.

Denver: Never.

Shepard: I think I've figured out this whole AJ being a dumbass wanting to propose to Allie in high school thing.

Denver: Yeah? Hit me with it.

Shepard: Convince him not to propose and to instead give her a promise ring.

Denver: Like promise to be virgins until marriage?

Denver: You know it's way too late for that, right? Those two bang like rabbits.

Shepard: Trust me, I know.

Shepard: But no, that's not a promise ring, that's a purity ring. A promise ring is more like a…pre-engagement ring.

Shepard: A promise of "forever".

Denver: Hmm…I think this could work.

Denver: I also just want to point out that some people DO have a FOREVER.

Shepard: A very, very small number of people, as at least 50% of all marriages end in divorce.

Denver: Your optimism is the highlight of my day.

Shepard: So you're saying texting with me is the highlight of your day?

Denver: If that's the way you need to spin it, sure. We'll go with that.

Shepard: Oh, it's spun all right.

Shepard: Anyway, I'm going to talk to AJ about it tonight. I know you already told Allie…do you think she'd freak if AJ changed it to a promise ring?

Denver: No. I'll just lie and tell her I got them mixed up.

Denver: Easy peasy.

Shepard: Lying to your best friend is that easy?

Denver: I lie to her all the time. She always asks me if the outfit she's wearing looks good and I always say yes.

Denver: Spoiler alert: it's a 50/50 shot.

Shepard: I'm 97% certain you just broke girl code.

Denver: *shrug* It's worth the extra 30 minutes we don't spend going through her closet for another outfit.

Shepard: SHAME!

Denver: Shep?

Shepard: Yeah?

Denver: Shut up.

Denver: I'm a little jealous of what Allie and AJ have.

Denver: There. I owed you a secret.

Shepard: Well, you're about to owe me another one…

Shepard: I'm a little jealous of them too.

Denver: GASP! You? Shepard Clark, the cynic?

Denver: Do I have the wrong number?

Shepard: Don't you tell anyone!

Denver: I'm shocked.

Shepard: That I want companionship?

Shepard: Just because I don't believe in forever or tying myself to one person for years and years doesn't mean I'm a robot and have no feelings or needs.

Shepard: It'd just be nice to have…someone, ya know. Not necessarily a traditional relationship, but someone I can talk to and count on to always be there. And someone I can kiss on the regular.

Denver: What about your "girlfriend"?

Shepard: Penny is great, but I can't really make out with her anymore.

Denver: Your fake girlfriend's name is Penny? That's awfully close to Denny…

Shepard: Don't remind me.

Denver: You said "anymore". I'm gonna need details.

Shepard: Penny and I used to ACTUALLY date.

Denver: What happened?

Shepard: We had sex.

Denver: I'm sorry but…WHAT?

Shepard: We lost our virginity to one

another, Penny realized she was gay, and that was that.

Denver: Is this why you don't believe in love? Because you turned your first girlfriend into a lesbian with your terrible sex?

Shepard: First, rude. Second, it's an interesting theory, but no.

Shepard: I don't not believe in love, just not forever.

Denver: Right, but your feelings are totally changing.

Shepard: Oh, are they now? Why is that?

Denver: Because you're totally falling in love with me and wanna spend the rest of your whole life with me. It's why you bug me every day.

Shepard: Don't make me laugh, Den.

Denver: Admit it—you've been thinking about our double wedding.

Shepard: You should see the scrapbook I have for it.

Shepard: Our colors are outfield green and baseball stitches red.

Denver: You know, I can see that being exactly what you want.

Shepard: Let's not forget our venue: the comic shop, right near the Captain America comics because he IS the hottest Avenger.

Denver: Is this your way of saying you'll be my Bucky? Because we ALL know Cap and Bucky are secretly lovers.

Shepard: AHA! You ARE a nerd!

Shepard: And no, because I call dibs on Captain America. You can be MY Bucky.

Denver: Deal, but only if you say it's forever.

Shepard: "It's forever."

Denver: Shep…

Shepard: Fine, Den. Forever. You'll always be my Bucky.

Shepard: I like Sinatra.

Shepard: Actually, I hardly listen to any modern music.

Shepard: Now you owe me another secret.

Denver: I honestly think that might have been the most shocking thing you could possibly say to me.

Denver: I, too, like Sinatra and don't listen to modern music, though not by choice. There's your secret.

Shepard: That doesn't count!

Denver: Are you kidding me? The only person who knows we're not allowed to listen to modern music is Allie. That most certainly counts as a secret.

Shepard: Fine. I think it's a cop-out, but I'll allow it.

Shepard: I'm curious though…what kind of music did you think I listen to?

Denver: I don't know…Justin Bieber? Yeah, you totally seem like you have Bieber fever.

Shepard: I'm starting to rethink our wedding album…

Denver: You said forever, Cap.

Shepard: Forever, Bucky. Forever.

Seven

SHEPARD

"I'm here to see Denny."

The receptionist sitting behind the counter drops the pen he's holding, and the phone glued to his ear almost slips from his grasp as his jaw hits the floor.

"I am going to need to call you back, Henry. There's a...well, someone important is here and I'm sure his time is worth a lot more than yours." He slams the phone down on the receiver and beams up at me. "How may I help you, dear?"

"Good morning..." I glance down at the nameplate on his desk. "Eric. I'm here to see Denny."

"Denny?" He purses his lips. "Ah, yes. Miss Andrews?" He leans forward, moving the pen between his fingers with curious, excited eyes. "Are you on her appointment book for the day?"

I quirk a brow. "I'm not, but I have a feeling I can talk you into making an exception for me."

He laughs, tossing the pen onto the calendar covering his desk and pushing his chair back to stand. "You'd be right. I'll take you to her." He struts around the desk. "Follow me."

Eric leads me down a hallway filled with fingers clacking against keyboards, shouts for more coffee, and a flurry of people bustling from desk to desk.

Tucked away in a corner in the back of the building, Denny's head is bent over her laptop, her eyes glued to the screen.

It reminds me of college, the two of us working on the school paper together.

I'd have to talk my dick down every day watching her work her magic in that computer lab. It didn't matter that she ignored me every chance she got; that never stopped me from watching her every moment I could, because watching Denver was pure gold.

She loved working on the paper, loved the chance to get creative, to voice her opinion while still giving the facts. She was a master at it, a far better writer than I ever was.

Wearing headphones, she's completely absorbed in whatever's on the screen in front of her, so she doesn't hear us approach.

Eric waves a hand across the screen and she nearly jumps out of her seat at the unexpected interruption.

"Dammit, E!" she shouts, hitting the space bar and pulling her earbuds out. She glares up at him with annoyance. "It's a good thing I'm wearing a panty liner—I just peed a little bit!"

He chuckles. "Sorry, but you have a guest."

Finally, she spots me standing behind him, and her face pales.

I can't help but serve her my famous grin. "Morning, Den."

Groaning, she drops her head into her hands and mutters, "Eff you, universe. Eff you."

She takes another moment to compose herself before looking back up and smiling sweetly—it's false sweetness, by the way—at Eric.

"Thank you for bringing him over here. I'll take it from here."

He turns to me and sticks his hand out. "It was great meeting you, Mr. Clark. I'm a huge fan of your baseball pants."

"Eric!" Denny admonishes.

I burst into laughter and shake his hand.

"Thank you for the compliment. It was great meeting you. I'm sure I'll be seeing you a lot in the upcoming weeks."

His perfectly groomed brows shoot into his hairline as he looks between me and Denny.

"And why's that, Mr. Clark?"

"Didn't you hear? Denny and I are a thing now. We're—"

"You ass!"

Denny launches out of her chair, clambering around her desk—I'm certain she hits her hip on the corner—and covering my mouth with her hand.

"Not. Another. Word," she instructs through clenched teeth.

I laugh against her palm.

She gives Eric another falsely sweet smile. "Thanks, Eric. So much." Her words drip with sarcasm. "I'll let you know if we need anything else."

The receptionist shakes his head and laughs, heading back to his station, probably not wanting to be witness to Denver maiming me.

I can't blame him. For someone so tiny, she sure can pack a punch.

Denny returns her attention to me, hand still covering my mouth, eyes ablaze.

"I will murder you in your sleep, Shepard Clark. I don't give a shit if you're some hotshot baseball player or not."

I lift a brow in response.

"Don't test me. Tell me you're not going to test me."

I dart my eyes down to her hand.

"I don't trust you. Shake your head up and down if you promise not to test me."

I do.

"Good. Now——"

Before she can finish her sentence, I dart my tongue out and lick her palm, laughing as she wrenches it away in disgust. She groans and wipes her hand against her jeans.

"I am so going to get fired for murder."

"Just fired? Not jail time?"

"If it goes to trial, I'll just explain how obnoxious you are. I'm certain I'll be able to sway several jurors in my favor."

"Not if the jury is mostly women."

"Those poor, delusional women." She wipes her hand on her jeans again like she can't get rid of the feel of my tongue against her skin. "Why are you here, Shep?"

"Dress shopping."

"Excuse me?"

"For tomorrow. Our date." I sigh. "Don't act like you forgot. I know you've been counting down the hours." I glance at the watch on my wrist. "We're down to thirty-three now, in case you were wondering."

"I'm not going shopping with you."

"Oh, but you are. I need to make sure you don't embarrass me with your...eccentric outfit choices."

"First of all..." She holds her finger up in my face.

I bite at her.

She grimaces in poorly disguised disgust. "Can you not keep your mouth to yourself?"

"I——"

Denny holds her hand up. "You know what, don't tell me. Anyway, how dare you judge my fashion sense! It's...it's..."

"Awkward? Confusing? Basically nonexistent?"

"No!"

"No offense, Den, but I ran into you last week while you were wearing brightly colored yoga pants, a sweater that was about four times too big, and no bra." I lean down. "And by the way, I was so happy to see that your nipples were enjoying my eyes on them."

A surprised gasp escapes from her lips then her breaths grow labored. She's rattled. She *likes* that my eyes were on her.

I liked it too.

Collecting herself, she crosses her arms over her chest like she's protecting it from my prying eyes, which is pointless because she's unfortunately wearing a bra today. I already checked.

"It was the middle of the night!" she reasons—or attempts to.

"All I'm hearing are excuses. Besides, us shopping together means your dress and my tie will match."

"I could always text you a picture."

"You still have my number?"

Her attention falls to the floor as she stammers through an uncertain, "N-N-No."

I can't tell if she's stammering because she's lying or because she's ashamed she deleted my number.

I have never wanted somebody to be lying so badly in my entire life.

"I still have yours."

Her bewildered gaze finds mine, searching to see if I'm being honest.

I am.

I haven't used it in…well, years, but I have it. I still have all our texts too.

Technology is kind of amazing in that way. Nowadays, you can save texts from years past, hold on to the memories of before—you

80

know, before you turned your own life into shit with your insecurities.

There were moments when I wanted to delete her from my phone, from my mind—because of my own shame, nothing to do with her—but I couldn't bring myself to do it.

Erasing her wouldn't erase my mistakes, no matter how hard I tried to make that happen.

"I have all our texts too," I confess, still holding her stare.

Her pupils grow, and I swear I've melted the ice around her heart by at least an inch.

She licks at her lips, her eyes dropping to my chest as she says, "I'll go shopping with you, Shep."

DENVER

I should have insisted on taking my own car.

As it turns out, when it comes to Shepard Clark, I'm still the biggest idiot around.

"What are we doing here? I can't afford this store." He pulls his steel gray truck into the parking lot of a high-end store about an hour south of where we live. "And on top of that, you never said we were going so far away. I have a job to do, you know. I didn't even tell anyone I'd be gone so long."

"You really think your boss will be mad if you're out shopping with me?"

"You say that like you're someone special."

He side-eyes me with a shit-eating grin. "You know I am."

"They make medicine for that, you know."

"For what?"

"Your constipation. Being so fucking full of shit all the time has to start hurting after a while."

His boisterous laugh echoes as he pulls into a parking space. He slides his baseball cap off and tosses it onto the dash, running a hand through his messy hair. "Get your ass inside, Andrews."

We climb out of the truck and trudge into the store I cannot even remotely afford to shop in.

"Welcome to Landry's," says the saleswoman who opens the door for us. "What brings you in today?"

Shep hitches his thumb back toward me. "Miracles. We need to make miracles happen."

I sigh. "Are you going to annoy me forever?"

He spins around, smirking. "Quit pretending like you hate it—and me."

"No."

"You didn't even look!"

"Because I don't have to. It's not the right color."

I stand before him in a pale yellow dress that I think looks stunning.

He doesn't. Again.

Why is he always so judgy about dresses?

I groan. "You have shot down literally every single dress I've tried on, which has been like fifteen. How much longer are we going to have to do this?"

He sits there with one leg resting on the other, a bored expression plastered on his face as he scrolls aimlessly through his phone.

His eyes, though—they're giving away his pleasure.

He's enjoying every single second of this torment.

Bastard.

"I've told you ten times: try this stack on and we'll be good to go."

"I am *not* letting you pick my dress for me. It's bad enough I'm letting you pay for it."

"You're seriously still upset I'm buying you thousands of dollars' worth of very fancy dresses that you get to keep *forever*?"

"Yes," I say stubbornly.

"You can barely say that with a straight face." He points to the mound of fabric beside him. "Try them and we can leave."

"And if I hate them? Then what?"

He sighs. "Then we can still leave."

I march over to him, snatch the dresses up, and tuck myself away in the dressing room for the millionth time this afternoon.

I shoot my boss another quick text, letting him know I'll be even later than expected, and then I send my intern one too, apologizing for abandoning her with the mountain of work I have to do.

Neither of them give a shit because I'm with *the* Shepard Clark. *Ugh. Spare me.*

I somehow manage to wrangle the zipper down—I am *not* inviting Shep in here to help—and pull the first dress off the hanger.

It's black and boring and I really don't want to try it on.

Surprise overcomes me when I slide the dress on and glance at my reflection in the mirror. It fits like a glove, accentuating my curves in ways I didn't know a garment could for people who aren't Blake Lively or Eva Mendes.

It's conservative with no cleavage showing and long sleeves, so there's not much that screams *sexy* until you come to the diamond-shaped cutout on each hip. It's enough to make the dress suggestive, but not enough to take away from the classy look.

As much as I hate to admit it, Shep was right. This *is* the perfect dress.

"I'd do me," I say with a shrug.

"I'd do you too. Now get out here and show me how right I was."

Sighing, I push open the curtain and step out.

Shep sits forward. He moves his eyes over me in a painfully slow perusal.

Hunger—it's there in his gaze as he pushes up from the chair and stalks toward me with purposeful strides. My heart rate is soaring higher and higher with each step, so loud I'm certain he can hear it as he comes near.

He doesn't stop until he's just a few inches from me.

Cinnamon. He smells like cinnamon. I fucking love cinnamon.

"It's my gum," he says, and I realize I've said it out loud.

Shit.

I don't realize he's reached out to me until his fingertips graze softly over my exposed hip, the touch causing me to jump.

"Does it hurt?"

"Huh?"

"The bruise—does it hurt? I saw you hit your hip on the corner of your desk when you attacked me."

I glance down at where his fingers are resting against my skin, and for the first time, I notice there's a purple mark forming.

He's right, I did hit my hip, but I was so caught up in the moment that I didn't care. Then during the hour-long car ride here, I was so focused on trying not to stare at him in his insanely hot baseball cap that I stared at my phone the whole time and forgot my hip was throbbing.

"I forgot about it. I didn't realize it was starting to bruise."

"You'll have to save this dress for one of our later events so it can heal."

I find his gaze again and turn my face toward his. He's no longer staring at my hip. His swirling green and brown eyes are locked onto my own.

"You look beautiful, Denver."

There's something in the way he says it, something that grabs at my heart and tugs on the strings. I don't know if it's the way he uses my full name—something he hardly ever does—or if it's the fire in his eyes that's sending his words straight into my chest.

"I..."

My lips are his sole focus now.

I could recite the phone book for him and I don't think he'd ever look away.

Worse? I don't think I'd want him to.

"How'd you know?"

"What?"

"How'd you know this dress was going to be the one?"

With reluctance, he draws his eyes up to mine.

"If you think for a second that while you spent the last five years hating me, I've been blind to your body..." His hand trails down my hip, dipping way too close to my ass.

God do I hate that I want him to keep going.

"To these curves..." He moves his touch upward, his fingertips teasing me at the base of my back. "To your sheer fucking beauty..."

Light, feathery touches dance up my spine. Goose bumps break out along my skin, though I don't think he notices.

I don't realize he's inched me closer to him with each dance of anticipation along my body until I feel his arousal pressed against my thigh.

His fingers curl around my neck, the touch hard and soft and everything I never knew I wanted, particularly from him.

"I'm not blind, especially when it comes to you, Bucky."

I watch as his mouth descends toward mine, and I do nothing to stop him.

"Oh, miss! That one is *stunning!* The young man has a good eye. He—"

The saleswoman pops up out of nowhere just before our mouths make contact.

Thank god.

"Oh my, I am *so* sorry. I didn't mean to interrupt, Mr. Clark. I-I—"

Shep pulls away, unwinding his arm from around my back, and I miss his warmth more than I've ever missed anything in my entire life.

I take three healthy steps away from him, smoothing down the front of my unwrinkled dress, and try to get my breathing back to normal, refusing to look over at him for fear I'll try to climb my way back into his arms.

Treacherous body.

"It's fine, Annabelle." He runs a hand through his hair and clears his throat. "We'll take this one."

"And all the ones in the room, too," I add.

I don't have to look at Shep to know he's grinning victoriously.

I flip him the bird and he laughs.

Annabelle, unbothered by our antics, claps her hands together and says, "Splendid! I'll get everything rung up."

She disappears to the front of the shop again, leaving us drowning in the sexual tension.

Finally, after what feels like hours, I muster the courage to look at Shep.

He's watching me, eyes still starving for me like I'm his prey, and I want to be caught so badly.

Before I do anything I'll be sure to regret, I dart back into the dressing room, yanking the curtain closed between us.

He laughs, and for the first time in a long damn time, I hate Shepard Clark just a little bit less.

Nine

Six years ago, October

Shepard: I still can't believe we pulled it off.

Denver: Dodged one hell of a bullet AND they're both happy. We're basically gods.

Shepard: Me, maybe. You, not so much.

Denver: You're right—goddess.

Shepard: Of what? Nerds?

Denver: Shep…

Shepard: Kidding, kidding.

Shepard: I saw your photos from last night. I don't think that dress was quite right for you.

Denver: Gee. Thanks so much.

Shepard: Don't get me wrong, you still looked hot, but it wasn't a perfect ten.

Denver: That doesn't help.

Shepard: Fine, fine. I'd still bang you even in your horrible dress. Happy?

Denver: So happy.

Denver: ^That was sarcasm, just so we're clear.

Shepard: I figured.

Shepard: How was your evening otherwise?

Denver: It was fine.

Shepard: Fine? Just fine? Did your date not wine and dine you?

Denver: She did not, which isn't surprising considering it was my sister.

Shepard: You have a sister?

Denver: A twin sister.

Shepard: OMG. All my porn dreams are about to come true. HALLELUJAH!

Denver: You are disgusting and I question my sanity every single day when I realize I'm still texting with you.

Shepard: No you don't. We're friends now. Just face the facts.

Shepard: I didn't know you were a twin. I feel like there's so much I do and don't know about you all at the same time.

Denver: That's because you never ask. So self-absorbed.

Shepard: I can't even argue with that.

Shepard: Fine. What's her name? What do you want to be when you grow up? Where are you going to college? Name a place you want to travel.

Shepard: Look at me, asking questions and caring. I'm so proud of myself.

Denver: And just like that, we're right

back where we started—you being an arrogant jerk.

Shepard: Answers—let's have 'em.

Denver: Fine. My sister's name is Montana, but she goes by Monty, and—this will really blow your mind—I also have a younger brother named Charleston, Chuck for short.

Shepard: That's…odd.

Denver: Coming from Shepard?

Shepard: Fair. Please continue.

Denver: I want to be a journalist.

Shepard: Really? You like writing?

Denver: I like giving the facts while voicing my opinion. It's important.

Shepard: As an athlete, I agree. College aspirations?

Denver: Honestly? Anywhere that isn't here. I kind of hate my home life. It's not that there is anything inherently wrong with it, my parents take care of us just fine, but it's…well, boring.

Denver: I'll probably follow Allie to college.

Shepard: Where's she going?

Denver: Take a wild guess.

Shepard: Wherever AJ is going.

Shepard: You do realize that's here, right? We both got accepted on baseball scholarships.

Denver: No.

Shepard: Yep. Looks like we'll be seeing a lot of each other, Denny.

Denver: I think I'm going to be sick.

Shepard: Be sick, dance around with excitement—totally the same thing.

Denver: Gag me.

Shepard: No thanks. I'm not into asphyxiation.

Denver: ANYWAY.

Denver: With how boring I find life here, you can imagine that I'd like to travel anywhere. Like, literally anywhere has to be better than here.

Shepard: I dunno...I hear Missouri is pretty damn boring too.

Denver: Fine, anywhere but Montana and Missouri. No states that start with M.

Shepard: I think you can swing that.

Denver: What about you?

Shepard: Baseball. It's my life. It's all that matters. As long as I'm playing, I don't care where I'm at.

Denver: Even Missouri?

Shepard: Okay, maybe not Missouri.

Shepard: Oh, and since I asked you, I only have the one older sibling, Zach. He's a genius and I admire the shit out of him.

Shepard: Total nerd though.

Denver: Is he hot?

Shepard: Watch it... I think he's about to get engaged, actually, to his college sweetheart. I don't really like her, but don't tell either of them I said that.

Denver: It's too late. I've uploaded that to the internets.

Shepard: I don't think you even know how to make a status update, so I'm pretty sure my secret's safe with you.

Denver: You're not wrong.

Shepard: I just still can't believe I didn't know you were a twin this entire time. I could have been working on getting a threesome set up. So many missed opportunities.

Denver: Omg

Denver: No. We are not doing this. I'm going to bed.

Denver: Good night, Captain.

Shepard: I hope you have sweet dreams. I know I will. Night, Bucky.

Denver: Hate. You.

Denver: Found your Halloween costume!

Denver: DOWNLOAD ATTACHMENT

Shepard: Holy shit. Hang on a sec.

Shepard: DOWNLOAD ATTACHMENT

Denver: NO. WAY!

Shepard: Yes! I bought it today. Was going to surprise you with it.

Shepard: And since I'm Captain America, you HAVE to dress up as Bucky. It's the rules, Den.

Denver: No way.

Denver: How can I look cute dressed as Bucky Barnes?

Shepard: Just do it. It'll be our own little thing.

Shepard: Pleeeeeeeease.

Denver: I'm sorry, are you trying to give me puppy dog eyes via text?

Shepard: Yes.

Shepard: Is it working?

Denver: Possibly.

Shepard: If you do it, I'll be your best friend forever.

Denver: That feels more like a threat than a reward.

Shepard: That might be the rudest thing you've ever said to me, and you have said a LOT of rude things.

Denver: I am not rude!

Denver: I'm honest. There is a difference.

Shepard: True. It's one of the things I love about you.

Denver: Ooooooh, love. Shepard Clark said love!

Denver: Told ya you were falling for me.

Shepard: I am not.

Denver: Bullshit.

Shepard: BULLSHIT bullshit.

Denver: BULLSHIT BULLSHIT bullshit.

Shepard: BULLSHIT Bu omg I don't think I can keep this up.

Denver: I win.

Shepard: I think I'm starting to hate you, Denver.

Denver: *love

Denver: Fixed it for ya. <3

Denver: Happy Halloween, Shep.

Denver: DOWNLOAD ATTACHMENT

Shepard: HOLY FUCK

Shepard: You are definitely one hot Bucky.

Shepard: I'm saving that photo.

Denver: Not for anything pervy, I hope.

Shepard: Of course it's for something pervy—why else would I keep it?

Denver: Gross.

Denver: I'm headed to a party. I expect a photo of you too, Captain.

Shepard: DOWNLOAD ATTACHMENT

Denver: OMG PUT SOME FREAKIN' CLOTHES ON!

Shepard: What? You said you wanted a pic. I'm not dressed yet.

Denver: I meant of your costume. THE
COSTUME.

Denver: No wonder you're single.

Shepard: I have a girlfriend!

Denver: A girlfriend I'd have better
chances with.

Shepard: That cut deep, Den. Super deep.

Shepard: Enjoy your party. I'll send a
real pic later.

Denver: I swear, if there is a single
dick in the pic…

Shepard: Well, there could only be one.
I'm not going to sprout another dick
in the next hour.

Shepard: Though that could come in handy
for our threesome…

Denver: BLOCKED

Denver: Brace yourself. I'm about to
admit something crazy.

Shepard: I'm ready.

Denver: You are a genius.

Shepard: I know I am, but care to elaborate on why?

Denver: I got SO many compliments on my Bucky costume last night. I'm pretty sure everyone thought the gender flip was the greatest thing in the whole world.

Shepard: I kind of figured you were…popular. I saw your photos on BookFace.

Denver: You did?

Denver: I didn't get any notifications from you.

Shepard: That's because I didn't like them.

Denver: Oh. Okay.

Denver: Did I do something wrong?

Shepard: Not at all, Den.

Denver: Then why do I get the sense you're mad at me?

Shepard: I'm not mad at you, I'm mad at me.

Denver: Wanna talk about it?

Shepard: Not tonight. I'm tired. Maybe later?

Denver: Yeah. Sure. I'll talk to you later, I guess.

Shepard: I'm glad you had fun at your party last night.

Denver: Are you though?

Denver: Shep?

Denver: Okay. Good night.

Ten

SHEPARD

Don't kiss her. Don't kiss her. Do not fucking kiss her.

It's the same thing that's been on repeat in my mind since yesterday in the dress shop.

It's the same thing I'm repeating now as she stands before me in a royal purple dress looking like sex wrapped in satin.

I loathe dressing up and rubbing elbows with people. It's stuffy and all they do is gloat about how much money they have in their pockets and who they know.

Don't get me wrong, I'm a cocky bastard when it comes to being a baseball god, but the rest of that shit? The money, the fame? I don't give two fucks.

I love baseball. I *need* baseball.

That's where the line is.

But this punishment my PR team and agent are making me endure?

It's almost worth it to see Denny in this dress.

I want to shove her back into her apartment and rip the overpriced garment from her body and make her scream my name...finally.

Instead, I hand over the bouquet of flowers I've brought for her.

"What's this?" She stares down at them, surprised.

"Flowers, for you."

"Well...well, thank you. I think." She runs her fingertips over one of the petals. "Come on in. I'm almost ready."

I follow her inside, closing the door behind me as she makes her way into her small kitchen.

She grabs a vase from one of the cabinets on the island and begins filling it with water. "What kind of flower is it?"

"Alstroemeria. It symbolizes friendship."

She glances at me over her shoulder, brows lifted high. "Friendship? Is that what this is?"

"I hope it can be."

"I-I...I don't know, Shep."

"We used to be really good at being friends, Den."

Shutting off the water, she turns to me, drying her hands on the towel sitting on the countertop. She regards me with cautious eyes. "We were, but we messed that up and let feelings get involved."

"We don't have to let them this time."

"Is that even possible?"

No. "Yes."

She nods and lets out a shaky breath. "All right. Let's do it then. *Friends.*" She tests the word out on her tongue like it's a foreign language.

In many ways, it is—for us, at least.

We started out as friends, sure, but it wasn't long before everything became...well, more.

I fell first, and hard.

But how could I not? She was smart and kind and funny. It didn't hurt that she was beautiful, too, and it didn't matter that she was over two thousand miles away.

I fell. I was ready for us, for a future.

Until I lost my nerve and wrecked us.

"We can be...*friends*."

There's a spark of hope that flares to life inside me.

"I'd like that, Den."

"Just try not to fall in love with me this time, Cap."

I wasn't prepared for tonight at all.

Not for the media hounds peppering me with question after question and not for all the fake smiles I'd have to plaster on my face.

I most fucking definitely was not prepared for Denny.

God, the woman oozes charm and wit and pure sex. I've spent half the night with my cock straining against my dress slacks.

Thank god the lighting is low and everyone is too captivated by her to pay me any mind, or else they'd be getting one hell of a show.

"Clark, where did you find this girl? I think I'm in love," says my teammate Joe, not giving a shit that his own date doesn't care much for his admiration of mine.

My jaw ticks and I bring my champagne glass to my mouth, sipping at it so I don't wring Joe's neck. "Don't you have a date for the night?"

He shrugs and leans in toward me so only I can hear. "She's a boring lay. Been there, done that, not interested in going back. But seriously, man, if you're not planning on keeping this broad around,

I'll gladly take her off your hands."

"I'd step away if I were you, Joe." Another teammate, Braxton, joins the conversation, and I appreciate the help. "Don't you know this is the same girl who got Gerard knocked out last month?"

Braxton was there that night, the only one able to talk some sense into me before I broke shit beyond any sort of repair. He was insightful enough to know it was about the girl Gerard was talking about, but how he knows Denny is that girl is beyond me.

His voice carries enough to catch many people's attention…including Denny's.

Standing on the outskirts of the circle, mid-conversation with another one of the guy's dates, she sends me a questioning look.

I avoid her stare, suddenly finding the bubbles in my glass very interesting as I take yet another sip.

I fucking hate champagne.

"Is that so?" Joe says, grinning. "You have one hell of a right hook."

"I know," I tell him, my voice conveying the message instead of my words. *Back off, dude.*

He gets it, loud and clear. Still grinning, he holds his hands up, backing away. "I'm tapping out. I saw the aftermath, and my face is way too pretty for that kind of reconstruction."

I dare a peek over at my date.

She looks confused, and I already know I'm going to be hammered with questions on the ride home.

Goddammit, Joe.

A reporter corners a handful of the guys, leaving just me and Braxton off to the side. The press knows better than to bother me too much.

"How'd you know that was her?" I say out of the corner of my mouth, not looking at him, eyes still settled on Denny.

"Because of this right here."

I glance at him, confused. "Let's use some real fucking sentences, shall we?"

"That right there, that small flick of a glance my way—it's one of about five times you've looked away from her all night. You might have introduced her as Bucky, whatever the hell that's about, but it's easy to see that's Denny."

He didn't go to college with me and Gerard, so he has no idea who Denny is…how important she is to me. None of the others that night knew either, not even Gerard, which is probably why they were so freaked out when I pounced on him for bragging about what an easy bang Denny was.

I don't try to act like I'm a good guy, don't hide the fact that I can be a huge fucking ass and have been one in the past. I've made massive mistakes, ones that have changed relationships with people I love. I've bragged about my conquests. I've treated women like toys. I might be a king, but I never said I wasn't an asshole too.

That said, I am trying to change, trying to be a better man, one worthy of love.

One worthy of Denver.

I just hope she can see that too.

Like I conjured her up, she appears in front of us.

Braxton steps toward her, holding his hand out. "Hi, I'm Braxton James. I play with this douchebag over here."

"Oh, I know exactly who you are, Mr. James. You have one hell of a batting average."

She takes his hand, and the strength of the champagne glass I'm holding is tested when he brushes his thumb over the back of hers in a not strictly friendly way.

Fucker.

"I'm Denver, or Denny to some, Bucky to this asshole, and I'm only here with him because he's blackmailing me."

"Blackmailing, huh?" Braxton looks my way. "Yeah, that sounds like him."

I flip him off and he laughs.

"I'm going to head out. Party's winding down and I've done my duty." He turns back to Denny. "If you need any rescuing, you just let me know. I'll take care of you." He winks at her, knowing he's getting under my skin, then pulls me into a bro hug, clapping me on the back just a little too hard. "Don't fuck it up, dick."

I push him away, glaring. "Get bent, Braxton."

He just laughs then says, "Great meeting you, Denver. Have a good night."

He disappears into the crowd and my jaw relaxes for the first time in several minutes.

We're left alone, and I know Denny is dying to shoot many questions at me, questions I'm not ready to answer just yet.

I'm spared when a few other players stop by to bid us good night, and then it's finally our turn to leave.

It's a rule with the players. We have a roster, rotating who gets to leave charity events first and last, spacing out our departures by at least fifteen minutes.

Tonight, Denny and I are second to last, and for the first time in…well, ever, I want to stick around the stuffy gala just to avoid a car ride with a beautiful woman.

"It's our turn," I tell her, having explained the roster on the way here. "I'll go grab our coats."

She says good night to a few people she's met this evening—because of course Denny, social butterfly that she is, would make friends at the gala—and I head to the coat check.

We're quiet the entire time, even standing there in the cool night air not saying a word as the valet pulls my truck around.

He hands over the keys and I give him a well-deserved tip for not messing my baby up.

I'm surprised when I turn around to find Denny sitting in the driver's seat.

I wrench open the door. "Fuck no. Move it, Bucky."

"Not happening. You drank tonight. I'm driving."

"I had a few sips of nasty champagne."

She holds her fingers up. "You had three. That's enough for me to not want you to drive. Get in and shut up."

"It's not even real alcohol!" I argue.

"A drink is a damn drink."

I did knock down three glasses, but I'm not drunk. If I were to drive right now, I'd be fine.

Which is probably exactly what someone who shouldn't be driving would say.

"Fine," I grumble, climbing inside. "But I swear, if anything happens to my truck, I'll kiss you."

Her lips twitch at what we both know is a non-threat.

"Just for that, I promise to drive extra careful."

She adjusts the seat, pushes in the brake, and hits the button to start the truck.

"I've never driven a truck before."

"I can tell. You look stiff."

She darts her eyes down to my lap. "You've looked stiff all night."

"I'm sorry—did you just admit to looking at my dick all night?" I smirk at her. "My, my, Denny. I didn't expect this from you."

"You know what, on second thought, maybe I *will* wreck this truck, put us both out of our misery."

"So you *want* me to kiss you?" I grin, knowing I have her trapped.

She groans. "I thought I told you to shut up, Shep."

Laughing, I unbutton my jacket and settle into the seat, shuffling around the heels she's thrown on the floor.

"Are you driving barefoot?"

"No."

"Then where are your shoes?"

"On my feet. Remember that bag I tucked into the back? It has normal people clothes in it for when we stop and grab burgers."

"I'm sorry, but for when we *what*?"

She lifts a shoulder. "Grab burgers. What part of that is hard to understand?"

"Did you have this planned?"

"Yes."

"What the hell?"

"What?" she says innocently. "I know you hate stuffy social gatherings, so I figured you'd be drinking. I also know they most definitely do not serve delicious foods at those things and therefore knew I'd be *starving* by the time it was over, and I *also* knew I would one hundred percent be ready to get out of this dress for the hour-long drive home."

She glances at me when I don't say anything.

"What? I like to be prepared."

"You just wanted to drive my truck."

"Yes, this was all one big elaborate scheme to drive this sexy beast."

I rub the dashboard. "She is sexy."

"She?"

"Yes. Shelia. Isn't she a beauty?"

"You're so weird, Shep."

"You're secretly into it, Den."

"Gag me."

"I thought we established that I'm not into asphyxiation."

"I'm about to gag you," she threatens.

"So *you* are into it. I'll make a note for later. Maybe it's something we can try together."

I'm not surprised when she reaches over and pinches my thigh...*hard*.

"Brat."

"You're secretly into it," she fires back.

DENVER

"Would you fucking quit it?"

"What?" I say through a mouthful of food. *Real attractive, Denny.*

"Moaning. It's annoying."

I grin. "Bullshit. Annoying is code for getting you all hot and bothered."

He rolls his eyes and takes another bite of his burger, which tells me my assessment is spot-on.

I stopped at the first burger joint I could find and forced Shep to buy me dinner as I changed into something much more comfortable.

My legs swing back and forth as we sit on the tailgate of his truck—because he wouldn't let us eat in the cab—as we finish off the last of our meals.

I stuff my face with another handful of fries.

"Hot, Den. Real hot."

I steal one of his fries just for his remark.

"Adding thief to your resume now, huh? Here." He hands me his milkshake. "Might as well take this too."

"You know what, I *will* take this, but only because you owe me an ice cream."

"I do?"

"Yes. You stole mine last week—or did you forget already?"

"Huh." He looks out at the parking lot, grinning. "Must have slipped my mind."

The lights are illuminating him in a way that makes him look like the god everyone seems to think he is.

Shep in jeans and a tee is hot enough. Shep sitting on the bed of a truck in a tux?

I might as well just throw my panties on the ground right now because *holy shit.*

Watching him work the room tonight was...unexpected. He was kind, polite, patient—basically the exact opposite of the cocky-in-a-not-so-sexy-way Shep I knew throughout college. Tonight, it was almost like he was the Shep I knew before.

The Shep I miss.

But the man he was tonight doesn't align with who he was last month...which is as confusing as it is concerning.

I've been trying to bite my tongue, but there have been so many questions rolling around in my head since we left.

What did that guy mean when he said I'm the one who caused the fight Shep was involved in last month? How would that even be possible? I wasn't anywhere near that area. Hell, we weren't even on speaking terms then. I still hated him.

Well, hated him as much as I could.

"Quit staring. It's rude."

Caught red-handed, I avert my gaze.

Just ask him.

"You can ask, you know. I've been waiting for it all night."

I sit up straighter, weirded out that he knows what I'm thinking. "Ask what?"

"Don't play games, Bucky. It doesn't suit you. You can ask what Braxton meant."

"What did Braxton mean?" The words tumble from my lips even though I'm scared of the answer.

"You remember Jacob Gerard from college? Played on the team with me?"

"I can't picture his face but the name sounds familiar."

I watch the muscles in Shep's jaw jump. "He remembers you, Den—quite well, actually."

"Okay," I say, stretching the word out, confused. "What about him?"

"Last month I was up north, hanging with some guys from the team and some from college after one of the games. Gerard was there. We were sitting around…" He pauses, trying to choose his next words carefully. "Let's just say we were talking about our college experiences."

The way he says it gives it away.

"You mean your college conquests."

He shuffles around uncomfortably, and I can't help but laugh.

"Trust me, Shep, I know you're not a virgin. The whole fucking college knew you weren't a virgin. No need to act shy about it now."

"You weren't exactly an angel yourself."

"You'd be real damn surprised," I mutter.

He's right, I wasn't an angel in college. I had my fair share of flings and fun, but I didn't sleep around as much as people tended to say I did. In fact, most of the guys I brought home with me just ended up getting to second base and that was as far as things went.

I knew they were running back and telling their friends they were scoring homeruns, but I didn't care, because I knew it was pissing Shep off.

Hence why I "dated" half the baseball team.

He'd get so mad every time he'd see one of his teammates with me. I loved to see the way his teeth clenched together, the nagging *that could have been mine* feeling that shone through his eyes.

Was it petty of me to flaunt that in front of Shep? Sure, but it was wrong of him to break my fucking heart too.

Fair is fair.

"What does that mean?"

"Nothing," I tell him. "Tell me what I have to do with what happened last month."

His knuckles turn white as he clenches the edge of the tailgate, staring out into the parking lot with rage and annoyance on his face.

"You might not remember Gerard, but he definitely remembers you. I had to sit through a rather detailed description of your…time together before he told us your name."

He's upset—fuming almost.

"And your asinine conversation earned him a good beating because…"

"Because it's you, Den!" he explodes, leaping off the truck. "Because I had to hear in excruciating detail about all the things that should have been mine!"

His? HIS?!

"You have got to be kidding me, Shepard. *You* ruined us!"

I take a few deep breaths, trying to calm myself, not wanting to let him get the best of me yet again.

"It was you," I repeat, quieter. "Not me. You don't get to be mad at me for moving on with my life, especially not when you *more than* moved on. If you think I haven't had to hear all about your escapades, you're dead wrong, buddy."

He stands there, breathing hard, chest pumping with adrenaline.

"Is that why you hit him? Because I had sex with him?"

"No. I hit him because he didn't respect you enough to keep his fucking mouth shut about it."

I'm taken aback by his words. "You say that like you've never participated in that kind of bragging before."

"I have." He nods. "You're right. But I'm not that person anymore. I *can't* be that person anymore. I have to be better. I've lost too much being that guy."

"Lost what?"

"Never mind," he mutters. "Point is, it wasn't okay for Gerard to do that shit, so I taught him a lesson."

"If you ask me—"

"I didn't," he interrupts.

I ignore him.

"I'd say it was just jealousy, not you wanting to teach him anything."

"Jealousy?" He laughs sardonically. "No, Den, that was definitely not jealousy."

"Sounds like it to me."

Suddenly, he's stalking toward me, not stopping until he's shoved himself between my legs. My lips part on an involuntary gasp and his fiery hazel stare is drawn to the movement. Heat floods my core as his scent hits me, all man mixed with just a touch of cinnamon. My cheeks burn where his hand cups my jaw.

I don't move. I *can't*.

I'm entranced. Captivated.

And so fucking turned on it hurts.

"I wasn't jealous, Den."

"N-No?" I stammer.

"No, because I know if I wanted to—and I mean if I really

fucking wanted to—I could have you, anytime, any place. You can't say no to me, Bucky."

"I can too."

"Bullshit."

"*Bullshit* bullshit," I whisper.

His lips fall to mine with a gentleness I wasn't expecting.

He pulls back, looking into my eyes, that angry fire now replaced by a yearning one.

Is this okay? they ask.

It's not okay…yet it's the most euphoric I've ever felt.

It's not okay…yet I want it more than anything I've ever wanted before, even though I shouldn't.

It's not okay…but in this moment, I don't care. I want it too badly to care.

I press my hand to his cheek, running my fingers over the stubble already growing there.

He takes it as the yes it is, and this time his lips aren't gentle. They're hard and demanding and filled with so much unvoiced want.

Want that's been bottled up for years and years.

Want that's been hidden behind facades and insults and lies to make ourselves feel better about what we really want.

Shepard Clark doesn't hate me. He never hated me.

And I never hated him either.

Our tongues twist together as I wrap my legs around his waist.

Through my thin leggings, I can feel his cock brushing against my wet pussy, and I wish there were nothing between us, wish he would lift us up into the bed of his truck and have his way with me.

Without warning, he picks me up, carries me around the passenger side, and pulls the back door open. He tosses me inside like I weigh nothing, and I scoot until I'm on the other side of the cab, shoving my overpriced dress onto the floor. He climbs in after me, not stopping until I'm lying underneath him.

"That's a lot better," he mutters before his mouth finds mine again.

His dick presses back against my center and the friction nearly sends me over the edge.

It's also enough to knock me out of the haze I'm in.

What the hell am I doing?

I can't do this, not with Shep, and certainly not in the back of his truck.

I push at him and he instantly pulls away, but that doesn't stop him from rocking his hips against me one more time.

"We have to stop."

He rests his head against my chest, his breaths labored and erratic, matching my own. "I know, but I *really* don't want to. My dick will probably fall off if we stop now."

I laugh at his dramatics. "Guess you'll just have to be dickless."

"I don't think you'd like me near as much then."

"I don't even like you now, Shep."

That's not a lie, and we both know it.

I don't like Shep, but I don't hate him either.

We're walking this thin line, the same one we've always walked, and right now it's too much. I don't know what to do with it, but I know for sure I don't want to do something I'll regret later...like letting him fuck me in the back seat of his truck.

He pulls back, sitting up and scrubbing a hand over his face. "You're right. Our first time can't be in the back of a truck."

"You say that like I was going to sleep with you."

He leans over to press a hard kiss to my lips, and I let him, our tongues quickly becoming a tangled web.

Before it can escalate—well, any more than it already has—Shep pulls away, grinning like he knows something no one else does.

"What'd I say about games, Den?"

I shove him away and he laughs.

"So while you were plotting your whole evening so you could drive Shelia, did you think about the fact that I drove us to the gala? From your apartment?"

Shit. I totally forgot about that.

"Yes," I lie. "I was going to Uber from your place to mine."

"You were going to call a car at this hour? And what—get murdered?"

He throws my words from last week back at me with a grin.

Can't believe I just kissed this asshole.

Actually, yes, I totally can.

He's hot and I'm horny. Anything will do right about now, even Shep...especially Shep.

Oh my god, shut up, Denny!

"I'm using this exact moment as justification during my murder trial."

"That sounded a lot like, 'You're right, Shep, that's just insane. Can I please stay the night? I promise not to molest you at two AM...or maybe I don't.'"

"Huh. That sounded *nothing* like that, especially the last part."

"Our lines are definitely getting crossed then," he says seriously.

"I'm not going home with you, Shep."

"What if I promise not to get frisky with you at two AM?"

"Or three...or four...or five, for that matter."

"Well, shit." He sighs. "There goes my whole plan for the night."

"Creep."

"You love it." He pokes my cheek. "But, seriously, Den, stay the night. We can sleep in separate bedrooms. It won't be weird at all. It's late, and by the time we get back, it'll be after midnight. I'm sure you're tired. Stay."

He's right. I *am* tired. Sure, he claims we don't live too far from each other and I *probably* wouldn't get murdered on the ride home, but I don't want to risk it.

There's just the unpleasant matter of staying in Shep's domain for an entire night.

That part might be tricky.

"We're friends, right? This is something friends would do."

"Would friends also make out in the back of a truck like horny teenagers?"

"Totally." No hesitation from him.

"Shep…"

"Just say yes," he insists.

I want to say no. I *should* say no. It's on the tip of my tongue…

"Yes."

I'm going to regret this in the morning, I know it already.

"You coming?"

I glance up at the looming building, unsure I want to walk inside.

When Shep said we live close to one another, he wasn't kidding.

He just forgot to mention that while I live in the *nice* part of town, he lives in the *fancy as fuck* part.

"I'm coming."

"Oh, you will be."

He chuckles then grunts when I whack him with my patched-up duffle bag.

"Good lord." He rubs at his shoulder. "What do you have in that raggedy-ass thing I'm pretty certain once belonged to a homeless person?"

"It did not!" I look down at my bag, which has seen better days. "It's just well loved."

"That's one way of putting it." He snatches it from my hands and leads us into the building, nodding at the security guard in the front lobby. "Evening, Jim."

"Mr. Clark, you're back late. Lookin' mighty sharp too. A date?"

"Gala."

"Oh goodness. Those things are always so stuffy."

"We raised a hundred thousand for charity, so it wasn't all bad."

"We did?" I say, surprised.

Shep ducks his head, refusing to meet my eyes. "It'll go to a baseball camp for kids with diabetes." He waves a hand. "It's no big deal. We donate all the time."

"We?"

He nods shyly, which is weird because shy isn't a word I'd use to describe Shep. "Me and a couple of other guys. I don't usually attend the events, but I always donate to them."

"I...I didn't know that."

He shrugs. "You didn't ask. Now move it. I have things to do."

"What in the world could you possibly have to do at almost midnight thirty?"

"Take care of Steve."

"Who's Steve? A neighbor?"

He guides me inside the elevator, ignoring my questions. "Good night, Jim."

"See ya later, Mr. Clark."

The elevator doors close, and the fact that we're alone suddenly hits me.

Panic begins to claw at my throat.

I'm going to Shep's apartment. I'm staying the night with him—willingly.

Am I insane?

The doors open and we step out of the elevator, turning left, not stopping until we reach the end of the hall.

I can't help but smile when I see the number on the door.

"23?"

He smirks, pushing the key into the lock. "I asked for it special."

It's been his jersey number for years. He used to say it was his lucky number because everything good in his life happened on the 23rd.

He was born on the 23rd.

His parents were married on the 23rd.

Rose met Jack on the 23rd.

He was 23 when he was drafted to the MLB.

He texted me on the 23rd.

23 is his version of fate.

"Take your shoes off, please."

He disappears down the hall as I walk into the entryway, surprised Shep is one of those *no shoes in the house* kind of people, and toe off my slip-ons.

His apartment is just as I pictured it. Dark gray hardwood floors cover the majority of the space, nicely contrasted with light gray paint on the walls. The furniture is all black, sleek, and modern.

It's clean, welcoming.

There's a scratching along the floors, a skittering that can only belong to one thing.

"Steve!" Shep shouts just as the puppy comes barreling around the corner, sliding right on top of my feet.

"You have a pug!" I stare down at the smiling dog, laughing as his tongue flops out of his mouth. "I've always wanted a pug!"

Shep already knows this.

Am I the reason he got one?

"Bucky, meet Steve Rogers Clark."

My eyes snap to Shep. "You named your dog Steve?"

He lifts a shoulder. "What? A guy can't name his dog after America's first Avenger?"

"Uh huh," I say, unconvinced that's why he did it. "Can I hold him?"

"Best I take him out to the balcony real quick so he can pee. I have one of those fake grass pads out there to train him." Shep scoops the puppy up. "Make yourself at home. I'll be right back."

He carries the pup outside, leaving me standing there. I notice then he's taken my bag somewhere, so I go in search, beyond ready to head to bed.

There are only three doors off the hallway, so I try the first one—bathroom.

I try the second—guest room, but no bag in sight.

Which means…

No. No, he did not.

I push open the door, and yes, just as I expected, Shep has put my bag on his bed—his *very* big bed, I might add. Other than the small tables on either side and the all-leather headboard, it's the only thing in the room.

Like hell I'm staying in here with him.

Although…it is very inviting.

I walk farther into the room, stepping up to the bed and pushing down on the mattress.

Oh fuck.

It feels heavenly.

Without thinking, I flop down beside my bag, sinking into the comforter and never wanting to leave.

"I'm moving in."

"I mean, if you really want to, you can, but you're gonna have to chip in for your portion of the rent. I accept sex, sex, and lots of fucking sex as payment."

I groan, pushing myself up to my elbows to find Shep standing in the doorway, holding Steve, and watching me with an amused smile.

Long gone is his suit jacket, and he stands there in a crisp white shirt, sleeves rolled up to elbows.

He looks lickable.

I hate that I think he looks lickable, but Shep and no clothes is all I can think about since he kissed me.

Shep kissed me. And I let him do it.

What was I thinking? I can't let him kiss me.

But…it wouldn't feel so right if it was something so wrong…right?

"Comfortable, Den?"

"I love your bed."

"I do too, but since I'm still feeling really goddamn charitable, I'll let you take the bed and I'll take the guest room."

"Deal."

His brows lift. "No arguments? That's a new one from you."

"I only have one condition."

He chuckles. "Of course you do. Name it."

"Steve stays with me."

"You're stealing my pug from me? Who am I going to snuggle with?"

"Use your imagination, Shep. Hand him over."

With reluctance, he nods. "Fine. Let me say good night first." He nuzzles the dog, letting him lick kisses all over his face. "I'm so sorry I'm leaving you with this crazy lady, Steve, but dad's gotta do it, okay? I'll make it up to you later with an extra long W-A-L-K and a bonus T-R-E-A-T." Another nuzzle. "Good night, bub."

He sets the pug down on the bed beside me, and Steve immediately trots up and rests on a pillow.

When I look questioningly at Shep, he shrugs. "What? That's his pillow."

I laugh, but it falls short when Shep fits himself between my legs, which are hanging off the edge of the bed.

Perfect fit.

Ugh.

He leans down, caging me in with his arms on either side of my head, holding his weight off me.

The *thump thump thump* of my heart is so loud it can probably be heard from miles away.

"W-What?" I whisper.

He pushes himself down farther, his nose connecting with the exposed base of my throat.

I bite down on my lip at the contact, doing everything I can to stifle the moan trying so desperately to leave my mouth.

Slowly, in the most painful manner you can imagine, he runs his nose up the column of my neck, not stopping until he's right under my ear.

There, he places the gentlest of kisses.

"Good night, Bucky," he murmurs in my ear.

Then he's gone, leaving me with a mess of pent-up frustration and a new realization.

No matter how much I know I should, there is no way I'm going to be able to walk away from him.

Twelve

Six years ago, November

Denver: Look, I'm just going to say it, okay?

Shepard: Um...okay?

Denver: What is your goddamn deal with me?

Shepard: What do you mean?

Denver: Don't give me that bullshit, Shep. Things have been off for weeks—since Halloween, actually.

Denver: Did I do something wrong?

Denver: I want to know because I want to fix this.

Shepard: You didn't do anything wrong, Denver.

Denver: You sure about that? Because you're making me feel like I did.

Shepard: You didn't. I did.

Denver: Oh goody. Riddles. I love those.

Denver: So we are clear...^SARCASM.

Shepard: Golly, glad you cleared that up, smartass.

Denver: Just stop playing games. I'm not into those.

Shepard: I'm not trying to.

Denver: You have one more chance to answer me or I'm finally going to block your ass.

Shepard: FINE.

Shepard: I... FUCK.

Denver: You fuck? Uh...congrats?

Shepard: No. Well, I mean, yes, but no. That's not it.

Shepard: This is just hard for me to say because it's really fucking stupid and I hate looking stupid.

Denver: I'm not going to judge you, Shep. I'll never judge you. You should know that by now.

Shepard: You will about this.

Denver: Try me.

Shepard: Fine. Okay.

Shepard: First…you didn't figure out how to take screenshots yet, did you?

Denver: EYE ROLL EMOJI. No, I didn't.

Shepard: Good.

Shepard: I was jealous.

Denver: Okay. Of?

Shepard: Your Halloween photos.

Denver: Because I looked way hotter than you?

Shepard: Quit making me laugh. NO.

Shepard: It's all those photos I was seeing with that guy's arm around you.

Shepard: I wanted to break it off and shove it up his ass.

Denver: That's…vivid.

Denver: You have nothing to be jealous of. That guy meant nothing.

Shepard: It didn't look like nothing.

Denver: I promise. It wasn't anything. He was just some guy I met that night. All we talked about was comics.

Shepard: So something you two have in common that we don't.

Denver: Quit your bitching. You and only you will always be my Captain.

Denver: I have to ask you something and I need a straight-up answer.

Shepard: I already know what you're going to ask.

Denver: Let me do it anyway?

Shepard: Okay.

Denver: Do you like me, Shep? Like as more than a friend?

Shepard: Yes.

Shepard: And it's really, really fucking annoying.

Shepard: I didn't mean to like you.

Denver: I know.

Denver: Told ya you were falling for me.

Shepard: Bucky?

Denver: Yeah?

Shepard: Shit up.

Denver: Give me your address.

Shepard: No. You're probably going to send me something weird.

Denver: It will only be as weird as you make it.

Shepard: Fine, but if you send me something weird, I'll have your address by that point and I'll send you something equally as weird.

Denver: I promise it's not weird. It's a Christmas present.

Shepard: We're doing gifts?

Denver: We are now.

Shepard: Christmas isn't for another month!

Denver: LESS than a month. Better start shopping.

Shepard: I'm sending you coal.

Denver: DOWNLOAD ATTACHMENT

Denver: ^I'll take that, please.

Shepard: I'm not buying you a puppy.

Denver: Not just any puppy...A PUG!

Denver: Do it and I'll be your friend forever.

Shepard: Keep dreaming.

Denver: Fine.

Denver: DOWNLOAD ATTACHMENT

Shepard: That is a $1,500 purse!

Shepard: I like you, but not that much.

Denver: Wow. I didn't know there were price limits on love, Shep.

Shepard: I said LIKE, not LOVE.

Denver: Keep telling yourself that.

Shepard: I will. It really helps me sleep at night.

Shepard: Speaking of sleep...I need to hit the hay. Apparently I need to get up early and hit the pavement if I want to get a job so I can afford your Christmas present.

Denver: I'll take a tan or black pug. I'm not picky.

Shepard: In the words of Aerosmith...DREAM ON.

Denver: Fine. Just make sure the purse is purple, you ass.

Denver: Good night, Cap.

Thirteen

SHEPARD

"Oh, fuck me," I mutter as I peer out the balcony door.

Denny's standing in the cold, the morning sun outlining her figure as she stares out over the horizon.

Steve sits at her feet, staring up at her like she's a goddess.

Watch it, Steve. I called dibs a long time ago.

She must have rooted around in my drawers because she's wearing one of my t-shirts—the number 23 stamped across her back is a dead giveaway—and a pair of my shorts that are way too big on her.

Guess she forgot pajamas in that Mary Poppins bag of hers.

Not that I mind. Seeing her in my clothes…well, it makes my already aching cock really fucking sorry it's not buried inside of her right now.

It could be, though.

I could march out there, scoop her up into my arms, and carry her back to my bedroom then spend the entire day inside her.

We both know I could do it. We both know she would let me.

And I want to…so fucking bad.

But AJ just called, and he and Allie want to do breakfast with their best man and maid of honor.

Duty fucking calls.

As if she can feel my eyes on her, she turns around and gives me a small wave.

I hold my hand up, telling her staying out there is fine. The last thing I need is for her to come in here and see my morning wood.

Coffee? I mouth.

She nods and turns back around to the view before her, paying me no mind as I continue to scroll my eyes over her body. So many curves, so much softness and sass rolled into one.

With reluctance, I turn away and head into the kitchen. I pull the canister of coffee from the cabinet and brew half a pot, which should be plenty for the two of us.

The balcony door slides open and Steve comes scampering inside, his feet barely getting traction on the hardwood floors.

"Morning, you little shit."

"Well, good morning to you too," Denny says.

"I meant this little traitor, but yes, good morning to you."

"Oh." She blushes. "Good morning. That coffee smells amazing."

"I know." I pull open the fridge. "I'm sorry to report that I don't have your coffee creamer here since I wasn't expecting you to stay over. I do have milk—will that do?"

"Ugh. I'll settle." She shuffles over to the island. "I hope you don't mind but I borrowed some of your clothes."

"Do you know how hot it is to see a girl wearing your clothes?"

"No. I'm usually annoyed when I find another girl wearing my clothes."

I roll my eyes, and she grins.

The coffee pot dings as it finishes up the brew and I pour us each a healthy cup of caffeine.

"What woke you up so early?"

Leaning against the counter, she blows on the hot java. "I'm naturally an early riser, though I probably could have slept another hour with your blackout curtains. I owe this early wakeup to Allie…again. She wants to meet and go over maid of honor duties."

"AJ called me too. They want to do breakfast in an hour."

She groans. "I know. I was hoping he'd have left you out of it though."

"Really? Even after last night?" I tease.

"*Especially* after last night."

"Does your mother know you lie this much?"

She pushes off the counter, sauntering into the living room. "I'm going to need more coffee to handle you today."

I watch as she pads around the space, looking at the knickknacks scattered along the custom shelving I have built around my flat-screen.

"You don't put your trophies out?"

"Nah. I'm full of myself, but not *that* full of myself."

"Could have fooled me," she smarts off. "You have a lot of balls."

"I hardly think two is a lot, but thank you."

She sighs. "A lot of *signed* balls."

"Ah, yes. I do. I got most of them when I was a kid, but I've managed to make a couple friends and score some extras in the last couple years."

"Must be nice to be famous."

"I'm hardly famous, Den."

"Around here you are. It's kind of annoying."

"Only kind of?" I tease.

"You're right—it's *massively* annoying. Do you know how hard it is to avoid someone when they're constantly thrown in your face?"

"So you're finally admitting you avoided me for four years?"

"I'd hardly call seeing you four times a week avoiding you."

"But you tried. You tried real fucking hard, always running out of class first, ignoring me at the paper, dodging me around campus. I once saw you enter a bar, make eye contact with me, and then leave— tell me *that* isn't avoiding me."

"Fine," she concedes, turning around to stare at me with hurt eyes. "I did try, but can you blame me, Shep? After everything?"

I look down at the cup in my hands, ashamed. "You're right."

"I know I am." She turns her attention back to the shelves. "It's nice to know you were watching me so closely though."

"It's impossible not to."

She pauses at my words, but only for a second.

When she stops at the last shelf, I don't miss the way her breath hitches, like she's surprised I kept her gift all these years.

"I've read them all multiple times."

Her shoulders rise and fall with her uneven breaths.

She likes that I kept the Captain America comics she sent me so many years ago. Even more than that, she likes that they're bagged and boarded even with being so well read.

Denny gives herself a small shake and strides toward the kitchen, setting her mug on the counter. "You should be keeping them in sleeves. I'll be ready to go in ten minutes."

"Oh my god, would you quit it? I didn't mess it up *that* bad."

"*This* is why I don't let people drive Shelia."

"You are so dramatic," she mutters in that smartass tone of hers I love. "Just drive. We're already late."

"We wouldn't be running late if you'd moved at more than a glacial pace this morning. You said ten minutes—that was definitely more like thirty."

"I had to do something with the rat's nest on my head."

I glance over at her disastrous-looking top knot. "Well, you missed a spot—or ten."

"It's *artfully* messy," she argues.

"How did you forget to pack pajamas but not an outfit for the day?"

She points to the bag she's holding on her lap. "That's what us girls call an emergency one-night stand bag. I didn't plan on needing pajamas."

"You're saying you planned on sleeping with me last night?"

She rolls her eyes. "This bag is not specific to our…situation last night. It's just a general one-night stand bag."

"Uh huh. You totally wanted to bang me last night, but I shot ya down. Couldn't let you take advantage of me in the back of a truck."

"I will yank Shelia right from your grip and run us into the nearest telephone pole."

"You wouldn't dare," I seethe, gripping the wheel tighter just in case.

"Try me."

I step on the gas, attempting to shave a few minutes off our drive…and keep Shelia safe from Denny.

There's a small yip sounding like it comes from the vicinity of the passenger seat as the car lurches forward.

Huh. Weird.

Ignoring it, I turn on the radio, and the sounds of Sinatra fill the cab.

"You still listen to this?"

I feel my cheeks begin to heat. "Yes."

"Are you still hiding your love of old-school music?"

"Yes."

She laughs. "I kind of like that I'm the only one who knows that secret."

"I did confess it to Zach, but he's not a real person, so you're still the only one. Not even AJ knows."

"Wow, I feel special," she says distractedly.

I glance over to see her slide open the zipper on her bag just enough to slip her hand inside.

"What are you doing, Den?"

"N-Nothing," she says, clearly guilty of something.

The bag moves.

I hit the brakes.

"Denver Andrews! Tell me you did *not* stuff my pug into your ratchet duffle bag."

"Well do you want me to lie to you then?"

"Denny!"

"What!" She unzips the bag fully and pulls Steve out, snuggling him against her face. "Look how cute he is."

"I cannot believe you right now."

"He was so lonely, Shep. I couldn't leave him in your apartment all by himself."

"We don't even have his leash."

She digs into the bag again, producing his leash, water bowl, and treats.

I shake my head, slightly annoyed but even more amused.

This woman, I swear.

"It's too late to turn back now. We'll be even later."

"How did I not notice this?"

She kisses Steve's nose. "Because you're a dumbass."

Surprisingly, Steve does a really good job in the car, Denny calming him down when we have to stop and his anxiety gets the best of him.

When we finally pull up to the restaurant, we're miraculously only ten minutes late.

Denny snaps Steve's leash on and gets out of the truck.

"Hope Allie and AJ don't mind sitting outside, Steve." She shakes her head at me. "Can't believe you're so codependent you brought your dog, Shep."

"I-I… You… You!" I sputter, dazed by her accusations. "I swear, Den, I'm going to kiss you today."

"I'll kiss you back." She winks. "Now go get us a table."

I shuffle inside, finding our friends and explaining to them the fact that we need to move this breakfast date outside because Denver is a psycho.

AJ finds it amusing. Allie's just confused about why we came together.

"What the hell is this?" she says to Denny as we all sit down at the new table outside.

Steve tucks himself into Denny's lap.

"This is Steve. Steve, meet Allie, your aunt."

"Oh my gosh, he is *so* cute. When did you get him?"

"He—"

"Just last night," Denny cuts me off. "Shep gave him to me as a gift. Isn't he just the sweetest?"

"What! You bought her a puppy?" Allie screeches.

"No, you nut. Your best friend is just insane," AJ tells her.

I point to my best friend. "What he said."

Though, if I'm being honest, I *did* buy the pug with Denny in mind.

I don't even want to admit how many hours I spent trying to find a way to get her that puppy for Christmas all those years ago, but I couldn't make it happen. I couldn't make the purse happen either.

So, I settled on sending her one of her favorite comics, signed. And coal, of course.

That pug never left my mind. When I found out I would be on disciplinary probation the rest of the season, I'd figured I'd have a long-ass time off to finally train a puppy, so I bit the bullet and here we are.

Denny covers Steve's ears. "You don't listen to a word they're saying about your new mommy. Meanies."

"Clinical," I remark.

Denver shields the dog's eyes and flips me off.

"Did you two ride here together?" AJ asks.

"We...did," I answer carefully, looking to Denny to see how she'd like me to answer that.

"I stayed the night after the gala. And no, before it's brought up again at a later point, Shep did not score a homerun with me. I'm not as clinically insane as he believes me to be."

Leave it to her to just put it all out there like that, like sex is completely normal breakfast conversation.

"Debatable," I argue.

"Hey! Be nice to my maid of honor."

"Tell your maid of honor she needs medical help and I'll consider it."

"He might not be *entirely* wrong, Denver," Allie admits with a smirk.

"Quit ganging up on me or I'll take my puppy and leave," she announces.

"*My* puppy."

She narrows her eyes at me. "For now."

Her lips twitch when I meet her stare, and I'm trying real fucking hard not to knock this table over and cover her mouth with mine.

Like she knows what's going through my mind, she lifts a challenging brow.

Oh fuck.

I scoot my chair into the table more, hoping to cover my growing dick.

Damn. What the fuck is wrong with me? It's like I'm fifteen and unable to control my boners all over again.

"Anyway," Allie says pointedly, interrupting our stare-down. "We're here to talk about important dates and duties."

She begins rattling off information, way more than I can process or care to process, and Denny takes it all in. She passes Steve to me, pulling her phone out and taking careful notes.

I order breakfast for Denny while AJ takes care of Allie, both of us way too afraid to interrupt them.

"So what gives, man?" my best friend asks quietly, the girls still absorbed by their discussion of flowers.

"What do you mean?"

The look he gives me says he doesn't buy my shit.

"It's just what Den said—she was tired after the gala last night and stayed over."

"Sure, understandable, but care to tell me why she was at the charity event with you in the first place? Last I heard you were taking Penny."

"Shh!" I whisper angrily, peering over at Denny and Allie to make sure neither of them heard that.

They aren't paying us a lick of attention.

"Keep that shit on the DL," I tell my friend.

He jerks his head back. "She doesn't know about that?"

"No, and I want to keep it that way."

"What are you up to, Shepard?"

"A bunch of none of your goddamn business."

My eyes drift back over to Denver, loving how animated and into the conversation she is. She's genuinely happy for her best friend, and I love that about her.

She once told me about her goals for life. She'd meet *the one* in college, they'd fall madly in love with just the right amount of angst in their relationship, and then when college was over, they'd get hitched, spending the rest of their days happy as fucking clams.

Or some shit like that.

I know she wanted that to be us.

I sure as shit screwed that one up.

"Just be careful, man," AJ says. "Last time you two were together it didn't end well. She wrecked you."

My eyes still focused on Denny, I tell him, "No, AJ, *I* wrecked us, and I'm not going to make that same mistake again."

Fourteen

DENVER

"I need you to not freak out when I tell you what I'm about to tell you."

"Well, that's super reassuring." Monty tosses her long hair over her shoulder. "Okay, I'm ready."

She sits across from me at the breakfast bar, another Wednesday already here, another stack of pancakes to be had.

I flip the one sitting in the pan, avoiding her curious stare.

"Wait!" She holds her hand up. "You're not pregnant, are you?"

"What? No! Babies are gross!" I shiver in disgust. "I'm *way* too diligent about that shit to get knocked up."

"Good." She sits back, looking relieved. "That's good. So, what's up then?"

I take a deep breath, ready to unleash years and years of secrets on my sister.

Luckily for me, I know she's way too nice to try to maim me for keeping my mouth zipped tight. Plus, she knows the kind of house we grew up in, knows why I needed to keep this secret.

At least I hope she knows.

"Okay, so, remember in high school how I told you I had this…pen pal?"

"I remember," she says.

"Well, remember when we started texting on my secret phone because I said buying stamps was getting too expensive?"

"Yes…though now I realize that doesn't make a whole lot of sense."

"No, it doesn't, especially considering those damn phone cards cost a whole hell of a lot more than a fucking stamp."

She laughs. "Very true."

I note the way she doesn't flinch when I use profanity, a huge step up from the Monty of last year.

I guess that's what happens when your prim and proper twin sister snags herself a tattooed bad boy…who also happens to be one hell of a sexy single dad.

If only I'd seen him first…

I move the finished pancake to a plate then slide it over to Monty.

"What about that though?"

"Well…" I drag out, pouring more batter into the skillet. "I was texting with a guy."

She lifts a cardigan-clad shoulder. She might be dating a bad boy, but the girl still dresses like she's a kindergarten teacher. "I kind of figured that much."

"He's…" I lick my suddenly dry lips and decide to just rip the band-aid off. "Fuck it. He's kind of the reason I moved across the country."

A crease forms between her brows. "I thought you moved to go to school with Allie."

"I mean, *technically* I did, but it was also because of him. He's best friends with AJ."

Her mouth drops open. "Oh. I wasn't expecting that."

"Yeah, well, I wasn't expecting him." I shake my head. "Anyway, I came out here to be with him. I—"

She holds her hand up again and I pause.

She swallows the food in her mouth. "Sorry. I had a question."

"Go on."

"When you say be with him, you mean…"

I sigh. "I was in love with him, Monty."

Her fork clatters to the plate and I glance over at her. She's shocked.

"But you didn't even know him!"

"Says the girl who met her boyfriend in a bar bathroom then proceeded to text him for weeks and weeks before falling in love with him."

Her shoulders sag in defeat.

"I didn't know him?" I challenge.

She shakes her head. "No, no, you're right." She stabs another piece of pancake and lifts her fork to her mouth. "Keep going."

I flip the pancake and continue. "Like I said, I was in love with him, like move across the goddamn country and leave my life behind kind of love. I was delusional."

"You were young."

"I was stupid," I argue. "I was so stupid because it turned out he didn't love me like I thought he did."

"What does that mean?"

The night of Shep's betrayal runs through my mind, but I refuse to relive that torment in story form with Monty.

The memories are bad enough.

"It's not important. We'll just say it didn't work out."

143

"But you'll tell me eventually, right?"

"Maybe when you're older," I tease. It's something I've always told her and something that's always annoyed her, because I'm only five minutes older than she is.

"Brat."

I point the spatula her way. "First, I cannot believe you just called me a brat. Second, now I'm really not telling you."

She rolls her eyes and I laugh. I've always loved the sassy side of my sister.

"Anyway, things didn't work out, so we went our separate ways, but I still had to see him all the time considering we attended the same college. Luckily Allie was kind enough to not try to force me to attend group dates with him, but that didn't stop him from whoring around campus." I grit my teeth together at the thought of seeing Shep with anyone other than me.

Not that I haven't seen it plenty of times—I have—but it doesn't make it hurt any less, even now.

"What does that have to do with now?"

"Well, he's kind of...back in my life."

"Because of the wedding, right? That should be over soon because your friends are loony enough to spring a wedding on everyone that's less than two months away."

"Breathe before you get yourself all worked up," I tell her, finding it very amusing how the thought of someone else rushing their big day makes *her* stressed out.

Only Monty.

"He's back because of the wedding, but there's more. I...well, I'm kind of whoring myself out for my career."

Her green eyes grow three times in size. "You mean you're sleeping with him for a *job*?"

"What? No! I'm sleeping with him because he's hot. The job part

144

is just a bonus." The words I just spoke hit me and I quickly backtrack. "Wait—no! I'm *not* sleeping with him."

"You're not?"

"No!" I nearly shout. "We made out last Friday and I stayed the night at his house—in a separate bedroom, though—but that's it. No other funny business. The only action I got was from Steve."

"And Steve is?"

"His pug."

She pushes herself off the barstool, slamming her hand down on the countertop. "He has a pug?! You go marry that man *right now*, Denver!"

Laughing, I busy myself with flipping my pancake onto my own plate and slathering some butter on the sweet deliciousness. Forgoing the syrup, I rip off a piece and stuff it in my mouth.

"I can't marry him. I haven't slept with him yet—what if he sucks in bed?"

She blushes. "You want to though."

"Huh?" I glance up to my sister, my mouth full of food, though that doesn't stop it from hanging open at her words.

"You want to," she repeats. "Sleep with him, I mean. Even after he hurt you, you still love him."

"I *do not* love him. I just…I think he's changed in the last five or so years. I'm not entirely opposed to giving him a second chance."

I can feel her eyes on me and do my best not to feed into the attention, tearing my pancake apart and stuffing piece after piece into my mouth.

"Do you think that's wise?" Monty says, and I note the worry in her voice.

I push off the counter with a heavy sigh, sliding my plate away from me, my appetite lost. "Probably not, but worst thing that happens is he breaks my heart again. I already know how to clean that mess up, so maybe it wouldn't be so bad."

"That's the dumbest thing I've ever heard, Denny."

"I know it is, but it's giving me the courage I need to finally go after what I really want from him—sex. Besides, we could always just do the whole no-strings-attached thing. We don't have to turn it into something more."

She laughs dryly. "Don't fall for that one. I did, and look where it got me."

"Where? Happy as hell? Madly in love with a walking, talking sex machine? Don't even try to complain about that."

Her cheeks heat again and she ducks her head. "Hush."

I gather our plates and rinse them off in the sink while Monty cleans up the mess I made with the batter.

"For what it's worth," she starts as she slides the butter back into the fridge. "I think you have a really good judge of character. If you think this guy of yours has changed, maybe he has. Go after it. See where it leads. Lord knows you need to find yourself a man and settle down soon before you become an old spinster."

"Oh my gosh, you catch yourself a man and suddenly we all need to immediately follow suit."

"I caught myself a man *and* a kid."

"How's that going anyway? Playing mom?"

She sighs contentedly. "It's amazing. I love the little rascal, and his dad."

"I love seeing you so happy, Monty. It's about time."

"I agree." She tucks the syrup away and closes the cabinet. "Now explain this…exchange you're doing for a job."

"Ah, yes, that." I load the plates and skillet into the dishwasher before turning to her. "Well, I promised him I'd be his date to some charity events and to the wedding—which, by the way, you're coming to—in exchange for him giving me an exclusive for the paper. He's notorious for not doing interviews, so it's kind of a big deal, like get me that promotion I've been after for months kind of big deal."

"That one with the cushy office?"

"That's the one, sis." I shoot a finger gun in her direction. "A few measly dates are *totally* worth the exclusive."

She opens her mouth but snaps it closed again just as quickly, shaking her head. Her lips tuck inward, like she's trying to keep them from moving on their own.

"Out with it," I demand.

"I-I...I..."

"Montana Andrews, tell me right now."

"Fine." She holds her hand up. "Fine. It's just that...is the interview worth the potential heartbreak?"

Is the promotion going to make things easier for me in my field? Yes. Is it going to give me a few extra bucks a month to squirrel away for my student loans? Hell fucking yes. Are the games I have to play with Shep in order to get it worth all that?

"I don't know, but I'm willing to find out."

She nods, her lips still pressed tightly together. "Just be careful, Denny."

I grin at her. "Where's the fun in that?"

Fifteen

Six years ago, December

Denver: You didn't.

Denver: PLEASE tell me you didn't!

Shepard: I don't know what I didn't do, but if you say I didn't do it, I definitely didn't do it.

Shepard: God, that was confusing.

Shepard: What are you going on about?

Denver: I got my Christmas present today. There are HOLES in the box.

Shepard: IT IS NOT CHRISTMAS, YOU HEATHEN! Last I checked Christmas was celebrated December 25th, and it is most definitely only December 23rd.

Denver: If you think I'm waiting TWO WHOLE days to open this, you're clearly on drugs.

Shepard: Cocaine. It's the rich man's drug.

Denver: I'M OPENING IT!

Shepard: SPOILER ALERT: it's not a puppy. I just put the holes in there to be funny and confuse you.

Denver: WAY TO RUIN THE SURPRISE!

Shepard: I got my gift too, but I've been waiting to open it like the goddamn gentleman I am. Does this mean I get to open it?

Denver: I'm 9% certain you're not allowed to say "goddamn" when referring to a Christmas present.

Shepard: Only 9%?

Denver: Ugh. I meant 97%. OBVIOUSLY.

Shepard: Of course. How could I not know

that?

Denver: On the count of three, let's both open them.

Shepard: Too late.

Denver: CHEATER!

Shepard: I was kidding.

Denver: One…

Shepard: Two…

Denver: GO!

Denver: Oh duck. HOLY DUCK, SHEP.

Shepard: I'm 9% certain I did not send you a duck.

Denver: Are they all signed?!

Shepard: Yes.

Denver: OH MY GOD!

Denver: But how?!

Shepard: I bought a Sharpie and signed them. Duh.

Denver: No you didn't. I see the letter of authenticity.

Denver: How did you get your hands on these?

Shepard: eBay. Did you know people are super nerdy and super into their signed comics? I had no idea there was that much out there.

Denver: This had to have cost a fortune. You really shouldn't have done this.

Shepard: It was nothing. I mean, sure, I'll be working until I'm 70 to pay off the debt, but it's no big deal. You're worth it.

Shepard: I hope.

Denver: Thank you. Seriously. This means the world to me.

Denver: Did you open yours yet?

Shepard: No. I'm waiting until Christmas because I'm a goddamn angel.

Denver: 9% certain, Shep. 9%.

Denver: So...did you open it?

Shepard: It is 7AM. Are you insane?

Denver: Um…IT'S CHRISTMAS! Wake your ass up!

Shepard: I told you Santa wasn't real. Go back to sleep. He won't be mad.

Denver: Get up and open it!

Shepard: How can you live thousands of miles away and still be so damn demanding?

Denver: It's a gift. Now move.

Shepard: I'm going, I'm going.

Denver: WELL?

Shepard: Will you give me a damn minute? It's really hard to pee with morning wood.

Denver: I'm sorry, but are you texting me while you're touching your dick?

Shepard: No. I'm not touching it. I'm sitting down.

Denver: You're SITTING to pee?

Shepard: It's easier in the mornings! STOP JUDGING.

Denver: I didn't say a thing.

Denver: What about now?

Shepard: I'm going to kiss you so hard.

Denver: That doesn't have the same effect now that I know you're madly in love with me.

Shepard: Like, Denver. I LIKED you.

Denver: GASP! Did you just use PAST TENSE?

Denver: ...but you're totally kidding, right?

Shepard: Guess we'll see.

Shepard: I find it very funny we both sent each other comics for Christmas.

Shepard: I love these. I've never read a comic before (my brother wouldn't let me touch his) so I'm pretty excited about these.

Denver: Did you open them?

Shepard: More demands. *eye roll* Hang on.

Denver: *waits impatiently*

Shepard: Well well well.

Denver: WELL?

Shepard: This might be my favorite Christmas present ever, and I once got a guitar AND an iPhone the same year.

Denver: Do you still like me?

Shepard: Yes, Denver. I still like you. I'm really fucking excited you're coming here for college.

Denver: That's four whole years I get to annoy you.

Denver: I'm coming early too. I got a journalism internship.

Shepard: The one for Bradford?

Denver: Yep.

Shepard: You're telling me we get to spend the entire summer together too?

Denver: No way!

Shepard: Best. Christmas. Ever. (Unless I end up hating you.)

Denver: I doubt it.

Denver: You're, uh, you're kind of my

best friend, Shep.

Shepard: You're kind of my best friend too. I don't call you Bucky for nothing.

Denver: Bucky and Cap were totally lovers, not besties.

Shepard: So you're saying you want to bang me?

Denver: OMG. No.

Denver: Merry Christmas, Captain.

Shepard: Merry Christmas, Bucky.

Shepard: We'll come back to that banging thing later.

Denver: It's almost midnight on the east coast.

Shepard: Wow. Thanks for telling me. All of our clocks actually stopped working.

Denver: Smartass.

Denver: I was telling you that because

being honest is my New Year's resolution and I have something I'd like to confess.

Shepard: Of course you're one of those people who believe in NY resolutions. Of course you are.

Denver: Shut up.

Shepard: Sorry (not). Confess away. I'm all ears.

Denver: I'm not going to pussyfoot around it like you did.

Shepard: I don't know…this feels like pussyfooting to me.

Denver: I like you too.

Shepard: I know you do.

Denver: UGH. That is NOT the right response, Shepard!

Shepard: Oh, I'm sorry. Let me act surprised then.

Shepard: Golly gee, I had NO idea. Wow. I'm SO flattered.

Denver: I lied. I hate you again.

Shepard: You could never hate me.

Shepard: So what are we going to do about this mutual attraction?

Denver: What can we do? We live over two thousand miles apart.

Shepard: There's always college…

Denver: There's always college.

Shepard: Is that, like, a deal?

Denver: Okay, I have another confession to make.

Shepard: What do I look like, the Pope?

Denver: No. He's way cuter than you.

Shepard: There are a lot of things about you that are suddenly starting to make sense.

Denver: QUIET!

Denver: See, I've always had this…plan: go off to college, fall madly in love with my soul mate, and get married when we graduate. I know you don't believe in forevers or soul mates or any of that, so it's really hard for me to say that's a deal…especially when it comes to you.

Denver: Is that going to be a problem for us?

Shepard: No.

Denver: You sure?

Shepard: I'm sure.

Denver: This scares me.

Shepard: Me too, but, Bucky?

Denver: Yes, Cap?

Shepard: I'd give forever a shot with you.

Sixteen

SHEPARD

"Where are you in the lineup tonight?"

"Second."

"Really? You mean I don't have to spend my entire Saturday night with you?"

"You say that like it's a bad thing."

She runs her eyes over my attire. "I mean, you do look pretty snazzy in that suit."

"Snazzy, huh? Not hot? Sexy? *Fuck*able?"

Red fills her cheeks, and it's one of the few times I've actually seen Denver blush.

I lean over, my shoulder brushing against her, my lips running along the shell of her ear. "Say I'm fuckable, Denver."

She sucks in a deep breath, holding it for far too long before finally letting it out and raising her chin up high.

She turns to me, meeting me head-on.

"You're fuckable, all right, but you're not getting any tonight."

My champagne glass disappears from my hand, she guzzles the contents down, and then she brushes past me with a triumphant glint in her eyes.

I shake my head, smiling, watching her immerse herself in a group of players like that's exactly where she belongs. As a journalist, it probably is.

I wonder how her article is coming along, what exactly it is she's writing about. I've had plenty of opportunities to ask her, but I can't say I care enough to actually do so.

I'm only letting her write it so I can spend time with her. She can write anything she wants. Tell people I wet the fucking bed for all I care—as long as by the end of this whole exchange of services, she's mine.

"I see you brought her back. A first for you, man."

Braxton appears beside me, holding out a new glass of champagne. I take it with no intention of drinking it. Like hell I'm letting Denver drive my truck again.

"Yep," I reply.

"Guess you haven't fucked it up."

"Not yet."

"You will."

I glare at him. "Thanks, dick."

He lifts a shoulder. "What? She's too good to be true, and too good for you."

"You say the sweetest things, Brax."

"Does she know what happened with your brother? That little hissy fit you threw?"

I tense at the mention of Zach and Delia and the second biggest mistake of my life.

"She doesn't," I say through clenched teeth. "And I'd like to keep it that way."

"You should tell her, let her decide if you're redeemable."

"I will…eventually."

Braxton grunts like he doesn't believe me.

Fucker.

I do plan to tell her, just not yet, not when things are going as well as they are. I'll do it before the wedding.

I hope.

My phone buzzes in my pocket and I pull it out, switching off the alarm.

"That's my cue. We're second tonight."

"Second? Lucky little shit." His heavy hand lands on my shoulder. "See ya next week."

I groan, mentally ticking off another event in my head.

Two down, just three more to go.

Since Gerard didn't press charges and because my coach finds me "valuable"—his words, not mine—I got out of the whole mess pretty clean, all things considered. I'm suspended for the remainder of the season, not allowed to participate in team activities, and must pay a nominal fine for making the team look like shit.

The club made me pay *damages.* I mean, seriously?

Whatever, it's understandable, but for my agent and PR team to force me to attend these charity events instead of just donating like I always do? Fucking deplorable.

The only good to come of it is the excuse to spend time with Denny.

I push through the crowd to find her, and my ears perk up when I hear my name.

"Are you dating Shepard Clark?" asks a redhead with perky tits.

"Dating?" Denny wrinkles her nose. "No."

"If you're not dating him then you must be related," another girl says. "Shep has never brought the same girl to more than one event."

If Denny is surprised by this, she doesn't show it.

She waves a hand, laughing. "We're most definitely not related either."

"Then what are you?"

"Well, to tell you the truth," she starts, leaning in closer to the girls. They all follow her lead, bending their heads together. "I'm only here because I feel sorry for him."

Oh, I cannot wait to see where this goes.

One girl grabs her chest, mouth dropping open. "Is he dying?"

"Is he off the team?"

"You're pity dating him?"

She nods, frowning. "I am. The reason you don't see him with the same date twice is because once girls find out about it, they don't stick around—no matter how big his wallet is."

"Is he scarred?"

"A weird birthmark?"

"Two left feet?"

They pepper her with questions and she continues frowning, shaking her head solemnly.

"Worse." She leans in closer. "He has a micro-penis."

"No!" one of the girls gasps.

Denny nods and holds her hand up, pinching her fingers together, telling everyone I have a three-inch dick.

"It's true." She shrugs. "It's a good thing he knows how to use his mouth or else I'd have been out of there so fast."

The girls clamor, all exchanging shocked comments, some going as far as saying they always suspected.

She takes a sip of her champagne, surveying the room, looking smug.

Until our eyes lock.

Until she sees the promise of revenge.

Her hands begin to shake. Her cheeks flush, lips part.

Just wait until you see what I can do with my tongue, Bucky.

"Where are we going? You just passed the burger joint."

"We had burgers last week. I'm craving p…"

In my peripheral, I watch as she clenches her thighs together, anticipating the word leaving my mouth.

"Pizza."

She releases a frustrated sigh. "God, it's hot in here," she says, playing like she wasn't waiting for me to say pussy.

Don't worry, Denny, pussy is definitely still on the menu for tonight.

"Does this mean we'll be eating back at your place?"

"Yep."

"Do you mind if we stop at Smart Shoppe first? I want to grab a few things."

"I already bought your coffee creamer," I tell her.

Her mouth drops open but she quickly snaps it closed.

"Well, I need other things. Besides, it's rather presumptuous of you to assume I'd be staying the night again."

"You are. We both know you are." I glance over at her. "Like you'll give up a night of snuggling Steve."

"Excellent point." She flips on the A/C, and I know it's because she's wound tight about our plans for dinner—well, *my* plans for dinner. "I'm still mad you wouldn't let me bring him."

"You're lucky I'm letting you anywhere near him after you tried to steal him *twice* last week."

She crosses her arms over her chest, putting her breasts on

display.

"I would have gotten away with it the second time if he hadn't peed in my duffle bag."

"He peed because he was getting kidnapped and was terrified."

"He gets his dramatics from you. You owe me a new bag, too."

I laugh. "You tried to steal *my* dog and I owe *you* a new bag? Keep dreaming."

We pull into Smart Shoppe. The event tonight was local, so the drive isn't much compared to last week…or next, which she has no idea is three hours away. We're also slotted to leave last.

She's going to *love* that one. I'll tell her later.

"Ugh, I should have changed before we left. I look ridiculous," she grumbles as we walk through the parking lot. "Oh god!"

She steps in a puddle then almost drops back into another one.

I grab her hand, stopping her before she can get her other shoe wet.

"What?" She peers down at our joined hands then back up at me. "Are you trying to hold my hand?"

"Don't be gross, Den. No. I'm trying to save you from stepping in yet another puddle." I tug her closer to me. "Come here."

I face away from her and bend my knees.

She just stands there.

Glancing over my shoulder, I roll my eyes. "Well, hop the fuck up."

"What? I am *not* riding you into the store."

I stand to my full height, turning toward her. "You might not ride me right now, Denny, but you *will* be riding me later."

She lifts her hand to smack at me and I grab it in midair, using the opportunity to drag her toward me and toss her over my shoulder fireman style.

"Dammit, Shep! Put me down!"

164

I bite her ass cheek. "Shush it."

"Oh my *god*—did you just bite my ass?" She hits me.

"Are you punching my butt right now?

"Yes!" She hits my cheek again. "How is it so hard?"

"Squats, baby. Lots of fucking squats." I do one right then, holding her like she weighs nothing—because she doesn't.

The biggest thing on Denny is her mouth.

"Oh, wow. I'm *so* turned on right now," she says sarcastically. "What is wrong with you? Put me down!"

I don't.

I carry her through the parking lot, smiling at the few strangers giving us weird looks, and I don't let her down until we reach the sidewalk.

She slides down my body, winded from yelling and beating me.

"I hate you."

I lean down, tilting my head like I'm about to go in for a kiss, and watch as her breaths quicken.

She wants the kiss.

I do too.

Problem is, if I start kissing her now, I won't be able to stop.

"Two things. One, you don't look ridiculous. You look fucking stunning."

Her pupils expand, and she darts her tongue out to lick at her lips.

"Two, what have I told you about lying, Den?" Forcing myself to back away before I fuse my mouth with hers, I step through the automatic doors and call over my shoulder, "You coming?"

She mutters something I swear sounds like, "I wish," and follows me into the store.

We look like goons, walking around the grocery store in fancy clothes. It's early enough for there to still be plenty of shoppers, and we're garnering an abundance of stares.

I let her wander around, loading her arms with random snacks and, of course, plenty of mint chocolate chip ice cream.

When she finally announces she's done, I pay for her haul and load the truck up.

We agree on a pizza—extra green olives for her—and head back to my place.

"Good evening, sir! Hello again, Miss Andrews."

Denny waves to the old man then looks at me, surprised Jim knows her name.

"I told him you'd probably be here with me a lot." I shrug. "Hey, Jim. How are the parents doing?"

"Fantastic, sir. Tiptop shape."

"That's good to hear. I'll see you tomorrow. Good night."

Jim bids us good night as the elevator doors close.

"His parents are still alive? He's so old," Denny remarks once we're alone.

"Not his parents, Steve's. He's who I bought Steve from."

"No way!"

"Yep." I press the button for my floor. "He gave me an amazing deal on him too. Turns out pugs are expensive as shit."

"I know. Why do you think I tried to get you to buy me one?" She winks as the elevator comes to a stop

We exit, and I lead her down the hall.

"Steve!"

Denny drops to her knees the moment I open the door, spreading her arms wide like she's waiting for my pug to come skidding around the corner at any moment.

He won't. I've crated him this time, since I discovered he peed in my shoes last time.

I stare down at her like she's lost her goddamn mind.

"You do realize he's in his crate, right? And that you're kneeling down on my floor in a thousand-dollar dress?"

She juts her bottom lip out, and I'll be damned if her plump mouth doesn't make my cock jump.

I want to see it wrapped around me. *Bad.*

Firmly, I grab her chin, tilting her face up to me.

Her breathing kicks into overdrive, her chest rising and falling with eagerness.

"The only time you should be on your knees in one of these dresses is for me, Denver."

I leave her sitting there, jaw slack and wanting more.

Soon, Denny. Soon.

Seventeen

DENVER

"Oh god," I moan loudly. "I don't think I ever want to stop." Another moan. "This is the best I've ever had."

Shep's head snaps my way. "Are you finished?"

"Almost."

I wink and take the last bite of my pizza, chew, and then swallow. Dusting my hands off, I throw myself back on his lush dark gray couch, satisfied.

"God." I pat my full stomach. "That was better than sex."

"I don't think you're having the right kind of sex."

"I don't think you're giving this pizza enough credit."

He shakes his head, grabs another slice, and dips it into the cup of barbeque sauce he's holding.

I curl my lip at the action. "I can't believe you're eating that. It's disgusting."

"Have you ever tried it before?"

Text Me Baby One More Time

"No, but it *sounds* disgusting."

He shoves a slice in my face. "Try it."

"If I try it and hate it, you owe me ten dollars."

"And if you try it and love it, I owe you an orgasm."

I sit forward, holding a hand up. "Wait—you're telling me no matter what, I win?" I snatch the slice of pizza from his hand. "Give me that."

I take a small bite, then another. Before I know it, I've annihilated yet another piece of pizza and eaten half his sauce.

Oops?

He sits, smug grin lining his stupid plump lips. "Told ya."

I roll my eyes and push myself off the couch. "Whatever. I'm going to change into jammies."

"I'm surprised you didn't do that as soon as you walked in the door."

"And eat cold pizza? No thanks."

I brush past him and snatch my overstuffed tote bag off the floor then head back to his bedroom.

Staying the night at Shep's is growing on me...and not just because of his ultra-comfy bed.

I like it here. It's quiet—way quieter than my apartment building—and cozy. Though the apartment is mostly made up of shades of gray, it's still inviting, pleasantly simple and modern.

Plus, there's Steve, who I might be growing a little too attached to.

I push open the bedroom door and stop dead in my tracks. "Shep!"

"What!" he hollers back.

"Get your ass in here."

"Nah. I'm comfy."

"Cap! Move that ass!"

169

I hear him sigh loudly, muttering as he shuffles down the hall.

"What?" he says when he's standing next to me.

I point to the bed. "What the shit is this?"

Laughing, he says, "That, Denny, is a dog in a suitcase."

"Whose suitcase is that? Yours?"

"No. That would be yours." He walks farther into the room, scooping Steve from the open rectangle and depositing him on the floor. The pup does not look too happy about being moved from his spot. "He was sleeping on your flowers."

"You got me flowers again?"

"I did."

I approach the bed, bringing the crushed bouquet up to my nose and smelling it. I don't recognize the blooms, or their scent. "What are they?"

"Amaryllis."

Remembering that last week the flowers he got for me had a meaning, I ask, "And they mean?"

"Beauty."

The single word lingers in the air, and a warmth trickles into my heart. It's that same warmth that's been working its way inside since Shep came back into my life. Slowly, every day we spend together, it's spreading.

Oddly, I'm finding that I like it.

I drag my fingertips over the suitcase. "You got me this?"

"I mean, my dog *did* pee in your other one."

"But I thought it was deserved because I was trying to kidnap him?"

"It was, but I still felt guilty. Besides, that other one was tragic looking. I couldn't let you stuff another one of those expensive dresses into it. It was painful to watch."

"They did barely fit…" I murmur, dragging the luggage closer.

"Shep, this is really nice."

"It's a hard case with those idiot-proof wheels."

"I did always want one of those."

"Yeah? Good. You're going to need it next weekend anyway."

"Next weekend?" I ask warily. "What's next weekend?"

"Another event."

"Why would I need a suitcase for that?"

He shoves his hands in his pockets, and I take a moment to admire how hot he looks in his black slacks and unbuttoned dress shirt, sleeves rolled up to reveal his muscular forearms.

I never thought forearms were sexy before, but damn does Shep have some nice ones.

"…on the roster."

I snap back to reality just as he finishes speaking. "Huh?"

"Quit checking me out and focus."

I put my hands on my hips and stare up at him. "Quit telling me what to do and just repeat what you said."

He rolls his eyes with a smile. "I said, the event we're headed to next weekend is three hours away and we're on the roster to leave last. I already have a room booked."

"You mean rooms, right?"

"Nope. *Room.*" He leans toward me, and I hate the way my heart starts pounding with his proximity.

What is with me tonight? Every little thing he says is getting me riled up.

I mean, to be fair, he is being very…forward. It's not that I'm not on board with forward, but there's no reason I should be squeezing my thighs together in anticipation of him saying *pussy*. I thought I was going to up and die when he grabbed my chin as I kneeled before him.

Now I'm overreacting because he's leaning in close to me?

I'm pathetic.

And really fucking overdue for that orgasm he promised me.

Yeah, that's all it is—sexual frustration. It has nothing to do with Shep himself. Impossible.

Keep telling yourself that, Denny.

"Two beds, Shep," I argue, even though I don't want to. I want to spend the night in the same bed as him so goddamn bad.

Wait...I do?

Oh hell. I *really* do.

I'm not Shep's biggest fan, but I'll be damned if my body doesn't think he's the hottest thing to ever walk this earth, despite how much my head is yelling at me to walk away from him and keep things simple between us.

"One."

"Two."

"*One.*"

Another step toward me, his lips only inches from my own. My stupid legs quiver, waiting for his mouth to drop to mine.

"And we're spooning."

Abruptly, he pulls away, spins on his heel, and leaves me standing there wanting more...for the umpteenth time tonight.

How I am going to survive this?

"You're drooling."

"I am not."

"Are too."

"I'm not even asleep, you ass." I pry my eyes open and stare at the TV, not watching what's happening on the screen.

Shep insisted on watching *Bob's Burgers*, and since I secretly have a huge crush on Bob Belcher, I didn't argue.

"Are you sure about that?"

"If I am, this is the worst dream I've ever had."

I go to pull my feet off his lap, but he puts his hand on my calf, stopping me.

"Where are you going?"

"Bathroom. Wanna wipe my ass for me?"

"That's the weirdest foreplay I've ever heard. No thank you."

"Then let me up."

"I will, but…" he draws out.

I groan. "What do you want, Shep?"

"Remember that ice cream you made me drive *way* out of my way for?"

"You mean way out of your way to the store that's on the way to your apartment? Sure, I remember."

"Wanna grab it?"

"I can do that."

I pull my feet away again and this time he lets go.

"But I get the mint chocolate chip!"

I haul myself off the couch and dart for the kitchen.

I don't make it far.

Those damn baseball player reflexes have him on me in seconds, wrapping his arm around my middle and hauling me into him.

"Nice try, shithead."

"Let me go."

"And give up my favorite ice cream to my arch nemesis? Not happening."

"Arch nemesis?" I pout. "I thought we were friends now."

He loosens his hold at the fake sadness in my voice and I try to wiggle away.

It's no use. He's too strong and not dumb enough to fall for my shit.

He shifts around, and that's when I feel it.

"I'm sorry, Shep, but is that your dick poking me in the ass right now?"

"Yes," he grunts as I push into him. "Fucking quit or I'm going to…"

"Going to…what? Kiss me again?"

Without warning he spins me, crushing his lips to mine. His tongue plunges into my mouth, twisting around my own, kissing me like he's never kissed me before.

My body sags against his and he uses the opportunity to lift me up. I wrap my legs around his waist, his dick sliding against all the right places as he carries me over to the island in his kitchen.

He drops me onto the counter, his mouth traveling down my chin and over my neck. He sucks and kisses and bites and I'm certain there will be marks on my skin tomorrow.

I don't even care. It feels too good to care.

Everything with Shep just feels too good.

His hands on my body. His lips on mine. Just being around him.

It's *too* good.

Which is why I can't help but give in, even when I know I shouldn't.

It's why I don't push him away as his hands trail up my legs, my thighs, and dive under the shirt of his I'm wearing, why I don't run when his fingers brush the undersides of my tits. If he's surprised to find I'm not wearing a bra, he doesn't show it.

It feels good.

Too good again.

But I don't care anymore. I need it.

Besides, it's just physical…right?

"God, I fucking love seeing you in my clothes," he practically

174

growls.

I knew last week he was enjoying the view, which is why I intentionally didn't pack pajamas for my overnight stay.

"Do you have any idea how sexy you are, Den? How hard I had to fight every day of the last five years to not touch you? To not pull you into the nearest empty closet and have my way with you? And tonight, seeing you in that dress…god, it was killing me."

He covers my nipple, sucking the hard peak through the t-shirt, and I nearly fall off the counter at the touch.

"Oh hell," I mutter. "Stop talking."

"No. You need to know this. You need to know how you've affected me."

I push him away, bringing his face up to mine. "No, Shep, I really don't need to know. I don't *want* to know, because if I know, it's going to make me all too aware of how bad an idea this is. I shouldn't be doing this—*we* shouldn't be doing this. I should have my guard up around you because you hurt me beyond belief. Yet, here I am, sitting on top of your counter wanting this more than my next breath. So, no, I *don't* want to hear this. I just want to *feel* good."

He looks like he wants to argue, to try to convince me I'm wrong, but that's the problem…we both know I'm not.

This is a horrible idea.

And we're going to do it anyway.

Like he flips a switch inside himself, he gives me his signature grin and says, "I can help with that."

His mouth closes around my nipple and he bites down—hard. I arch into it, wanting more, needing more. He complies with my demands, sucking on me until I can't take it anymore.

"Shep."

That's all it takes and he's pulling at my bottoms. The shorts of his I'm wearing slide off me with ease, leaving me sitting on his kitchen counter in nothing but my t-shirt and panties.

His large hands splayed across my thighs send my mind reeling, and I squirm at the thought of him burying his head between them.

His eyes meet mine, *starved*, wanting this as much as I do.

He doesn't voice his question out loud, but I see it anyway and spread my thighs in answer.

With a grunt of approval, he hauls me to the edge and I fall backward, my back resting against the cool countertop.

My legs shake as he pushes them apart even farther and I feel his eyes on me, on my light pink lacy boy-shorts.

"This is what you were wearing under that dress all night long?"

"Y-Yes."

"Fuck, Den."

"You should see the ass."

With ease, he flips me around until I'm facedown on the counter, arching me until my ass is in the air.

"Hashtag no filter, huh?"

He lifts the edge of my underwear, just enough to see the bite mark he left there earlier, and he kisses it. The gesture sends my heart into overdrive as he flips me around again, jerking me back to the edge of the counter.

Maybe it's the anticipation driving me nuts as he stares down at me, fingers on the edge of my panties. Slowly, he pulls the fabric aside, exposing me to him for the first time.

"Give me your hand," he instructs, never taking his eyes off me.

I slip my hand into his, not questioning him.

He replaces his fingers with mine so they're holding my underwear back then gives me the most wolfish grin.

"Hold these for me."

And then his head disappears between my thighs.

"F-Fuck me," I stutter as his tongue sweeps over my skin.

"Later," he teases, using his fingers to spread me open even more. "Goddamn, Den. I knew this would be good, but I didn't think it would be *this* good."

His mouth covers me again and I'm so fucking mad at myself because this is what I've been missing for the last five years.

His tongue covers my clit, swirling with the right amount of pressure. He uses his shoulders to push my legs apart, spreading me to the point of my underwear digging painfully into my thigh, but I don't care.

He dips his tongue inside me then moves to my clit again, sucking and pulling it into his mouth as he slides two fingers in.

Suck, pump, suck, pump.

I can't handle it.

I release my panties and pull myself up, missing the feel of his tongue against me the moment I move.

"Finger me like you mean it, Shep."

I crush my mouth to his, loving the taste of myself on his lips as he quickens his pace and pistons his fingers in and out, sweeping his thumb up to rub circles on my clit.

It's almost enough to send me over the edge, but not quite. I need more. I need it harder.

"More."

"My fucking hand is cramping."

"Utilize those baseball player muscles and finish this, Shep." I press a quick kiss to his lips. "If you can."

With a growl, he withdraws his fingers as he shoves me backward again. I smack against the counter, relishing the pain in my shoulder blades as he spreads me wider than I could have imagined and covers my pussy with his mouth one last time...*through* the fabric.

I combust beneath him, riding his face as my orgasm rages through me.

"Holy hell," I rasp out, pushing myself up onto my elbows and looking down at Shep once my breathing returns to normal.

"You're welcome."

I groan and swat at him. He grabs my hand and pulls me until I'm sitting up.

"Hi," he says.

"Hey."

He gives me a self-satisfied grin. "So, you were saying something about how I know how to use my mouth?"

Eighteen

Five years ago, February

Shepard: I just want to put this out there because I feel like it's super important to remind you of this.

Denver: Okay...

Shepard: Valentine's Day is a commercial holiday and I will NOT be participating in it.

Shepard: No cards. No chocolates. And definitely no flowers.

Denver: You saying you're NEVER going to buy me flowers?

Shepard: Not never, but when I do, they're going to mean something. They won't be a "holiday" obligation.

Denver: Duly noted.

Shepard: So that means tomorrow when VDay rolls around, don't be upset that I didn't send you anything.

Denver: Wait a second—why would you send me something?

Denver: OH MY GOD. Are we dating and I didn't know it?!

Shepard: No.

Shepard: But we have intentions to date.

Shepard: I feel like that's the same thing.

Denver: It's…close-ish.

Shepard: I'm not seeing anyone else.

Shepard: Well, not anyone other than Penny.

Shepard: But since I still don't have a vagina, that's not working out.

Shepard: While we're on the subject…does it bother you that Penny and I are "dating"?"

Denver: If I'm being 9% honest with you, I do think it's a little weird because I don't really know how into the fake dating you two are, but I also understand it.

Shepard: We don't kiss.

Denver: Yes, we've established that.

Shepard: Sometimes we hold hands, but it's not in a…sexual way.

Denver: You can hold hands in a sexual way?

Shepard: Definitely.

Shepard: I'll show you one day.

Denver: Okay, but only because I'm intrigued.

Shepard: And because you like me.

Denver: Sometimes.

Shepard: Quit trying to take it back.

Shepard: Anyway, that's about the extent

of it. She just comes over once a week for dinner and I accompany her to dances. We're more like siblings than anything else.

Denver: So you and Zach also hold hands?

Shepard: All the time. Especially when we're watching something with bunnies.

Denver: Excuse me?

Shepard: He's scared of them. Don't ask.

Denver: Please tell me I can meet him one day.

Shepard: We'll see.

Denver: Can I just say I think it's kind of cool of you to be so protective of your friend and give up your single man status for her.

Shepard: What can I say? I'm a gentleman.

Denver: Oh, Shep. I don't know if I'd use that word to describe you. Utter shithead, maybe, but not gentleman.

Shepard: You say the sweetest things to me sometimes.

Shepard: If it makes you feel any better about Penny, she told me at Christmas she plans to dump me before school's out. I've been practicing my fake crying for weeks.

Denver: I'm sorry to hear that.

Shepard: So...uh...are you seeing anyone else?

Denver: I'm not. Not even fake dating anyone either.

Denver: Though I did just turn down someone who asked me to the dance tomorrow.

Shepard: I want to feel bad that you're not going and experiencing that, but I'm also really fucking happy you turned him down. I don't think I could handle knowing someone was dancing all up on you all night long.

Denver: He still picks his nose. I didn't do it for you, Shep. I did it for myself. Quit being so full of yourself.

Denver: (okay, that's a lie, I did it for you)

Shepard: So you're telling me you're into nose-pickers? That might be a deal-breaker.

Denver: Well, this was fun while it lasted.

Denver: One more thing though…

Shepard: Shoot.

Denver: You said no cards, chocolates, or flowers…

Shepard: No pugs either.

Denver: *cries*

Denver: Why do you torture me?!

Shepard: God, Bucky, forever with you is going to be so much fun.

Denver: DOWNLOAD ATTACHMENT

Denver: YOU ARE A LIAR!

Shepard: I am not.

Denver: You do too believe in Valentine's Day!

Shepard: I have no idea what you're talking about.

Denver: You said you weren't sending anything, but you did. You're a closet romantic.

Shepard: I said I wouldn't send a card, chocolate, or flowers.

Shepard: Or a pug.

Denver: But you sent me pug-shaped cookies?

Denver: You loooooove me.

Shepard: I tolerate you. On a good day.

Denver: Uh huh. You wanna kiss me.

Denver: UGH. Why'd I say that? Now I want to kiss you.

Shepard: WHAT ARE YOU DOING? STOP IT.

Shepard: Shit. Now I can't stop thinking about kissing you.

Denver: I'M SORRY!

Denver: Kind of.

Denver: You totally have a boner now, don't you?

Shepard: Pft. No.

Denver: You know, I heard your dick shrinks half an inch for every lie you tell.

Shepard: I don't have a boner!

Denver: It's perfectly natural, Shep. Even ladies get boners—in our nipples.

Shepard: Stop talking, Denver.

Denver: Oooh, using the full name huh? You're totally thinking about my nipples, aren't you?

Denver: Bet that boner is real painful right about now.

Shepard: Quit saying boner!

Shepard: You're too exhausting for me to have one right now.

Denver: You'll have one later. I'm certain of it.

Denver: Shep?

Shepard: What?

Denver: Boner.

Shepard: GODDAMIT!

Nineteen

SHEPARD

"Do you want bacon, eggs, and toast or waffles?"

"Biscuits and gravy."

"That wasn't an option."

"Well it should have been." She sips her coffee—which is loaded with her own creamer—and eyes me from across the kitchen island.

Memories of her moaning as she rode my fingers and face flash through my mind, making my cock jump to attention.

After she came down from her first orgasm, I brought her to another. When she tried to drop to her knees to reciprocate, I refused, tucked her into bed, and took the coldest fucking shower of my life.

I wanted to bury my dick inside her more than anything last night, but I didn't let myself take it there, craving the anticipation us going away next weekend brings.

Besides, it was only three weeks ago that Denny hated me. I want to make sure when I finally fuck her, it's not a hate fuck. I want to make sure it's because she's finally admitting she wants me too.

I want her to admit she never hated me.

"Who doesn't have the ingredients for biscuits and gravy?"

"Normal people."

"You know, I have this friend who always listens to rap music while she and her boyfriend make breakfast. They call it Breakfast and Beats and it's the cutest thing ever."

"Sounds cheesy." I down the rest of my black coffee and set the dirty mug in the sink. "We're not doing that."

"We can listen to Sinatra or Michael Boobie."

"*Bublé*, and it's still a no."

"You're no fun."

"I'm not?" She shakes her head. "Well I was going to suggest we order delivery and stay here all morning. You can feast on biscuits and gravy while I feast on your pussy."

Her lips part on a small gasp and she crosses her legs together tightly.

"But since I'm no fun"—I lift a shoulder—"I guess going out for breakfast it is. That's too bad, too. I can't do the things I want to do to you in public. It's just gonna have to wait."

It's right on the tip of her tongue to beg me for…well, my tongue.

But, Denny being Denny, she doesn't.

Instead she pushes her shoulders back, takes a sip of her coffee, and says, "You're buying."

I shake my head, fighting a laugh as I make my way down the hall to get dressed for the day, leaving her sitting there regretting her decision.

I slide into my bedroom, not bothering to close the door, and strip down to my underwear while I root around in my drawers for something to wear.

"You know, we could always—what in the hell are you wearing?"

I spin around, trying to cover myself, but it's no use.

She darts into the room, pulling my hands away.

"Are you wearing *pug* underwear?"

"N-No!"

"Is he lying on a pizza floatie?"

"He's not!"

She laughs, holding my arms out and inspecting me.

"You *so* are." She looks up at me, eyes smiling. "You are on a whole new level of messed up, Shepard."

"It's Doug the Pug!" I say in defense.

Steve pushes the door open, sauntering over to Denny like she's his owner. She scoops him up and snuggles him close to her chest.

"Come on, Steve, you don't need to see this." She nudges her nose against his and says quietly, "Your dad is a freak, but he's *our* freak."

Ours.

And that's the first time I get a boner in front of my dog.

"Mmm…"

"Why do you always sound like you're having an orgasm when you're eating?"

"You would know, wouldn't you?" She shoves another bite of her gravy-slathered bacon into her mouth.

Why, yes I would.

She chews and swallows then sits back in the booth, looking stuffed. "I was famished. Thanks for breakfast."

"You're welcome. I'm just glad we could come to an agreement on leaving Steve at home."

"I still think it's bullshit you made me leave him behind. He's lonely!"

"Which is why I set him up in the living room with a view of the TV and his favorite show on, as requested." I hold my finger up. "Nay, as *demanded*."

"It's not the same as snuggles," she argues. "Come on, we better get going if we're going to make it to the decorations store." She sighs. "I can't believe I have to spend the *entire* weekend with you two weekends in a row."

"Well if *your* best friend wasn't insisting on a shotgun October wedding, we wouldn't have to."

"Oh my gosh!" She clutches her chest. "I didn't even think to ask her—is Allie pregnant? Is that why they're rushing this?"

"I think they're just in love."

Slowly, a smile stretches across Denny's lip at my words. "My, my. Are you saying you believe in love now?"

I shrug. "My feelings might have changed over the years."

"Yeah? What changed your mind?"

You.

I wish I had the balls to say it out loud, to tell her that the moment I fell in love with her six years ago was the moment I started believing.

I'll never forget pacing around my room, freaking out when I realized I'd fallen for her.

Zach was home for break during college. He was there with his girlfriend at the time and watching them be all lovey-dovey was getting to me, so I was texting Denver an excessive amount to avoid them. He caught me smiling at one of her asinine texts and, thinking it was Penny—like everyone else did—he teased me like big brothers do.

"Aw, I see you're texting your girlfriend again. Someone's in love." *He puckered his lips and made the most obnoxious kissing noise.*

"Yeah, so?" I shot back without thought.

191

My automatic response kicked me in the ass and I ran to my room, calling AJ and asking him to explain what love felt like.

It was the most awkward fucking conversation in all our years of friendship, but when it was over, I had my answer.

I was in love with Denver Andrews, a girl who lived over two thousand miles away, a girl I'd never met and only knew via text. I'd never heard her voice or her laugh, but I already knew I loved them.

Still, that didn't stop me from completely screwing things up for us.

That's what happens when doubt and worry creep into your head. You do really stupid shit—shit you can't fix, shit that takes years to heal, shit that can fuck you up and turn you into a person even you don't recognize.

I know, because that's what happened to me.

I made one mistake and it snowballed into several more. I couldn't stop it. It didn't matter who I was hurting in the process because no matter what I did, they couldn't hate me as much as I hated me.

I realize how fucked up that kind of logic is.

"How's the article coming along?" I ask, changing the subject on her, not answering her question because I'm not interested in lying to her.

She takes a sip of her orange juice, which she insisted on getting along with another coffee *and* a water. Surprisingly, she's had most of all three. "It's going."

"What exactly are you writing about?"

"You."

"Right, but what about me *specifically*? My stats? My career?"

"No baseball stuff, actually. I want the community to get to know the golden boy they adore so much. I…" She runs her fingers over the condensation on her glass, not meeting my curious eyes. "I want them to get to know the Shep I used to know…if he still exists," she adds quietly.

"He does."

She doesn't say anything for the longest time, her attention still focused on her cup.

I shovel a few more bites of food in, unsure of where to take this conversation after that.

She guzzles the rest of her juice like there's secretly vodka mixed in there and nearly slams her glass down onto the table.

Finally, she looks at me. "I'm starting to believe that."

Hope sparks inside me.

Hope I've longed for.

Hope I desperately need when it comes to Denny.

Hope that gets fucking crushed when I look up and see Zach. He's tugging his girlfriend along behind him, about to walk directly by my table.

We lock eyes.

His harden, and I try to not cower.

He turns to Delia, whispering something to her. She glances to me and nods. They quicken their pace, planning to waltz by without saying a word.

I don't blame them.

"Delia!"

She whips her head Denny's way just as they're pushing past us.

"Oh my gosh, I haven't seen you in forever!" Denny scrambles out of the booth, throwing her arms around my brother's girlfriend.

"It's so funny running into you here," Delia says, her eyes flashing to me as she hugs Denny back. The glance is quick, only lasting a moment, but I see panic there.

Unnecessary panic, I might add.

Feeling awkward, I throw a few twenties onto the table and stand too, not missing the way my brother slides a protective arm around Delia's waist and pulls her to him.

"Denver, this is Zach. I know you heard all about him last year."

Denny shakes my brother's hand. "Nice to meet you, Zach. I look forward to one day seeing your Harry Potter underwear."

"Oh, you haven't yet?" He acts like he's about to unbuckle his belt, and Delia knocks his hands away.

"Quit it." She laughs. "I'll show her pictures later. Zach did a Harry Potter boudoir shoot for me. We'll have to get together so I can show you the goods."

I clear my throat, trying not to laugh, because *of course* my brother did that.

Denny speaks up. "Oh, where are my manners? Have you met Shep Clark yet?"

No one moves or says anything.

"Did you guys hear me? *The* Shep Clark." She rolls her eyes teasingly. "He's kind of a legend around here."

Heat fills my cheeks and I shuffle my feet, clearing my throat. "Uh, Bucky?"

"Yes, Cap?"

"This is Zach."

She crinkles her nose at me. "I'm aware. Delia just introduced me to him."

"No, Den, this is *Zach.*"

I see the wheels spinning in her head and the moment everything connects for her.

Only AJ knew about Denny and me, so when she moved out here for college and I fucked things up, that was that. We went on with our lives like the other didn't exist, doing everything in our power to ensure that beyond the paper a few days a week, we didn't have any contact. She didn't run in the same circles and it wasn't common knowledge

194

that Zach and I are related, so they never met.

Until now.

"Shit up!" she hollers, attracting a few curious stares from other patrons. "You're kidding, right?"

"Not at all. Denver, meet my brother. Zach, this is Denver Andrews."

"Andrews?" His brows shoot into his hairline. He looks at Delia and she nods. "Huh." He tilts his head and squints at Denver. "I guess I can see it."

"What am I missing here?" I ask.

"Denver's twin sister Monty is dating Robbie," Zach explains. "Delia and Denver know one another from college. They were in a few classes together."

"And because I never want to feel like the fifth wheel, I've been turning down their offers to hang out for forever," Denny adds.

Oh fuck. This just got a whole lot more complicated.

"How do you two know each other?" Delia asks, the worry clear in her voice.

I don't know how much Denny does and doesn't want to reveal about our history, so I go with the safest response I can think of. "We go way back."

"Yeah?" Zach asks, and I know what he's really saying: *How many hours is way back, Shep?*

"We've, uh, we've known each other for about six years now," Denny says quietly.

Zach, the brainiac that he is, calculates this in seconds and his eyes show his surprise.

"That's your senior year."

"Yep," I answer.

"Are you from here, Denver?"

"You know she's not," Delia says. "She and Monty are from

Montana."

"I'm...surprised they've known one another so long, is all," he says coolly, and I know he has a whole lot of fucking questions to ask me.

If he ever gets up the gumption to spend more than two minutes in a room with me, I'll gladly answer them.

"It's a long story," Denny says, waving her hand. "We'll have to get together some night and talk about it."

Was that an implication of a future for us?

"Well, this has been rather...enlightening," Denny says, laughing. "But Shep and I have to split. We have a few best man and maid of honor duties we need to attend to before our phones start blowing up." She gives Delia another hug. "It was good seeing you, Delia. We'll have to catch up soon."

Delia's eyes slide my way again. "Yes, we will."

My stomach turns, my pancake and eggs begging to come back up at the thought of Delia and Denny sitting down together at some point. I know for a fact Delia does not have a single nice thing to say about me.

Not that I blame her, since I did something really fucking shitty that I can't take back.

Which leads to my current situation: a stilted relationship with my brother and his girlfriend—who, as it turns out, is pretty goddamn awesome.

I'm the only asshole in this situation. I know it, they know it, and soon Denny will know it too.

"It was good seeing you, Zach," I say genuinely, because despite what I did to hurt him, I *do* love him. I've always looked up to him.

He grunts in response, waving goodbye to Denny and ushering Delia through the restaurant without another word to me.

"Well, that was fun," I remark once they're out of earshot.

"Fun? Try awkward as hell." She whacks me in the arm. "Why didn't you tell me your brother was so hot? I wouldn't have wasted my time with your ass."

I laugh, shaking my head at her.

"I have questions, though. Don't think I don't."

"I kind of figured," I say on a heavy sigh. "Later, though, okay? I want to enjoy the rest of the day."

"But soon, right?"

"Sure. Soon."

I want to prolong this as long as I can, because I know once I tell her the truth, it's going to change everything for us. Our versions of "soon" are drastically different.

The pit in my stomach grows. The moment I tell Denny about the dumbass thing I did, we're done, and I won't be able to blame anyone but myself.

I was a sleaze ball who did a really shitty thing. I can't change that. I can't take that back—though I wish like *hell* I fucking could.

"Before the wedding?"

I gulp and nod. "Before the wedding."

God, I hate me.

Twenty

DENVER

"I'm scared shitless of spending a weekend away with him."

There.

I admitted it out loud.

"Given your history, I don't blame you," Allie says, frowning.

I glance over at her, her face filling my phone screen as I continue cramming all my clothes into my new luggage, courtesy of Shep.

"Are those your 'get lucky' panties?"

"You have 'get lucky' panties?" Monty whispers…rather loudly, I might add.

"Is that Montana?"

My sister pops her head into the frame and waves to Allie. "Hey."

"First, hi. I had no idea you were there or I wouldn't have interrupted your sister time."

"It's totally fine," Monty says, brushing off her apology.

"Second, are you telling me you *don't* have special undies you wear when you want your hot-as-fuck boyfriend to bang the shit out of you?"

Monty's face flames red. "I-I-I—"

"Oh my gosh, I think you've broken her, Allie!" I scold. "It's okay, Monty, you don't have to answer my horndog of a friend."

"Robbie prefers that I don't wear any panties at all. He thinks they just get in the way," my sister admits, staring at her hands, which she's wringing together in her lap.

Allie and I exchange a glance and then burst into laughter at how mortified Monty looks.

"Don't be ashamed of that, girl. Own it!"

Monty smiles tentatively, blushing harder, if that's even possible.

"Anyway, no, they aren't my 'get lucky' panties," I say, trying to save my sister from further mortification. She may not be a virgin anymore, but she's still *very* virginal. "I'm too scared to pack those."

"You could also go without…that's what your sister does," Allie says with a devious smirk.

Monty covers her face with her hands. "Stop it!"

"I'm kidding, Monty. I'm actually really proud of you. I'd give you a hug right now if I could, but I'm busy stomping around this mall, trying to find a decent cake knife."

"Did you not like what they had at the bridal store?" I ask

"I did, but my pocketbook didn't." She sighs. "Never mind all that. Why are you so afraid of the panties? I thought for sure you two would be banging like maniacs by now. There's so much sexual tension there—always has been."

"Well, we're not. I…don't know if I'm ready for that with him just yet, after everything."

"I mean, you did let him go to town on you on the kitchen counter."

"What!" Monty shoots off the bed. "I eat breakfast there!"

I wave her off. "Not my kitchen counter, his."

"Oh." She sits back down. "Okay. Carry on then."

"Just because I let him do"—I glance to Monty then back at Allie—"things to me, that doesn't mean I'm ready for sex."

"Aren't you though? It's been *ages* for you."

"My body is saying to bang the crap out of him, but my heart? That's the part that's scared."

"And with good reason." Allie nods. "Okay, I get it, but…you've been doing the no-strings-attached thing for years. Why not give that a shot with Slug?"

"Ew. His name is Slug?" Monty chimes in.

"No, it's a nickname. We don't dare speak his real name," Allie tells her.

I still remember the grit of his teeth the first time I called him Slug because he knew exactly what it meant—that I hated him. It didn't matter that deep down we both knew I could never truly hate him; the intent was the same.

Now, though, I couldn't call him Slug even if I tried.

"Denny?" Allie prompts me.

"I…"

I'm not sure I can do that with Shep. He's more than a no-strings commitment. He always has been, and we both know it. Hell, even Allie knows that.

If I sleep with Shep, I'll be handing him my heart on a silver platter to do with as he pleases.

I just have to hope he doesn't destroy it again.

"I'm just going to say something here, and I could be totally off base, but I could be right. I have a feeling I'm right because of twintuition and all that."

"Are you going to spit it out anytime soon?" Allie presses.

"Sorry," Monty mumbles. "Anyway, I think since you've hidden this Slug guy for so many years—I mean, almost nobody knows about him—you had a reason for doing so. You care for him, a lot more than you're willing to admit to others and to yourself, and that's totally fine. I just think there's a reason you haven't jumped into the sack with him yet. He means more. *It* will mean more. Therefore, you can't just do the no-strings-attached thing."

"That is literally what was just running through my mind," I say quietly, stunned.

Monty sits there looking quite proud of herself.

"Is that true, Denny? You're still into him like that?"

I glance to Allie, worrying my lip between my teeth, and give her a short nod.

"Ha!" She pumps her fist into the air, dancing around like she just won the lottery. "AJ totally owes me twenty bucks!"

"What the hell, Allie!"

She stops her dancing, her breathing erratic because my best friend is a spaz. "What? We knew you two were still into each other. Did you know he called AJ the other day to talk about it? Did you also know Penny was supposed to be his date to all these events but he canceled on her so he could invite you instead? You two are in *love*." She draws the word out, making kissing noises at the phone. "L-O-V-E!"

She starts crooning Nat King Cole, and I so desperately want to push that little red button and shut her up.

I don't hate Shep anymore.

But I don't still love him either.

That's not possible…right?

"Allie!"

"Oh my gosh, I was trying to sing for you, you brat!"

Monty picks up singing where Allie stopped, and I throw the nearest pillow at her, smacking her right in the face.

"Vindication!" I yell as she tosses it back, missing me. "And I totally wanna slap you both. I *do not* love him."

"Uh huh." Allie rolls her eyes.

"Whatever you say," Monty agrees.

I point to Monty then the door. "You, out." Then I look at Allie. "I'm hanging up."

"I love you…but not as much as you love Slug. Okayseeyabye."

She hangs up as my finger hovers over the button.

Monty falls back onto the bed in a fit of laughter. I grab the pillow again and cover her face, suffocating her.

"Ah, I can't wait to be an only child."

"We still have Chuck!" I make out despite her voice being muffled.

I lift the pillow for just a second, giving her a sinister grin.

"For now."

Twenty-One

Five years ago, April

Denver: DOWNLOAD ATTACHMENT

Shepard: What is that?

Shepard: Is that a dog crate?

Denver: It is. I found it at a garage sale for $5. I bet a pug could fit inside with plenty of room to spare.

Shepard: It totally could, especially if it's invisible. Lots of room to spare.

Denver: You are a dream crusher.

Shepard: Hey, I'm not saying you can't buy your own pug one day. I'm just not buying you one.

Denver: Uh huh. We'll see about that.

Denver: Do you know how many dicks I'd have to suck on the street corner to buy a pug? Good thing I didn't throw out my hooker heels from homecoming.

Shepard: At least ten.

Denver: OH MY GOD. So you WANT me to whore myself out?

Shepard: I mean, it's a pug, Den—who wouldn't whore themselves out for a pug?

Denver: I've been thinking...you should fly out here.

Shepard: Yeah? That would be kind of cool.

Denver: It would be, because then I could slap the shit out of you.

Shepard: Wow. Tell me how you really feel.

Denver: I don't think I can type for that long.

Shepard: I'm going to assume that's because you love me so, so much.

Denver: Sure. We'll go with that.

Shepard: Wait, did you buy the dog crate?

Denver: …yes

Shepard: I'm rethinking so many things right now. You're insane.

Denver: Uh huh. You're just looking for an excuse to get out of our…arrangement.

Denver: You know, that sounds SO weird to say, like we're in some sort of arranged marriage.

Shepard: It does feel a little weird.

Shepard: But it also feels weird calling you my girlfriend or some shit like that.

Denver: Yeah, that's taking things too far, especially since we haven't met.

Shepard: Besides, I've definitely been cheating on you for months with my other "girlfriend".

Denver: Fair point.

Shepard: What about…mine?

Denver: No.

Denver: Too barbaric.

Shepard: Fine, fine.

Shepard: Dibs! You're my dibs!

Denver: Hmm…I like this.

Denver: I think we can roll with this. Besides, that makes all this seem a whole lot less serious.

Denver: Not that this isn't serious, because it is, but you get what I mean.

Denver: I think.

Shepard: If anyone gets it, I get it.

Shepard: How in the hell did we let this happen?

Denver: It was totally my charm and wit.

Shepard: Pretty sure you fell for MY charm and wit.

Denver: Oh, please. You're the one who fell in love first.

Denver: LIKE! I mean like.

Denver: Shep? Did I lose you?

Shepard: I'm still here, Den.

Denver: Sorry, I didn't mean that.

Shepard: You should.

Denver: Huh? Should what?

Shepard: Mean that. You should mean that.

Denver: Oh.

Shepard: Yeah. Oh.

Denver: Well, hell, now I'm never gonna get a pug.

Shepard: What?

Denver: How am I going to whore myself out knowing you're in love with me?

Shepard: I'm...sorry?

Denver: You should be! I really wanted that pug.

Shepard: Bucky?

Denver: *grumbles* What.

Shepard: I'll buy you a pug.

Denver: WILL YOU REALLY?

Shepard: Yes. Now quit talking about whoring yourself out.

Shepard: You know, for someone who isn't allowed to do a whole lot of things normal teens are allowed to do, you sure do have a wild imagination.

Denver: I blame Allie.

Shepard: I could kiss Allie right now.

Denver: You're totally thinking about blow jobs, aren't you?

Shepard: Nah.

Shepard: Also, yes.

Denver: Cap?

Shepard: Hang on, I'm trying to concentrate.

Denver: Oh my god, quit being weird!

Shepard: One more month, Bucky. One more month.

Denver: One more month until what?

Shepard: Until I kiss you so goddamn hard.

Denver: You countin' down the days?

Shepard: Maybe.

Denver: 32.

Shepard: Now who's in love?

Denver: Me.

Twenty-Two

SHEPARD

The sound of my favorite Sinatra song *I've Got You Under My Skin* fills the cab as we cruise down the highway, and I can't help but grin because this song is just so fitting for us.

"What are you smiling about?" Denny asks.

I shake my head and lie, "Just that I can't believe you still have that dog crate."

"I mean, you're welcome."

"Did you even have a dog over the last five years?"

She shakes her head, running her hand over the pug curled in her lap. "Nope. I was saving it for Steve."

"And what did you do with it in the meantime?"

"Threw a piece of plywood on top, covered it with a blanket, and called it a shelf."

I give her an incredulous look.

"What?" she says. "I was a broke-ass college student! I mean, I *had* just picked up my entire life and moved two thousand miles away from home for some boy I love."

I stop breathing.

Love?

"Loved…w-with a D—past tense," she says, trying to play it cool but failing miserably as she stammers the words out.

Huh.

"What was that? You want my D?"

"Don't make me vomit, Shep."

"Can you really say that given how many orgasms you've had from my tongue alone?"

She brushes an invisible hair away from her face, shifting in her seat. "I…suppose that's a fair point."

"That's what I thought. You're welcome." I glance over at her. "I don't know how you think we're going to sneak him into the hotel."

"I brought my movie theater purse."

"Movie theater purse?"

"You know, the bag you take to the movies so you can shove all your snacks in there, like a burger and fries."

"You take a burger and fries into the theater?"

"Once." She shrugs like this is the most normal thing in the world. "Sometimes you're just extra hungry and trying to catch that cheap movie night and you're running out of time, so you improvise. It happens."

"Remind me to stop taking you out in public."

"Oh whatever. You're just jealous *you* don't have a movie purse. Besides, you can still take me to the movies. It's dark in there, so no one will know we're together."

"Is this your way of asking me to take you to the movies?"

She taps at her chin and Steve huffs when she stops petting him. "I wouldn't argue with a real date."

"Real date, huh? So breakfast the other morning doesn't count as a real date? Or what about taking you to all these galas? Dress shopping?"

"All of those were obligations."

"Breakfast was an obligation?"

"Yes. You give a girl an orgasm, you're obligated to feed her breakfast. Don't you know the rules?"

I laugh. "Clearly I don't."

"No wonder you haven't settled down after all these years."

I was waiting for you.

"I mean, besides the fact that you were so obviously pining over me."

I eye her. "Is that so?"

"I said obviously, didn't I?"

"You saying you paid attention to me?"

"I'm sorry, but have you seen your ass? You might have been a total dick to me, but that doesn't mean I don't have eyes, Shep."

I cough out a surprised laugh. "I mean, it's nice to know you still used me as man meat all these years."

"Are you implying I flicked my bean to thoughts of...." She shudders. "*You?*"

"I wasn't, but since you brought it up, I can only assume it's true."

The wheels in her head are spinning as she tries to figure out how to lie her way out of this one. It's obvious in the way her eyes brighten with embarrassment.

"W-Well, it's not," she finally manages to utter.

"Uh huh. Whatever you say, Den."

"Shepard!" She shoves her finger in my direction. "Take it back!"

"Nah. I kind of like the idea of you...how did you put it? *Flicking your bean* to the thought of me."

"Shepard!"

I reach forward and crank up Sinatra.

"This isn't over!" she yells over the crooning.

Not by a long shot.

"Are you trying to give me a heart attack, Den? Do you *want* me to walk around with a raging fucking hard-on all night?"

She smiles at me sheepishly. "It's just a dress. Calm yourself."

"Just a dress my ass," I mutter as she focuses on getting her earring in the hole while I let my eyes roam over the beauty in front of me. "The way you look tonight… It's… *Damn.*"

She smiles as I quote Sinatra to her and take in her delectable figure.

She's wearing the black cutout dress…*finally*. I could pat myself on the back for how well I did with picking that one out. I knew the moment I saw it hanging on the changing room door it was *the* dress for her. I had to slip Annabelle an extra hundred bucks for her to take it from the other woman, and it was worth it.

Especially for the way it hugs her ass.

It's moments like these I want to punch myself for giving us up all those years ago—not the moments of having my eyes on her ass, but these small ones.

Us in a hotel room, getting ready for yet another event.

Steve curled up on the pillow. It was comical watching her try to sneak him inside in her purse, not knowing I paid extra to get us a pet-friendly room.

Denny's makeup is sitting next to all my crap on the counter.

All the small things and moments leading up to the big ones—I missed them all, and I'm a fool for letting my fears and doubts get in the way.

"Are you done?"

"Huh?" I pull my eyes off her backside and meet her amused stare in the mirror.

"Are you done staring at my ass?"

I pull myself from the bed and stalk toward her. I love the gasp that leaves her lips as I pull her close to me.

"You weren't lying about that boner thing."

"Not even a little bit."

"You're right—*that* is far from little."

I groan when she wiggles her ass against me. *Tease.*

I pull her in tighter, stopping her from moving any more because if she doesn't quit, we won't be making it to the gala, and I paid a whole hell of a lot for those spots tonight.

"If you think I won't be staring at you *all* night long, you're wrong, Den. I plan to stare…"

She catches my burning gaze in the mirror, catching on to the intensity inside me, the building desire—the threat of stripping that dress from her body right this fucking moment.

Her chest pumps up and down with anticipation.

"To touch…"

Her eyes follow my movements as I trace my fingers along the edge of the cutout, and her flesh breaks out in goose bumps. I fucking love it.

"To taste."

I pull her face toward mine, capturing her lips in a hard kiss, devouring her mouth in a decidedly not gentle manner.

She's definitely going to have to redo her lipstick after this.

She whimpers when I pull away, and I trail my lips down her neck, sucking the skin below her ear between my teeth. It's going to leave a mark, and I don't give two shits. Let everyone see it.

I called dibs on Denver Andrews a long damn time ago, and nothing about that has changed.

With reluctance, I drag my lips from her perfect skin. She hates it too, pushing against me, wanting me.

Patience, Den.

Her eyes flutter open and our gazes meet in the mirror.

"And to fuck."

The fire in Denver's eyes blazes to life

"Understood?" I finish.

She nods, and I walk away before I can't.

"Funny running into you here."

"Jesus fuck, Brax. Do I have to see your ugly mug at every one of these events?"

He winces. "Afraid so. I owe the coach the hours for helping me out of something last year. I'm on gala duty for the entire season."

"Well, thank god it's almost over. These things are expensive."

"You're telling me." He grins. "It's all worth it though. You should come to the Christmas one where we give out gifts to the kiddos. Seeing their little faces, man…it's worth every single penny."

"How much did we raise tonight?"

"Nearly $150k."

My brows shoot up. "No shit? Damn. I'm proud of us."

"Me too."

"You bring a date?"

"Nah." He takes a sip of the soda he's nursing. "I'm not really looking to get into dating right now. I'm trying to stay focused on my career."

My attention drifts over to Denny, who's yet again yakking it up with new friends. I'm a little thankful Penny was willing to bow out; we're both too antisocial in these settings. Denny, though—she thrives.

"I thought that was best once too. Made a lot of mistakes because of it, missed out on a lot of years with someone who made my whole world move." I draw my eyes away from my biggest mistake and look to my teammate. "I was wrong, though—real goddamn wrong, Brax."

He flicks his eyes to Denny. "She know that?"

"I think she's finally starting to get it."

"Good. Just—"

"Don't fuck it up?"

He laughs, holding his hands up. "Hey, man, I'm just saying. Guys are morons sometimes. We're prone to fucking shit up."

"Trust me, I know."

"Good luck, dude. I'm first on the roster and I just got my reminder. I'm out of here." He claps me on the shoulder. "Oh, and by the way, I'm fairly certain she's over there telling people your dick is only a few inches long again."

"Goddammit."

Tossing back the last of the champagne—which I still fucking hate—I make my way over to the woman in question just in time to hear some of the shit she's spewing.

"And then he said, 'It's not about the size of the boat, it's the motion in the ocean.' I knew I couldn't leave the poor guy after that played-out line. It was obvious he was desperate for someone to stick around."

She sighs sympathetically, and all the girls around her titter with their own half-hearted comments.

The way these girls are eating this up…it's comical how easy they are.

A few ladies throw sad smiles my way, those ones that say, *Good thing your pockets are deep.*

I clear my throat, pushing away the urge to laugh when one's eyes widen upon spotting me standing behind Denver.

"Bucky." It takes everything I have to keep my face straight and the humor out of my voice.

"Excuse me, ladies." She spins on her heel, a smirk playing at her lips. God, I want to kiss her so bad right now because I know exactly what game she's playing at. "Yes, Cap?"

"May I have a word?"

"Sure thing."

I grab her elbow and hurriedly steer us from the room. She laughs the whole way there, waving at some of the friends she's made in the last few weeks.

"Ma'am, is there somewhere quiet my guest and I could talk?" I ask a server who passes by us.

"We aren't really allowed to let guests use any of these rooms."

"Please, she's just told me she has herpes and we *need* to discuss it."

Denny's laugh echoes off the walls. The server's mouth drops open, looking between me and my date, confused as hell, I'm certain.

With a shaky finger, she points down the hall. "There's an empty storage room down there, but don't—"

"Thank you, that will do."

"G-Good luck," the poor woman murmurs as I drag Denny away and toward the room.

The moment I click the lock into place, I press her back against the door, caging her in between my arms.

Suddenly, she's no longer laughing.

"Last time you did this I proved I could most definitely use my tongue."

She nods.

"And this time I assume you're looking for something too?"

She nods again.

"What did I tell you about games, Denver?"

"That they don't suit me." She lifts a shoulder. "It's interesting, though, because I keep winning them."

She's not winning this round.

Twenty-Three

DENVER

Shep crushes his mouth to mine, stealing away anything else I had to say.

I love that he caught on to my game, and I love even more that he's falling right into my trap. I haven't been able to stop thinking about his promise to fuck me since we left the hotel room.

That was two hours ago.

That's two whole hours of squeezing my thighs together and trying to push the thoughts away so I don't embarrass myself in a room full of strangers.

Two hours of pure torture.

I guess that's nothing when you compare it to the years we've spent apart and the pining that occurred. I tried so hard to ignore him, to move on, to do anything but think of Shepard Clark, but it was no use. The universe pushed us together too many times to count, and it was pure agony.

So, yeah, I *could* survive a little longer without Shep fulfilling his promise, but that doesn't mean I want to.

I shove my hands into his suit jacket, clawing at him and pulling him as close to me as possible, craving the feel of his body against mine.

We have too many clothes in our way.

"Pull your dress up," he says, like he's reading my mind.

Shep falls to his knees, and it's a good thing he's holding on to my hips because I nearly fall over at the sight.

If there's one thing I've learned about Shep, it's that he *loves* eating me out.

Which is good, because I love it too.

Slowly, enjoying the anticipation, I shimmy until the dress is around my hips, lucky the material has a little give to it.

"Seriously, Denny?" He nearly pants once I'm bared.

"What? I didn't want panty lines."

"Fuck." He scrubs a hand over his face. "I could strangle you for walking around like this all night."

"There you go talking about asphyxiation again."

Without another word, he parts my lips with his tongue, finding my clit and sucking it into his mouth.

A loud moan escapes me, and he pulls away, grinning up at me with wet lips.

"You might wanna dial that down, Den."

"You might want to shut up and keep proving to me just how good you are with your tongue, Shep. You wanna—oh, *fuck*!"

He uses his thumbs to part me as he works me over with his mouth, and *holy hell,* I could stay in this closet with him forever.

I rock against him and he loves it, letting me ride his face and his tongue until I'm sitting on the edge of pure fucking bliss. I have to press my hand over my mouth to quiet my whimpers as an orgasm threatens to shoot through me.

Just as I'm about to explode, Shep pulls away.

"What the—"

He stands, his hand covering my mouth before I can say another word.

"What was that about winning?"

"I hate you," I hiss.

"It's a fine line between love and hate, Bucky."

My heart races. Those words might be the truest ones he's ever spoken.

I've known for a long time now Shep and I weren't finished. Even when he humiliated me all those years ago and turned away from me, I knew in my heart of hearts it wasn't over. We could never be over.

Because fate had other plans.

That's the only way to explain the way the universe kept pushing us together.

I drop my hands to the belt on his waist, the clinking of the metal as I unbuckle it echoing off the walls like gunshots in the otherwise quiet closet.

"Tell me you have a condom, Shep."

Without another word, he pulls his wallet from his back pocket, producing a foil packet.

"Thank god."

"I'm about 9% certain you can't talk about God during sex."

I shove his pants and tight black boxer briefs down his hips, curling my hand around his cock once it's free.

His eyes fall shut as he sags forward, catching himself with one hand against the door as I work him over.

"Oh fuck," he groans. "I don't think you can keep doing that, Den. I'm already too close."

"Then do something about it."

He grins and says, "Only if you go back out there and tell those girls my cock is *definitely* bigger than three inches."

I stroke him again. Another groan.

"Shep?"

"Yeah?"

"Shut up and fuck me."

He uses his teeth to rip the condom open then covers himself within seconds.

Before I know it, he's wrapping my leg around his hip and thrusting into me in one swift move.

"*Shiiiiiiiiiiiit.*" He draws the word out on a hiss.

I wrap my hands around his head, threading my fingers through his hair and holding on as he pumps in and out of me at a pace that's going to ensure neither of us last very long.

Good. We can save the soft and slow for later.

"Holy shit. This is better than I could have imagined." He drops his forehead to mine, brushing soft kisses against my lips. "Have you ever thought about us, Denny? About what it would be like for me to be inside you?"

"Y-Yes."

"And what you imagined—was it better than this?"

"Yes."

He pulls back, still thrusting inside me. "Why?"

My shoulder blades press against the door and I know it's going to leave a bruise, but I don't care. Despite my answer to his question, I wouldn't trade this for anything.

"Because you loved me."

His movements stop, and I hate that he stops. His fingers collide with my face, pulling my attention to his. It's dark in the closet, but our eyes have adjusted enough for me to know he's staring at me with pain and desire and confusion in his expression.

I'm giving it all right back to him.

After what feels like a lifetime, he drops his forehead back to mine and pumps into me harder than ever, and I love every goddamn second of it.

Our pants fill the room, so loud that I know if someone were to walk by the door right now, they'd know exactly what we're doing.

I reach between us, rubbing circles over my clit, so close to release. By the change in his breathing, I know he's there too.

His lips trace along my ear.

"You say it would have been better if I had loved you."

His voice is hoarse, almost harsh, and he doesn't quit moving inside me.

I don't say anything, because I know he's not expecting an answer.

"Well I have news for you, Denver."

Another thrust. Another groan.

"I never fucking stopped."

My whole world falls apart around me.

Twenty-Four

Five years ago, May

Denver: DOWNLOAD ATTACHMENT

Denver: I made it!

Denver: Is it just me or is the east
coast ridiculously humid? I feel like
I'm trying to breathe under water.

Denver: Hey, you good? I texted
yesterday and didn't get a response.

Denver: Allie and I went shopping for things for the apartment today. She bought half of Target.

Denver: Shep?

Denver: Well, just text me back whenever you have a chance. I'm sure you're swamped.

Denver: I'm starting to worry. I haven't heard from you in days.

Denver: Is everything okay?

Denver: I tried calling. I know that's not something we do, but I had to try anyway.

Denver: Just please let me know you're okay.

Denver: Okay, so this is my last text. If you're not answering, there's nothing I can do about that. Allie and I will be at the party Friday night. I'll see ya if I see ya. Good `night, Shep.`

SHEPARD

"Why in the fuck would you invite her?"

"Uh, because she's my girlfriend's best friend, and the girl you're into. Obviously, dickhead." AJ rolls his eyes and takes a long pull off his beer, not caring about the clear irritation in my voice. "What's your deal, dude? All of a sudden you're not into Denny anymore? What gives?"

Oh, I'm into Denny. I am *very* into Denny.

Some would say I'm *too* into her.

I love her.

And that's scary as fuck.

I'm so deep in this weird long-distance thing we have going on that there is no way it could possibly be healthy. It scares me…big time.

So much so that I stopped responding to her texts last week. I tucked my tail like a fucking pussy and hid from her and my feelings.

It's too much for me, too intense.

I want it too badly.

What if it doesn't work out? What if we don't work out? What if I'm not what she wants? The fallout of that is going to be a whole lot worse if we continue to get attached.

So, I'm doing the responsible thing—ending it before it can go any further.

"You're not running scared, are you?"

I glare at my best friend, annoyed he knows me so well. "Shut the fuck up, AJ."

"I'm just saying, you should at least give it a shot with her. She's a cool chick."

"And what if she hates me?"

"Oh, she's gonna hate you all right, especially if you fucking ditch her after she moved out here for your ass."

"She didn't move out here for me. She moved for Allie."

"Whatever you two morons need to tell yourselves." He takes another drink. "I'm gonna head to the back room. Just send Allie that way when she gets here, which will be any moment."

"Why don't you go get your girlfriend yourself?"

He shakes his bottle. "Because I'm fucking out of beer, that's why."

I flip off his back as he spins around.

"Stop flipping me off."

"I hate you!"

He laughs. "Liar. Go get the door."

I realize then the doorbell *is* ringing.

My fingers begin to tingle, and I have to count backward from ten so I don't run in the opposite direction.

Just do it, Shep. Get it over with.

I push my way through the bodies, trying not to freak out the entire trek to the door.

I don't give myself time to pause or think. I just pull the door open and face Denny for the first time ever.

Fuck me.

She's *gorgeous*—stunning, even. Her photos on social media don't do her justice. Her dark hair is pulled into a messy braid that's sitting on her shoulder, and her green eyes are so much brighter than I could have imagined.

I shake myself from my stupor and fix my eyes on Allie, willing myself not to glance at Denny again.

"What are you doing here?"

I know what the fuck she's doing here. I'm just biding my time, making this last as long as possible because apparently I love to torture myself.

She just stares at me, so I step aside, waving them in. "He's in the back."

I don't miss the look Allie gives Denny, or the one Denny gives her before she tries to catch my eye.

I don't let it happen because I know I'll break if it does.

With a sigh, Denny grabs Allie's outstretched hand and lets her best friend drag her through the mass of bodies.

I let them disappear into the crowd, watching her as she's swallowed up by the crowd.

I need a moment. I need to think. I need to make sure.

No. No thinking. Just do it.

I march toward the back room, determined. The guys in the room eye her, and I want to punch every fucking single one of them.

Instead I lean against the doorframe, my arms crossed over my chest so my fists don't snake out on their own.

"Who you here with, doll?"

Doll—ugh. Fucking pet names.

"I'm with—"

"She came with Allie," I interrupt.

I don't know why I say it, but I can't take it back now, especially not since I can see the hurt in Denny's eyes.

She doesn't like that I didn't say she's here with me. In fact, she hates it.

Good. Maybe I can make her hate me too. That'll make this easier.

"Yep." She points a shaky finger at Allie. "I'm here with her—

only her."

Her words sting, but I don't let it show.

I can't. I *have* to walk away now. I don't have a choice. It's either break it off now or go down in flames, and I've never been one to play with fire.

"Since you're free, you want to dance?"

She glances to me again.

I don't back down.

"Sure. I'd love to," she says, a cheery fake smile on her lips.

He pulls himself from the chair. "I'm Cade."

She slides her hand into his extended one, and the contact makes me reel. It's even worse when he pulls her toward him and she crashes against his chest.

He grins. "Just thought we'd get that out of the way before we go make sweet love on the dance floor."

God fucking dammit.

She smirks up at him playfully, eating out of the palm of his hand. "Sweet love, huh? That's where you're going with this?"

Cade loves her mouth, which is complete fucking bullshit because that's *my* mouth to love.

I have to turn away before I do something I'll regret, like beat the shit out of my teammate for trying to steal my girl.

Someone slams into me, stumbling and spilling a beer on my shirt.

Great.

"Oh em gee! I am *so* sorry, Slug." I try not to flinch at the nickname. "I didn't see you there."

Sure you didn't.

"Whatever. Wanna dance?"

I don't even glance at her or wait for her to answer, my eyes are too busy tracking Denver through the room.

My blood boils when Cade slips his arms around her waist. I do the same thing to the girl in my arms because if I don't, I'm going to fucking lose it.

Denny's gaze finds me again. *Why does she have to keep looking over here?*

I see it, even from across the room—I see the hate and the rage burning through her.

Good, Den. Good.

Cade nuzzles her neck. I mimic him. Everything he does to Denny, I do to the girl in my arms. She hates it, physically hates him touching her. I can see from here she wishes it were me.

She wants me like I want her, and I want her a whole hell of a lot.

I realize in that moment I *have* to follow through with this, because Denver Andrews could fucking break me.

She pushes free of Cade again, sending him a smile and then running from the room.

I waste no time chasing after her. I have to make sure I take this all the way.

I find her standing at the bottom of the stairs, and everything inside me screams that I should go to her and wrap her in my arms and take away all the pain.

But I don't.

Instead I say, "You should leave."

She spins around, mouth dropping open in surprise.

"L-Leave?" It comes out a strangled whisper. "What do you mean? I just came out here to breathe, not to leave."

"I meant what I said." She studies me hard, long enough to know I'm not joking but not long enough to know I'm lying, internally pleading for her to stay. "You should leave," I repeat.

"Why?"

"Because I fucking said so."

230

I cannot believe this is happening, can't believe I'm doing this.

I was wrong. This was wrong.

It hurts. It *fucking hurts* and it wasn't supposed to hurt. This was supposed to prevent the pain, not ignite it.

"Why are you doing this?" she asks quietly, barely holding back tears. "Did I do something wrong?"

I drop my gaze from hers, knowing I need to before her tears break me down. "We both knew this was coming."

"Did w-we?" Her voice cracks, and I hate that it cracks. "Because I sure didn't expect this. I came out here for *you*—for *us*...for *dibs*. We've talked about this for months. I most certainly did not expect this."

My eyes fall closed for a moment, and a future where Denver leaves me flashes through my mind.

That pain is much worse than this pain.

"You did, Denver."

The use of her full name startles her; I know by the way her breaths quicken.

"You knew I wasn't cut out for commitment from the beginning," I push on, and the longer I talk, the angrier she gets. "Whatever you built this up to in your head is your own fault. I can't do this." I flick my finger between us, driving the point home. "Whatever this *was*, it's over."

The fury blazes in her eyes.

Good. Be angry. Hate me, Den. Hate me like I hate me right now.

And she does. She hates me. I can see it.

Without another word, she turns on her heel and continues down the walkway.

"I mean it, Denver. This is over."

I can't tell if I'm trying to convince her or myself.

"I heard you loud and clear...*Slug*."

My breath hitches, and I know she hears it.

She did it. She called me *Slug*.

I know in that moment. I know.

Cap and Bucky? We're officially done.

And the pain is everything I didn't want.

Twenty-Five

SHEPARD

"You got us *locked* in a closet because you couldn't keep your dick in your pants!"

"I didn't hear you complaining a few minutes ago when said dick was inside you. All I heard was lots of moaning and heavy breathing, maybe a few cries for 'more'."

She smacks at my chest and I laugh, causing her to strike at me again.

I don't understand how she can be upset right now. What we just did? That was *mind-blowing*.

I should be committed to the crazy house because I have no fucking clue how I spent so many years not touching her.

"Murder, Shep! I will murder you!" Denny bangs on the door. "Help! I'm going to murder him, and I am way too cute for jail!"

"So dramatic." I roll my eyes even though she can't see me. "Let me see if Braxton is still here."

I pull my phone out, scroll through the contacts, and tap his name just as the overhead light flicks to life.

"Goddamn, woman!" I shield my eyes. "That's bright!"

"Well?"

"Well what, you impatient little shit? It's still ringing."

Denny huffs, crossing her arms over her chest and tapping her foot. I can't help but laugh at her again. She looks so fucking cute when she's upset, especially when she's still rocking that post-orgasm glow. Her hair is a mess, her dress is wrinkled, and it's obvious she's been up to no good.

The line trills in my ear and I'm about to hang up when I finally hear Braxton's voice fill the speaker.

"You already fucked it up, didn't you?"

"First of all, fuck you. Second of all, no—well, not in the sense you're thinking at least. Please tell me you're still here."

"Hell no. I bounced quick. I *do* have a life outside of philanthropic events, ya know. Why? What's up?"

I groan. "Fuck. Well, see, what had happened was…"

His deep laugh fills the line. "Nothing good ever starts with those words."

"I kind of sort of locked myself…and Denny…in a closet."

He's quiet…quiet enough that I think he's hung up, so I check the line.

Nope, he's still there.

"Braxton?"

"I'm sorry," he says through laughter. "But did you two *fuck* at a charity gala?"

"I…" I try to come up with a lie, but nothing sounds right, so I settle for the truth. "Yes."

"Oh shit." More laughter. "You're a mess, Clark, a real fuckin' mess. If the coaches caught wind of this…"

234

"I know, I know. I'd be out on my ass, but it was a necessary risk to take."

"Was it? Couldn't have waited until you got back to your room?"

"I'm sorry, but did you *see* that dress?" I whisper into the phone. "You know what, don't answer that."

"I'm shaking my head at you, Clark."

"Yeah, yeah."

"Maybe try calling Joe? He's still there, second to last to leave."

"Son of a bitch," I complain through gritted teeth.

That bastard Braxton laughs again.

"I am thinking really hard of turning around right now, though, if that makes you feel any better. I'm so tempted to do it just to see Joe let you out."

"I'm hanging up on you, dick."

"Good luck, Clark."

The line goes dead.

"He can't help us?"

I shake my head at her. "Nope."

"Do you have any other teammates here?"

"None that I want to call."

She marches toward me, holding her hand out. "Then I will. Gimme."

"No way!" I clutch my phone to my chest. "Not happening."

"You *will* call someone to get us out of here, or this"—she twirls her fingers between us—"will have been a onetime-only thing."

I smirk at her. "Oh, Den. We've waited *years* for this to happen—we both know I don't have to do anything other than crook my finger at you to get you back in bed."

"Want to test that theory, Cap?"

"I'd bet double on it."

She grits her teeth because she knows I'm right, and then she

235

lunges for my phone again.

Naturally, she misses.

Thank you, baseball reflexes.

She turns back to the door, banging loud and hard. "Help us!"

"Quiet! If my coach finds out about—"

"You fucking me in a closet while you're supposed to be raising money for charity?"

"Yes, that. If he finds out, I'm fucked. We need to handle this discreetly."

She raises her hand like she's about to bang on the door again, hard green eyes penetrating me across the small space. "Then you better start dialing, Shep."

"You're crazy."

She lifts a brow.

"Don't worry"—I wink—"I like it."

With reluctance, because I know he's going to give me intolerable amounts of shit, I scroll until I find Joe's number and hit call.

"Are you calling me from inside the building? Where'd you disappear to?"

"I, uh, I kind of need your help."

"Oh, this is going to be good."

I hear the smile in Joe's voice and now *I* want to kill me for doing this to us.

"I'm locked in a closet."

"I'm sorry, you're in the closet and you need *my* help getting out? I'm flattered, Clark, but I don't bat for that team."

"Joe…" I pinch my nose. "I'm not alone."

"Who are you with? That girl you brought?"

"Obviously."

He hoots in laughter. "Oh wow, man. That's ballsy considering all the trouble you're already in. What a dumbass."

"I don't need a talking to, Joe. I need help out."

"Where are you?"

"If you go out of the room through the main door and make a left, we're down at the end in the small storage closet."

"Give me five."

He ends the call.

"Is he going to help?"

"Yes, but it's going to come with a price."

She gives me a lopsided grin. "Was it worth it?"

I want to toss a witty comeback at her, a saucy grin, something flirtatious and fun and light—but I can't.

There's something that's bugging me more than I'd like to admit, and if Denny and I are going to have a future together, I need to start bucking the fuck up and talking to her about my insecurities—the same ones that drove me away from her all those years ago.

"I don't know, you tell me, Ms. It's Not As Good As I Imagined."

She ducks her head, and I can tell the reality of what we just did is hitting her for the first time.

I make my way over, wrapping an arm around her waist and drawing her close. Gently, I place two fingers under her chin and bring her face up to mine.

Her cheeks are still flushed from her orgasm, a sheen of sweat still covers her forehead, and even her makeup is looking like it has seen better days.

She's still so fucking beautiful though.

"Did you mean it?" she whispers.

"More than anything."

"I want to believe you."

"Then do."

She sighs, closing her eyes against my stare. "I've heard you say that before, Shep. I've heard you tell me you mean it then in the end, you didn't."

"I've always meant it, Den, even then. Even when I pushed you away, I meant it."

"Then why?" She drops her head to my chest. "Why couldn't we be together?"

I press a gentle kiss to her temple. "Because I'm a fucking pussy when it comes to love. I'm petrified to have my heart broken. I don't want to experience that same earth-shattering pain my mom felt when my dad died. So, I run and I hide and I push people away, especially the people who mean the most to me."

"I'm not going anywhere, Shep. I never planned to go anywhere."

"I know that now."

"I can't do this with you again if all you're going to do is break my heart."

For a moment, just one single moment, Zach and Delia flit through my mind, but I push them away.

I pull Denny's face back up to mine, forcing her to look me in the eyes.

"I won't."

I'm a liar.

The saddest part? We both believe what I'm saying.

It's nearly twenty minutes later when there's a tapping at the door. "Clark?"

"Oh thank fuck," I mutter, pushing off the wall. "Joe, dude, I never thought I'd be so happy to hear your voice."

"Say that again, just a little louder. I don't think the microphone caught that."

"I lied. Go away."

"No!" Denny shouts, running to the door and yanking on the handle. "Please let us out!"

"Not until Clark tells me I'm the best shortstop on the team, *and* that I have the biggest dick."

"Your cock is massive and you're the best shortstop!"

"Thank you, sweetheart, but I need to hear it from Clark's mouth."

"That was the sickest thing I have ever heard leave your mouth, and you talk a lot of shit," I tell Denny quietly. "You need to take it back."

"Fine, I take it back, but *you* need to say it. I'm starting to feel like I'm suffocating in here. If that's the price you have to pay then pay up."

"Clark? I'm needed back at the party. It's now or never."

"Say it," Denny pushes.

"Fuck," I groan. "You're the best shortstop on the team and you have the biggest dick!"

Joe cackles and turns the knob, pulling the door open. His grinning face fills the doorway.

"'Sup, buttmunch?"

I grab Denny's hand and shove past him.

The applause starts, the noise filling the otherwise empty hallway.

Several guys from the team are standing out there, all hooting and hollering as Denny and I make our shameful exit.

"Way to go, Clark!"

"Yeah! Nice going!"

"You're the real MVP!"

Denny being Denny, she starts high-fiving and fist-bumping the guys, apparently feeling real goddamn proud of herself.

Fucking hell. I duck my head and pull her forward as fast as I can.

When we get to the last player, Denny yanks herself out of my grasp and turns to the crowd.

"I'd like to take this moment to address some rumors you might have heard about Shepard Clark—rumors spread by me."

They all listen with rapt attention, amused smiles on their faces. *Bastards.*

"I was wrong to tell everyone Shep's penis is only three inches long. That was a miscalculation on my part."

What is she doing...?

She gives me a quick wink. "It's clearly four."

With that, she bows, and then she sashays down the hall, leaving me standing here with my mouth agape and all my teammates in tears of laughter.

"I vote we keep her," Joe says.

A smile creeps across my face as I stare after the woman who just fucked me in a supply closet, made me confess my love for her, and then told all my friends I have a four-inch dick like it was nothing.

I vote we keep her too.

Twenty-Six

DENVER

I was right. Casual with Shep would be impossible.

Every feeling I've had about him in the last five years reared its ugly head the moment he slid inside me.

I felt the love, hate, adoration, the rage, and the hurt—all of it. With every thrust, every gentle touch…it was all there, begging to burst from my chest.

And when he asked me if it was what I'd always imagined? I couldn't bring myself to lie to him, not while he was inside me.

Which is why I beelined to the bathroom after our tryst. I need time to breathe, a moment to myself to wrap my head around the fact that he'd said he never stopped loving me.

How is that possible when he hurt me so much? How is it possible that I still love him even through all that?

Is that what fate is? Loving someone even when you know you're not supposed to? Knowing they have the power to destroy you yet still opening your heart to them?

If so, maybe Shep was right to fear fate. It's scary as hell.

I finish cleaning up my makeup and smoothing down the flyaways that have escaped the intricate bun I have my hair tied up in. Once I decide I don't completely look like I've been ravished, I make my way back to the main ballroom.

Sliding back into the crowd, I accept a glass of champagne from one of the waitstaff.

"When we get up to that room, your ass is mine."

His warm hand slides his body against me, and I smirk against the glass I have raised to my lips.

"Wow, we're already progressing to anal? You move fast, Shep."

He shakes his head. "I never know what to expect from your mouth, Denny."

"Is that good or bad?"

"Good—most of the time."

"When don't you like it?"

"Well, when you tell everyone I have a four-inch dick, for instance."

I try not to laugh. "You're right—three was much more believable."

"Dammit, Denny," he mutters, pulling me close and laying a kiss on my cheek. "I'm keeping you this time."

I turn into him, catching his hungry eyes with mine. "Are you?"

"If you'll let me, Bucky."

I take another sip of alcohol, needing the confidence.

"We'll see, Cap. We'll see."

242

"What are you doing?" Shep asks as I drop to my knees when we enter the hotel room. He chuckles. "Steve is in his crate—and you're the one who put him in there."

"I'm not down here for Steve."

His eyes darken. "Den…"

"Didn't you say I could only be on my knees for you in one of these dresses?"

He swallows thickly and nods.

I've never been one for giving blow jobs. It always felt like work, not play. This, though, feels different.

It's Shep, so I should expect nothing less.

I don't look away from him as I work his buckle open, don't blink when the sound of his zipper echoes off the walls, and refuse to look away even as I draw his slacks and boxers down his thighs.

I don't dare close my eyes as I take him into my mouth for the first time.

His hiss of pleasure fills the room as I begin to suck him, and a pressure is already beginning to build between my legs.

"No," he instructs with a strained voice as I begin to close my eyes. He wraps his hand in my hair, pulling until there's just a bite of pain to keep me looking at him. "Don't you fucking dare, Bucky."

I don't dare.

He moans when I take him deeper, and the moisture between my legs builds to an embarrassing level. I wish I'd thought ahead and pulled my dress up so I could at least rub my clit, but this isn't about me. It's about him, and I'm sure it won't take much to cajole Shep into round three.

His breathing grows ragged and I can tell he's already getting close.

"Fuck, this is so embarrassing. I'm about to come."

I pull off him but continue stroking, giving him a lazy grin. "I can stop, if you want."

"I swear, you're trying to kill me." He bites at his lip, pushing into my hand and stifling another groan of pleasure. "If you don't keep sucking, I'm taking it out on your ass."

"So much talk of ass play tonight."

"Den?"

"Yes, Shep?"

"Suck."

I take him into my mouth again, breathing through my nose as I take him deeper than I have before. His legs shake, and I hum with a thrill at his reaction.

"*Fuckfuckfuck*," he mutters.

He pulls my hair tighter and the move nearly brings me to orgasm, all without him even touching me below the waist.

"Den, unless you want me to blow my load down your throat, move."

I don't move.

"Last chance," he grits out.

I pull back but don't let him go, working him until he empties himself in my mouth.

I release him, sitting back on my haunches, feeling satisfied as he collapses against the door, his breathing ragged and raw.

"Jesus, Den."

"What did I say—"

"9%," he huffs out on a strangled laugh. "I know."

"Quit licking my feet, Shep."

"Why would I lick your feet?"

"Um, because you're a freak."

"True, but I'm not *that* big of a freak." He turns toward me, and I feel his breath on the back of my neck. "Two things: one, I'm too tired to lick your feet—you've worn me out with all the orgasms—and two, did you ever stop to think it might be Steve licking your feet?"

I don't know how he had the energy to roll over just now. I couldn't move even if I tried.

I didn't have to wait long for Shep to return the orgasm favor. Once he regained his composure, he scooped me up off the floor and hauled me into a steaming shower, where he showed me that shower sex *can* be fun.

Then he showed me that sex on a bed is great too, and that's where we've been ever since, too worn out to move.

"First, Steve knows I hate that. Second, are you telling me if you weren't too tired then you *would* be licking my feet?"

Though I'm not facing him, I know he rolls his eyes. "Go to sleep, Den."

"Snuggle me first."

"I don't snuggle."

"You also said you don't do commitment…or love…" I trail off.

He groans and wraps his arm around me, being the big spoon to my little.

"Can you tell me something?"

"Can you promise me you'll go to sleep after I tell you?"

"Yes, and unlike you, I stick to my promises." He pinches my ass with his free hand and I yelp, trying to wiggle away, but he holds me tighter. "There's that ass play you've been promising all night."

He shakes his head. "What do you want me to tell you, Bucky?"

"Was it something I did or said?"

I don't have to elaborate. He knows exactly what I'm referring to.

They're the same questions I asked him all those years ago, standing on that porch.

Did I do something to push him away? Did I say something to make him run?

"No, it wasn't you." He presses a kiss to my neck. "Zach and his fiancée broke up."

"Now that I know he's Delia's Zach, I just cannot imagine him engaged to anyone else."

"It didn't last long, and it scared me. They were together for years before getting engaged. They were supposed to be that couple that made it through college. They didn't, though. They failed, and I was terrified we would fail too."

"You didn't even give us a chance, Cap."

"I know." Another kiss. "But all these doubts started creeping in. What if I wasn't good enough for you? What if I couldn't make you happy? You were moving across the country for me—what if I didn't give you everything you needed? What if I wanted baseball more than you? There was so much I didn't have answers for."

"That's life, though. We don't have answers for any of it."

"Tell that to eighteen-year-old me, because I sure as shit always thought I had all the answers. I was the king of the fucking world."

I laugh. "You still think you're the king."

I feel his smile against my neck. "Guilty, but I was wrong then, Den. I was wrong to project all my insecurities onto you. It's something I've done time and time again. I've made that same mistake several times after…us, but I'm ready to own up to it. I'm ready to face it."

I roll toward him, snuggling close and searching for his eyes in the dimly lit room. "What changed?"

Shep buries his face in the pillows. "Yurhunnawaf."

"What?"

"Yurhunnawafatme."

"English, Shepard—do you speak it?"

He turns to me, grinning. "Say what again. I dare you. I double dare you."

I wrinkle my nose. "Um, what?"

"Oh god, you haven't seen it." He rolls away from me, pulling himself out of bed...naked. He moves around so fast that Steve falls off and darts under the desk, cowering in his bed. "Well"—he tosses his hands up in the air—"this was good while it lasted. I'll be taking my dog and leaving now."

"Don't you dare touch Steve!" I shoot up to a sitting position, pointing at him. "I've seen *Pulp Fiction*. Now get your ass back in bed."

"Oh, thank god," he says as he exhales. He shakes his head, sliding back under the blankets. "I thought we were done for."

We snuggle back down into the same spots we were in before.

"Tell me."

"Fine, but no laughing."

"Is *that* what you were saying? That I was going to laugh at you?"

"Duh. Anyway, it was Allie and AJ. They, uh, they're the ones who made me believe."

"In?"

"Love. Fate. All that other bullshit you subscribe to."

"So then Santa, Valentine's Day, *and* the dangers of mixing Pop Rocks and Coke?"

He laughs, remembering what he said to me all those years ago. "Yes, all that bullshit."

"How?"

"They made it." He brushes away a hair that's fallen over my eye. "They made it through college, AJ's baseball career, and all the other shit. They did it."

I lean into him, getting close enough to where he thinks I'm going to kiss him, then against his lips, I whisper, "I called it."

He chuckles when I pull away. "You did. And it just got me thinking about us..."

"And everything we missed."

"God, there's so much."

"We could have at least three pugs by now."

"Is Steve not enough for you, Den?"

"You can't just ask a girl how many pugs is enough. That's barbaric."

He laughs, and I roll onto my back and can feel him staring holes into the side of my head.

"What?" I ask.

"Last month, when I almost lost my career over one stupid decision, it made me realize all the other things I've lost to stupid decisions."

"Like?"

"The respect of my parents. A relationship with my brother. Some friends. And the biggest one of them all..." He pauses then exhales a shaky breath. "You."

"I'm right here, Shep."

"I'm right here too, and I'm not going anywhere—not this time."

I don't say anything else.

I stare at the ceiling for a long time, so long that Steve begins to snore from his corner of the room.

Not Shep, though. He's still awake...waiting, staring.

I roll back toward him, capturing his hazel stare with my own.

"I'm not going anywhere either, but Cap?"

"Yeah?"

"No bullshit this time?"

"No bullshit. Until the end of the line."

My eyes widen. "I think I just came. You quoted Captain America to me."

He winks. "You're welcome."

And then I smother him with a pillow.

Twenty-Seven

SHEPARD

I've never been the type to talk about my feelings, always keeping shit bottled up because it's no one's business but my own. Last night, talking to Denny so openly about how abso-fucking-lutely terrified I am of heartbreak was a first for me. It was the most real I've been in a long time, probably since I had a screen and two thousand miles separating us.

I wasn't lying when I told her I still love her. How could I possibly stop? Of course I fucking love her. I just didn't have the goddamn balls to put my heart on the line back then.

Now in the car on the way home, I peer at her out of the corner of my eye, admiring the way her lashes fall across her cheeks, loving the freckles that dot the bridge of her nose, the upturn of her plump lips, which are the same color as her nipples.

"I can feel you staring."

"No you can't."

"Can too, ass."

"Ass? Is that any way to talk to the guy who gave you a wild night of pleasure?"

"You might have fucked me, Shep, but I'm still a little mad at you."

The word *fuck* leaving her lips makes my dick jump, and this is *so* not the time for that shit.

I clear my throat. "Why's that, Den?"

"For then. For screwing up our dibs. For making me chase after you and then abandoning me."

"I—"

"You never told me why."

I dare a peek at her. She's still resting against the window, eyes still closed like she can't look at me for this conversation, and I can't say I blame her.

I kind of want to kiss her for it because I don't think I can stand to look at her right now either.

"I was scared."

"*I was scared.* That's your big reasoning for pretending I didn't exist when I packed my life up and moved across the country for you? Leaving me completely on my own and scared out of my mind?" The irritation in her voice is clear.

"It's the truth, Den. I told you last night I was scared to go through what my mom did. I was fucking terrified as shit that I could fall in love with someone I'd never met before, frightened out of my goddamn mind that someone could mean so much to me." I squeeze the steering wheel tighter. "The only thing I was ever passionate about was baseball. That was it for me. That's all it was ever supposed to be."

"We were young, Shep. You had your whole life for baseball."

"I had my whole life for love, too. I wasn't supposed to find it then, not when I had a career ahead of me, a future I couldn't dream of wrecking."

"Yet you almost did last month…without me. You could have had me *and* baseball," she argues.

I shake my head. "Not then. I couldn't afford the distraction. It was either go after my lifelong dream of playing in the big leagues or chase after a girl I'd never met."

"I hate the way you say that," she says in a small voice. "Like what we had didn't mean anything."

"It meant everything, and that was the scariest part of all of it," I tell her honestly. "If it had come down to it, I would have walked away from my dream for you. That scared me to no end."

"You wouldn't have walked away from baseball."

I laugh. It's dry and dark and sad even to my own ears. "But I already had."

She sits up in her seat, finally looking up at me. "What do you mean?"

"I was recruited by another school with a better team."

"What!" she yells so loudly she wakes Steve, who begins scrambling up her chest, whining like mad.

She cuddles him close. "Shh, shh. Sorry, buddy, didn't mean to scare you. Your dad just dropped a big, unexpected goddamn bomb on me and I'm about two seconds from kicking his ass."

"I could totally take you," I tell her.

She glowers at me. "Don't test me right now, Shepard."

Denny scoops Steve into her arms and slides him into the crate in the back seat. She tucks a blanket around him and closes the door, not turning back to me until he's snuggled in tight.

Spoiled little shit.

"Explain."

"What, no *please*?"

"Shepard…" she warns, her tone enough to send a chill down my back.

I let out a long breath. "I already said it: I was recruited by a bigger, better school. I was days away from telling them yes."

"What happened?"

"You sent me that acceptance letter for Christmas. I called them the next day and turned them down."

Her mouth drops open and she shakes her head, staring at me like I'm fucking insane. "But…but…why in the hell would you do that!"

"You. Us. *Dibs*. Because you were coming to be with me."

"What about AJ? He was coming too."

"Right, but AJ is a baseball guy. He knew how big a deal it was to be recruited by that school. He was telling me to go for it."

"Why would you do that, Shep?" she begs, desperate for answers. "Why?"

"I already said why: because of you, because I loved you, Den. I wanted to be with you."

"Then why did you abandon me? Why did you ignore me? I showed up to that party and you shut me out—literally! Not only did you break my heart, you embarrassed the shit out of me. Why? A classic case of cold feet?"

"It got real."

"What did?"

"Dibs." I motion between us. "*We* got too real. You being there…it scared me. What if I wasn't what you wanted or expected? What if we didn't work out? What if we failed? What if I regretted not taking that offer?"

"Sure, Shep, sure, but what if you were everything I expected and hoped for? What if we did work out? What if we didn't fail? What if you didn't regret it for a second? What if the fucking Pope shits in the goddamn woods? There are a lot of what-ifs in life." She shakes her head. "Being chickenshit isn't a reason to walk away from something."

My knuckles turn white against the wheel.

She's right. I *know* she's right.

If I could go back and change everything, I would. I wouldn't push her away. I'd fight through my struggles. I'd fight for us.

But I can't change it. All I can do is make it up to her.

"I know that now. If it makes you feel any better, the only decision I've regretted the last five years is not giving us a chance, not giving up that school. It was us…always us."

She crosses her arms over her chest and lets out a sardonic laugh. "Good. You should. We would have been fucking amazing together."

I chuckle and glance over to her, enjoying the way her lips twitch, like she's made herself laugh with her own sarcasm.

It's typical Denny: fun, not perfect by any stretch of the imagination. She knows *exactly* who she is.

And I'm a goddamn fool for giving her up.

"We still can be, Bucky."

Her gaze shifts my way and I catch her green eyes for a moment before she turns away and whispers, "I know, Cap, and that's what scares me."

"What are you doing this Friday?"

"Did you just ask my *dog* what his plans are this Friday?"

"What? *Noooo!*" she drags out. "But also maybe."

"You have some serious problems." I grab Denver's suitcase from the bed of the truck and drop it to the ground. "He's not busy."

"Oh. Huh." She reaches into the truck to grab Steve, and I have the best view of her ass as she stretches across the cab. "Good to know."

I press myself against her when she stands, and I'm certain she feels just what the view she gave me has done to me.

"Neither am I," I say, my lips against her ear.

Her breaths come out stuttered. "Th-That's nice, Shep." She steps away. "Quit trying to bang me again."

"Don't you mean again again again again ag—?"

"How many times are you going to say again?"

"As many as it takes to catch up to how many times we…banged? Is that the right word?"

"Ugh," Denny groans, pulling Steve free from his crate and turning to face me. "Shut it."

I laugh and take a step away from her to keep myself from tossing her right back into my truck and keeping her forever.

"Why'd you wanna know what Steve is doing on Friday?"

"Gala, duh."

"We're off until after the wedding."

"Really? You mean I *don't* have to spend the next two weekends with you?"

"*Have* to? No. *Want* to?" I lean into her. "You want to spend time with me, especially after this weekend. Don't play, Den."

We didn't talk about our past any more on the ride here. We left everything we had said hanging in the air between us, especially that part about us having a future together.

I want one—I've always wanted one—and it gives me so much hope that Denny does too.

"How about we call a truce? Try for that future we missed out on?"

"You mean the one you stole from us?"

"Den…" I rub a hand over the back of my neck, trying to relax the knots the tension of the past few hours helped form. "I'm trying here."

"I know. That wasn't fair. I mean, it totally was, but I shouldn't have said it." She kicks at invisible rocks on the ground to avoid my eyes. "Sorry," she mumbles.

"Don't apologize to me, not after everything."

She lifts her head. "Truce?"

"Only if you agree to a date with me one night this week."

She beams at me. "I'd like that."

"What?" I raise a brow. "No pretending to hate me? No declaring you don't want to be seen in public with me?"

"Nah. We called truce. Besides, if we're going to the movies, it'll be dark. The movies don't count as public." She winks then grabs her bag from my hand. "See ya later, Shep."

"Denver?"

She quickens her pace but yells over her shoulder, "Yes?"

"Aren't you forgetting something?"

"Can't imagine a thing."

"Are you seriously stealing my dog right now?"

Steve barks in her arms. She moves even faster, her suitcase bouncing off the uneven pavement behind her.

She sends me a worried glance. "Nope!"

"You trying to get me to come inside?"

"Not a chance."

"Denver?"

"Maybe!"

I take off at a sprint, and catching her is easy. I curl my arm around her waist and pull her to me. She gasps out a laugh.

"Fine, fine. You caught me."

"You're the world's slowest runner."

"I'm holding a damn puppy *and* pulling my suitcase because *someone* didn't carry it up to my apartment for me."

"All you had to do was ask," I whisper into her ear.

She drops her suitcase at our feet. "Fine. Shep, will you please carry my suitcase for me?"

"*And?*" I prompt.

She huffs in faux annoyance. "And please come inside?"

I grin at her. "I thought you'd never ask."

We spend the rest of the day locked inside her apartment.

Twenty-Eight

Present day

Denver: HELP! She's kidnapped me and won't let me go.

Shepard: If I have to suffer through tux shopping with AJ then you have to suffer through dress shopping with Allie. Besides, aren't girls supposed to love this kind of shit?

Denver: Stereotype much?

Denver: Actually, I love dress shopping. Just not with Allie. This is pure torture.

Denver: She is SO picky.

Shepard: I think she's allowed to be picky about her wedding dress.

Denver: But she looks amazing in everything. She could wear a damn trash bag and still look amazing.

Denver: I know, I know. I'm just being bitchy.

Shepard: Everything okay?

Denver: Yes. I'm just tired.

Shepard: And whose fault is that?

Denver: Yours. Definitely yours.

Shepard: I beg to differ.

Shepard: "Oh, Shep! Keep doing that thing with your tongue!"

Shepard: "Yes, yes, YES! Right there, Shep!"

Shepard: "MORE, SHEP!"

Denver: OH MY GOD. ARE YOU FINISHED?!

Denver: And don't you dare say ALMOST!

Shepard: Then this conversation is

over.

Denver: THANK GOD.

Denver: Also...can you maybe do that thing with your tongue again tonight?

Shepard: You hussy.

Shepard: Tomorrow. After our movie date?

Denver: Or before. I mean, whatever floats your boat.

Shepard: Fuck. I wish I could kiss your dirty, sexy mouth right now.

Shepard: And your neck.

Shepard: Those tits too.

Shepard: Fuck it. I'll kiss all of you. Even your feet.

Denver: See, I knew you were a freak.

Denver: Quit bothering me. I'm trying to dress shop!

Shepard: One more thing...

Denver: No. Go away.

Denver: Fine. What?

Shepard: Never mind. You ruined the moment.

Denver: Tell me.

Shepard: Nah.

Denver: Shep!

Denver: SHEPARD!

Denver: Ugh. I am going to murder you. It's a good thing I look good in orange.

Shepard: Do you want to do dinner before the movie or after?

Denver: I thought I was dinner.

Shepard: You're right. After sounds good.

Denver: I was kidding. Let's go before. I had to skip lunch today so I'm certain I'll be ravenous.

Denver: Okay, okay. You got me. I wasn't really kidding, but I WILL need sustenance at some point.

Shepard: I am so lost right now.

Shepard: Dinner before or after?

Denver: YES. God, Shep. Just feed or eat me. WHY IS THIS SO HARD?

Shepard: I'm really starting to rethink this whole "we should try again" shit.

Denver: But are you really?

Shepard: Nah. I kind of like the chaos.

Denver: Good answer.

Shepard: Why'd you have to skip lunch?

Denver: I'm behind on my deadline on some articles about some sort of famous baseball star.

Shepard: Make sure you mention his dick length in there. It's super important for all his adoring fans to know this information.

Denver: *solid four inches* NOTED.

Denver: Any other requests?

Shepard: Nah. I'm actually really excited to read it. And also a little nervous.

Denver: Why nervous?

Shepard: I know I'm not the world's nicest person. I know I've been a sleaze ball. I know I hurt you. It's hard to wrap my head around what you could possibly write about me.

Denver: You're also not the sleaze ball you once were. Sure, you tried to pick a girl up in a grocery store a few weeks ago, but people change. You're in a…well, I wouldn't say relationship, but a committed "let's see where this shit takes us" thing. (Which, by the way, is an exclusive thing. Keep those four inches to yourself and to me, thanks.) As for us…clean slate, remember?

Shepard: A few things coming your way…

Shepard: I am very impressed that we just had The Talk without actually having it. (And, by the way, we're on the same page. Keep those beef curtains closed to anyone but me.)

Denver: OH MY GOD. NO. WHAT THE FUCK,

SHEPARD?

Denver: DO NOT EVER CALL THEM BEEF CURTAINS AGAIN!

Shepard: Ham wallet?

Denver: WHY IS IT ALL MEAT?

Shepard: Taco shack?

Denver: Better…slightly.

Denver: God. I need to go scrub my eyes out.

Shepard: I'm not sorry.

Denver: Oh, you should be.

Denver: But in all seriousness, you don't need to be worried about the article. I like the Shep I'm getting to know now.

Shepard: So you like me?

Denver: I tolerate you.

Shepard: You liiiiiiiiiiiike me.

Denver: YOU ARE OKAY.

Shepard: Do you…like-like me?

Denver: See above.

Shepard: But also yes, right?

Denver: *grumbles* yes

Shepard: Ha. Knew it.

Twenty-Nine

DENVER

"Anemone."

I reach for the flowers Shep's holding out for me and bring them to my nose.

"They don't have a scent," he tells me.

"I noticed. That's...odd. Thank you for my non-smelling flowers." I pull the front door open wider. "Come on in. I'm almost ready."

He doesn't budge.

"Don't you want to know?"

"Know what?"

"What they mean?"

"Ah," I say. "Yes. Tell me."

A wolfish grin stretches across his face as he leans down close to me, his lips hovering dangerously close to mine. I can feel his breath tickling my senses and I want to press my mouth to his so badly, which is kind of sad because it's only been two days since I last saw him.

"Tell me," I say again.

"The wait is all part of the fun."

I know exactly what he's trying to do: get me all hot and bothered and then leave me hanging and waiting all through our date.

Not tonight.

"It's anticipation, isn't it?"

His lips quirk up in the corners. "Maybe."

I lift onto my toes, bringing myself closer to him but still not letting our lips touch. His pupils widen, and I hear the hitch in his breath.

Shep wants this kiss just as badly as I do, but I'm determined to best him at his own game, so no kiss for him.

I brush my mouth against his, so soft and quick I know he'll be certain he's imagined it.

"Shep?"

He grunts in response.

"Two can play that game." I step back, leaving him standing in the doorway.

"Goddammit," he mutters before he finally steps inside and closes my door, shaking his head at my antics.

I smile, making my way into the kitchen to get my new bouquet of flowers in some water.

"Is that what you're wearing for our date?"

Glancing down at my outfit, I begin to worry. "What's wrong with it?"

"Nothing, surprisingly. You look normal. And sexy."

"Ass." I flip him the bird and dump the old flowers from him into the trash. "It's jeans and a t-shirt—you can't mess those up."

"To be fair, I think that's called a *blouse*, not a t-shirt."

"Technically, it's a called a mind-your-own-fucking-business."

"They must have a difficult time marketing those." He smirks.

"Or a swimsuit coverup. Same thing."

"You're wearing swimwear on our date? In October?"

I lift a shoulder and fill the vase I'm holding with water. "What? It's my get lucky shirt."

"You're telling me you wear this for others?"

"I have, yes."

"Does it work?"

"Like a charm."

"And is that what you're trying to do tonight? Get lucky?"

"Obviously." I fluff the flowers, arranging them so they look cute and full. "I thought you knew I only keep you around for orgasms."

"Damn. Here I thought it was my charm and good looks."

"I mean, you're cute and all, but that charm? That's not getting you very far."

"Words hurt, you know."

"Not when they're true." I wink at him then make my way down the hall to my bedroom to grab my things.

"Real shit ain't funny!" he calls, but I hear the laughter in his voice anyway.

I work on putting the finishing touches on my hair, coating it with another layer of hairspray and checking to make sure my makeup is on point.

It's weird how having Shep in my apartment feels so normal now, especially when a month ago he wasn't even on my radar.

Well, that's a lie. He's always been on my radar. I had just learned to ignore the blipping coming from him.

I can't anymore, though. It's not possible, not after everything these last few weeks.

On Sunday when he chased me inside, I felt like the happiest girl in the world, like I used to feel when I'd sneak my cell phone into my closet at night and text with him. My heart would beat in my chest with anticipation as I waited for him to text me back, relishing the thrill that would run through my veins when I'd hear someone on the stairs.

The forbidden aspect of texting with Shep might have been what started our entire relationship, but it was him who kept it going. He captivated me with his words and wit, and I knew almost right away I'd found someone special.

I had no idea he'd break my heart, but I knew no matter what, it would beat for him.

Young love isn't always right, but when it is, it's the rightest kind of right there is…and if my heart is telling me one thing, it's that Shep and me? We're right, and I'm ready to fight for it.

"We should just stay in tonight!" he yells from the living room. "That way I can ravish you on the couch."

"Not a chance!" I snatch my bag off my bed and make my way back down the hall. I stand in front of the TV, holding it up. "I already have my movie purse packed."

His brows shoot up. "What do you have in there?"

"Nothing yet. We're hitting the dollar store for some candy. Scoot. We have a show to catch."

"You do know I signed a *massive* contract with the MLB, right? Meaning I do have some money in my bank account?"

"Sure, but where's the thrill in *buying* candy?"

"I thought the movie was supposed to be the thrill, not actually getting into the theater."

"Move your ass, Shep." I put my hand out for him to grab. "You're wasting valuable candy-choosing time."

"It's weird," he says, putting his hand in mine and letting me do all the work to pull him up. "I've known you for a long time now, yet I'm still learning things about you."

"I like turtles."

"What?"

"I like turtles—sea turtles. They're the cutest little creatures ever. I still cut the plastic on my six-packs of soda because I can't stand the thought of a little baby sea turtle getting stuck in one."

He stares at me, unblinking.

"What?"

"I'm going to kiss you now."

"What? Why? Because I—"

His mouth covers mine and I don't hesitate to move my lips against his. He pushes his tongue against mine and we're pulling at one another like we didn't just do this two days ago.

I can't get enough of him. He can't get enough of me.

It's scary and thrilling all at once.

The kiss is hard and hot and over way before I want it to be.

"God." His forehead drops to mine. "I don't think I'll ever get tired of kissing you."

"I don't think I want you to." I swallow the lump in my throat. "Why'd you kiss me?"

"Because you're cute, Den. And because I really fucking wanted to."

The smile stretches across my lips. "Good enough for me."

"Are you eating the popcorn one by one?"

"How are you supposed to eat it?"

He shoves his fingers into the bucket then crams a handful into his mouth. "Vike vis."

"So classy, Shep."

He swallows and nods toward my purse. "Funny coming from

you. I cannot believe they didn't check your bag. It's obvious you're carrying half the candy aisle in there."

"And…" I dig through my purse, rooting around until I find what I'm looking for. "Half the chip aisle."

"Nobody brings chips to the movies."

"I was hungry! You refused to feed me before the movie."

He yanks the bag from my hands and pulls out a box, shaking it my way. "Chicken nuggets, Denver—you made me stop and get you chicken nuggets!"

"What?" I snatch said nuggets from his hand. "I was hungry! I told you to feed me *before* the movie."

"I couldn't get reservations until after."

"It's obvious I would have settled for the dollar menu, Shep."

"I swear, for the next fifty years, I'm only ever taking you to places with dollar menus."

I freeze, my chicken nugget hovering just inches from my mouth. *Is he saying…*

"Just shove it in your mouth, Den. I meant what I said."

I laugh, devouring my last-minute dinner and chewing not only on it, but also on his words.

The next fifty years with Shep? While it sounds exhausting, it's not entirely unappealing.

Almost makes it hard to believe we were sworn enemies just a few weeks ago.

Now I'm sitting next to him in a dark theater contemplating a real-life future with him.

Fate is weird.

"First of all," I start once I swallow, "that's what she said. Second, that…uh, that doesn't sound half bad. I mean, I don't know about fifty. That's going to make me super old and I'd rather not have wrinkles, but I wouldn't complain about spending *some* time with you."

"So you love me—noted."

"I never said that."

"You didn't have to. You implied it."

"How?"

"Shh!" He holds his finger up to his mouth. "The movie is starting."

"We're the only people in here!"

"No you're not!" someone yells from the other side of the theater.

We're seated in the very back row, tucked away in a dark corner. This guy must be in the same spot on the other side because when I peek around the projection box, I don't see him.

"Oh, and one other thing: no one eats chips during a movie! It's loud and obnoxious. Just eat those chicken nuggets I can smell from here and skip the chips."

"I-I… Okay."

"Shh! The movie is starting!" the stranger says impatiently.

Shep shakes with laughter next to me and I toss a glare his way.

"What?" he whispers. "I told you to skip the chips."

"Shut up, you ass!"

The movie begins playing, but I can't focus on the screen. All that's running through my mind is Shep and a possible future.

I want to be with him. If I'm being damn honest with myself, I've always wanted to be with him, even when I hated him…except when I think about Shep, commitment doesn't come to mind. The heartache from before does.

Is he that same guy he was then? Has he actually changed? I've watched him over the years, a different girl on his arm every day. He never settled down, never tried. He can say he was waiting for me all he wants, but that doesn't make it true.

"Stop thinking so loud or we're going to get yelled at again," he says in my ear.

"I'm not thinking."

"Yes, you are. You're worried I don't mean what I said."

"How'd you know?"

"Because I know you, Den. I've always known you, better than anyone else in the whole fucking world."

He pushes up the armrest between us then takes the purse and food and shoves them into the empty seat next to him.

He hauls me onto his lap and suddenly I'm straddling him.

"What are you doing?" I whisper.

"This movie sucks."

"It's just the previews."

"I've *heard* it sucks."

The bright screen illuminates the glow in his eyes, and I know just what he's after—*me*.

"Shepard Clark, are you trying to get me to make out with you in a movie theater?"

"Yeah. I mean, I was hoping we'd be alone, but this is close enough."

Then he's kissing me. And I'm letting him.

Spreading my legs farther apart, I sink down onto him more, wrapping my arms around his neck and tangling my fingers in his hair. It's soft, messy as always.

He drags his fingers down my back and his touch feels like the sun itself brushing against me. His hands dip into the waistband of my jeans and I suddenly wish I had worn something else—something with easier access.

He voices my thought against my lips. "Why couldn't you have worn a skirt?"

He trails his mouth from my mine, down my chin and over my neck, sucking at that same place below my ear. I've had a permanent hickey since he discovered it and I'm not complaining.

I can feel his cock straining against his jeans under me and I grind down on him, swirling my hips, causing him to gasp.

"You witch."

"Watch it," I mutter. "I'm on top—I'm the one in control here."

He chuckles lowly. "It's so cute you think that."

Without warning he pops the button on my jeans, and I realize I didn't even notice his hands were anywhere close to my center.

With deft movements, he slides one into the waistband of my undies, and I have to catch the gasp that tries to leave my lips when his fingers brush against my swollen clit.

"Shh," he rumbles. "Keep quiet."

He works me over, rubbing tight circles until I'm about to combust then pushing two fingers inside me.

Shep swallows my gasps and moves his tongue against mine as he thrusts his fingers in and out of me. The orgasm hits me out of nowhere and I ride his fingers until every last shiver runs through me.

My heart rate works to even out as I sag against him, feeling satiated and exhausted and so fucking high all at once.

He pulls his fingers from my center and I relish the emptiness. When he brushes against my clit once more, I bite my lip to keep from making a sound.

I watch with rapt attention as he draws his hand up to his mouth and sucks both fingers inside.

Oh holy fuck…

He pops them free and winks. "Guess you were right about me having you for dinner after all."

I can't help the stuttered gasp that squeaks out.

"Are you two fucking?"

The moment is broken at the interruption.

"No!" Shep hollers back, lips twitching. "This trailer is just really intense!"

"It's for a kids' movie, but whatever," the stranger says.

We burst into laughter, not caring how loud we're being.

"Shh!" he says again.

We laugh harder.

I rest my head against his chest. "I want this to last forever."

I don't know why I say it, but I do know I mean it.

"I think I'd like that."

"This scares me, Shep."

"Me too."

"I can't help but keep thinking—"

"What if?"

I nod. "Yes."

"There are a lot of what-ifs in life. Being chickenshit isn't a reason to walk away from something," he says softly, repeating my words from our heated conversation in the truck. "I'm done being scared, Denny. I promise."

"Your version of a promise scares me too."

He doesn't say anything, and I don't know if that's a good thing or not.

Thirty

SHEPARD

"Bro, will you please quit pacing? You're starting to make me nervous."

"You *should* be nervous. You're getting married tomorrow."

"Nah, man." AJ smiles, shaking his head. "All I can think is *finally*. I still can't believe I let you talk me out of doing this in high school. Do you know how many years of being husband and wife we'd have under our belt already?"

"You thanked me back then. You can't take that back."

"You're right—waiting totally made us stronger."

"Like you and Allie ever needed to be stronger."

"I'm sorry…was that a compliment on my love life?"

I shoot him a look. "Shut it."

He laughs. "Uh huh. We both know you're a closet romantic."

"I am not."

"Tell that to Denver. You buy her flowers with special meanings and hand-deliver them to her at work."

"Once! I did that once!" I argue.

"Once is enough." He winks. "Seriously, sit the fuck down. You're freaking me out."

I've been pacing my kitchen and scrubbing the counters that are already way too fucking clean for nearly two hours now.

That's what I do when I'm nervous: pace and clean. My teammates are constantly poking fun when I'm pacing the dugout and sweeping the floors. The announcers eat that shit up, but they'd never know what a sign of stress it really is.

"What's rolling around in that big head of yours?"

I toss the rag onto the counter and force myself to take a step back. Folding my arms across my chest, I exhale a steadying breath.

"Come on, man. Talk to me."

"What if she hates me after she finds out about…"

"You being the biggest fucking tool on the planet and screwing over your brother's gal?"

I wince. "Yeah, that."

AJ's been pushing me to tell Denny about Delia from the start. I told him I would before the wedding.

But the wedding's tomorrow and I haven't said a fucking peep about it. I can't bring myself to. Things are going well—like ridiculously so—for us and I don't want anything to screw that up, especially not some stupid mistake I made almost two years ago.

I know I need to tell her, though. It would be wrong not to, and I know I'm making such a big deal out of it because of how Denny is going to react to the news—badly.

"You gotta do it, man. Just rip the band-aid off before she finds out from someone who isn't you."

"Why do I have to tell her at all?"

He narrows his eyes at me. "You know why—because you were

way in the fucking wrong and she needs to know the kind of person she's letting into her life."

"But I'm not that person anymore."

"I know you're not, I do, but that doesn't mean you didn't do it. That doesn't mean it never happened just because you're not who you were back then. Sorry, bro, but this is like if you had an arrest record for assault and didn't tell her about it." He snaps his fingers together. "Oh, wait, you do have one."

I'm quick to correct him. "Not true—he didn't press charges."

"You're right, just a destruction of property charge and a suspension from the MLB." He rolls his eyes. "My bad."

"But the difference is she already knows all that and she's still into me."

He pushes himself off the couch and joins me in the kitchen. He rests his hands on the counter across from me, staring at me with hard eyes.

"What?" I grind out.

"You want this time to be different, yeah? You want things to not get all muddled and fucked up like they did last time? Want to build a future with her?"

"More than anything."

No hesitation.

That's exactly what I want.

"You want to be *worthy* of her?"

"Yes."

He points at me. "Then *you* have to tell her."

"Why can't I just sweep it under the rug and never speak of it ever again?"

"Because that, my friend, is the pussy way out, and you aren't a pussy."

"You sure? How much pussy does one have to eat to become

one?"

AJ pinches the bridge of his nose. "Dammit, Clark. You're exhausting."

"Weird—your mom said the same thing last night."

"Shep…" he warns.

I hold my hand up. "Fine, fine. I'll tell her, but if she dumps my ass, this is on you."

He laughs, but there's no humor in it. "No, this is on you—entirely. Remember that."

It's a bitter pill to swallow, but I know he's right.

Fuck him for being right.

I have to tell her. Tomorrow. Before the wedding.

AJ pushes away from the counter and retreats into the living room, throwing himself back down on my sofa that cost way too much money and clicking play on the movie he was watching.

"Now beer me! Let's get fucking drunk. I'm getting hitched tomorrow!"

"No, Shep, we *cannot* skip our best friends' wedding."

"You sure about that? They won't even know we're missing."

"You're right, they won't miss the best man and maid of honor at all." She rolls her eyes. "We're not skipping."

"But…you look so hot."

She bites her lower lip, raking her eyes over me like the only thing she wants to do is see me in this tuxedo. "You don't look too shabby yourself."

Another slow perusal.

Her eyes catch the smirk lining my lips and she shakes herself out of her sexual stupor.

"Dammit, Shep! You almost had me."

I reach for her, pulling her close and bringing my lips to my favorite spot below her ear. "I could still have you…"

She sighs, sinking into me. "Maybe just a quick—*no!*" She pushes herself back, swatting away my attempts to bring her back into my arms. "Stop being so sexy!"

"I can't. It's a curse."

"Shep!"

"Denny!"

She laughs and shakes her head at me. "Come on, we need to get out there. The ceremony is starting soon."

"I'm telling you, they could totally do this without us. There are only like fifty people here. They've got it under control."

"You're just horny."

"Yes. Next question."

"I didn't ask a question."

I slap my palm against my forehead. "Duh. Sorry. Tits on the brain."

She picks up the bottom of her dress and pushes past me, dodging my hands as she walks by.

"Move it, Clark. Now."

I sigh. "Fine. Let's get this over with."

"Maybe we can sneak off during the reception—*after* we greet all the guests," she adds when she sees me perk up. "You still need to meet Monty, and I am *dying* to meet your Titanic parents."

My gut grows heavy, that swirl of nerves from last night coming back full force.

I tried every way I could think of to bring it up casually this morning on the truck ride over to the venue, but I couldn't do it. Nothing was sounding right.

Hey, Den, turns out you were right all these years—I'm a fucking tool.

Or...

Yo, Den, so a few years ago I sent a naked picture of my brother's girlfriend to a few friends on the baseball team.

Nothing was fitting for the moment. So, I kept my mouth shut.

Now that we're about to walk out there and face everyone, I have the distinct feeling that maybe blurting it all out would have been better.

Please don't let this be the end...

"The end?" Denny says.

I snap my gaze her way, realizing I said that out loud.

She smiles at me and it's one of those genuine expressions, the ones where everything is going just perfect in your life and nothing can touch you.

"It's not the end. It's just beginning." She extends her hand my way. "Come on, Cap."

Thirty-One

DENVER

Shep's been acting weird all week leading up to the wedding. It's not been overly obvious, which I think is more concerning.

He keeps staring at me like he's never going to see me again.

He's doing it right now from across the room, watching me as he sips on his whiskey. I bet he's thrilled to finally have something other than the putrid champagne they serve at all the galas.

"He's staring over here really hard. It looks..." Allie gulps loudly. "Sexual."

"That's because he's hoping we can sneak off into a closet somewhere. I kind of promised him we would."

"You are *not* having sex at my wedding!"

I smirk at my best friend. "We'll see."

She shakes her head, smiling. "You incorrigible little hussy."

"Oh, please. Don't act like you and AJ won't be sneaking off later too. Just think of this as research—we'll scope out the best place and report back. You're welcome."

"There's a room down the hall, kind of small, but you can totally make it work," Delia chimes in, coming to stand next to me.

"Already?" I raise a brow at her.

"What? Have you seen Zach? That nerd pushes all my buttons." She laughs and waves to her boyfriend, who's across the room and definitely looks like he was just having sex.

"*This* is why we're friends," I tell her. "Allie, this is Delia. She's dating Shep's brother, Zach Hastings."

I've been wanting to say hi to Zach and Delia all night and finally meet Shep's parents, but every time I approach the subject or try to drag him over that way, he distracts me with kisses or cake.

I can't resist either.

Allie's eyes widen. "Two things, and I'm addressing these in order of importance. One"—she turns to Delia—"you snagged a hottie. He reminds me of a grown-up Harry Potter."

"He kind of does, huh?" Delia agrees. "Congrats on your wedding. The ceremony was beautiful."

"Thank you." Allie blushes. "It was a long time coming."

"What was two?" I ask.

"Oh!" She whirls on me. "You! You just called him *Shep*. You're totally in love."

"Zach's hotness was more important than you accusing me of being in love with Shep?"

"I'm sorry, but have you seen him? Not to be a creeper, Delia, but *damn*."

Delia laughs and shrugs. "What can I say? I got the best wrong number ever."

"And you," Allie says to me, "can hush. There was no 'accusing' going on. I *know* it's true—you're full-blown in love with him. It's like high school all over again."

"High school? But you and Monty didn't move out here until college." Delia's looking at me, brows creased and confusion covering her face.

"Oh, you didn't know? Those two met in high school and fell in love when they lived over two thousand miles apart."

"You're shitting me."

"Nope," Allie continues. "Shep used to pretend to date this other chick all throughout high school, but he and Denny were busy swooning over one another. I followed AJ out here for college and she claims she followed me, but I know she came for Shep. Then that prick dumped her the moment she got into town. God, I'm still so pissed at him for that," she adds.

"Huh. This is all very…enlightening. What happened?"

"He dumped her."

"We were never dating," I interject.

Allie rolls her eyes. "You were practically dating."

"But not officially."

"Are you two dating now?" Delia asks.

"We're…taking things slow."

"As slow as two people who bang as often as possible can," Allie says. "You love him."

I drop my head to avoid Allie's smirking face, staring into the drink I'm taking my sweet time with.

I never fucking stopped.

Shep's words from our time in the closet ring through my head, because they're the exact ones I want to use right now.

I've loved Shep from afar for years, even when I wanted to hate him so, so badly.

I peer up and catch Delia staring at me with the strangest look in her eye. It's a mix of uncertainty and hope and something I can't quite place my finger on.

I lift a brow at her in a silent question.

"I would just…be careful with Shep. He's—"

"A total fucking asshat," Zoe interrupts.

"Zoe! You made it!" Allie throws her arms around her friend's neck and squeezes tight. "Thank you so much for coming."

"Like I'd miss your wedding. Stop it."

It's crazy that I never met Zoe in college, her being Delia's best friend, but we finally met when Robbie and Monty were doing their dance around one another and I mistook her for Robbie's date. We've been friends since.

In fact, it was my idea that AJ and Caleb get together to coach a little league team. Zoe, Allie, and I have had plenty of opportunity to bond over the season, so I'm a little surprised this is the first time I'm hearing Zoe talk about Shep.

"Do you know Shep well?"

"Know him well?" Zoe groans. "Ugh. Don't remind me of that mistake. He wined and dined me and then banged and dashed—his signature move."

I know Shep wasn't perfect in college. He had quite the reputation, but so did I. I never expected him to be celibate.

"Whatever, though. I didn't expect anything different from *the* Shep Clark." Zoe points to Delia. "But I did expect a lot more out of him than what he did to my best friend."

My gaze snaps to her and she's looking at me like she's in pain.

I don't know if it's the memories or the fact that she's wishing she didn't have to tell me what I don't know.

"Delia?" I say.

"It's not pretty, Denny," she warns.

"Tell me anyway."

She and Zoe exchange a look.

"You didn't tell her?" Delia asks her.

"I didn't know I needed to."

Delia sighs, her eyes falling back to me. "Are you sure? It's probably going to change things for you two."

The thudding in my chest picks up pace and pure panic begins to race through me.

I watch them, their faces filled with worry and dread and total fucking pity.

I *hate* pity.

"I feel like I'm missing something very important over here. What are we talking about?"

"I think we're about to break your sister's heart," Zoe says to Monty.

"Oh. Maybe I *shouldn't* be present then."

She begins to turn away, but I clasp her hand, keeping her close because I feel like I'm going to need all the strength she can offer me.

Monty squeezes me back, letting me know she's not going anywhere.

"Tell me. *Please.*"

"Okay." Delia clears her throat. "I, uh, sent Zach a naked picture when we first started dating. The pervert was bugging me about sexting and I finally gave in by sending him a nude. It was this really cute, tasteful shot of just—"

"Can you focus on the story, D?" Zoe interrupts her.

"Oops. Sorry." She shakes her head. "Anyway, we were at Zach's parents for Thanksgiving and I was kind of giving him the third degree for being a dick to my bestie because of girl code." Delia pauses and laughs. "Funny, considering Zoe ended up with my ex, breaking rule number one."

"You snooze, you lose." Zoe waves her off.

My ears begin to clog with the rhythmic *thump thump thump* of my overactive heart. Bile begins to rise in my throat, and suddenly I wish

286

I hadn't crammed so much cake in my gob because I'm certain it's about to come back up.

"Anyway," Delia continues, "Shep, uh, got ahold of the photo after borrowing Zach's phone."

"Oh god." The words tumble from my lips and I have to slap my hand over my mouth so the puke doesn't follow.

Delia winces. "I'm sorry, Denny."

"Are you saying…" Allie trails off.

"Say it, Delia." I squeeze Monty's hand tighter, bracing myself for the words. "I need to hear you say it."

"I don't want to. Zoe, you do it."

"No way. Shep is your demon, not mine."

"Hesentthephototohisfriends," Delia finally rushes out in one breath.

The thumping stops and fire replaces the beat as my breath catches in my throat.

I was wrong.

Shep hasn't changed.

He's still the same *slug* he's always been, and I've fallen for his games once again.

"There you are. I've been looking all over for you." Shep slides an arm around me. "What are you doing out here all by yourself?"

I'm standing in the gazebo where Allie and AJ exchanged their vows two hours ago.

I had to get out of there after Delia finally confessed what Shep did to her. My stomach was twisting and turning, and I couldn't stand to be in that room of happy people for another minute.

Though every bone in my body is screaming at me not to because I love the way he feels against me, I step out of Shep's hold, creating the distance this conversation necessitates between us.

He looks dejected and hurt, but so am I.

Only I *deserve* to feel that way because of his betrayal. He doesn't.

Shep shoves his hands into his pockets, rocking back on his heels and staring at me with worry.

"Is, uh, is everything okay?" he asks quietly.

Turning away from him, I rest my arms on the banister of the gazebo and stare out into the sunset on the horizon. It's like the sun is setting on our relationship or whatever the hell this is we're doing.

"Bucky?"

"Don't."

He exhales heavily. "You talked to Delia."

The ice in my voice must be a dead giveaway for him, and I think what hurts the most is that he was expecting this, that his mind automatically goes to that.

"Is that why you've been so cagey this week? Why you were weird when we ran into them at the restaurant? Why you won't take me near your parents?"

He takes a moment to answer, and I can't help but wonder if he's trying to think up a lie.

"Yes," he finally says. "That's why."

"How did I not know?"

"No one does, really. It was kept quiet because of my baseball career."

"Why didn't you tell me?"

"Because it's embarrassing as fuck, Denny. I made one of the biggest goddamn mistakes of my life in a moment of simple jealousy and I can't take it back."

I spin to face him. "How could you do that to her?"

"I was stupid."

"*Beyond* stupid, Shep. That's a massive invasion of privacy."

"I know that."

"It's disgusting and crude and so harsh it hurts to look at you right now."

He winces like I've just punched him in the gut, and maybe I have with my words. He deserves every hit.

"If it makes you feel any better, I've lost nearly everything because of it."

"It doesn't. It would make me feel a whole lot better to know you aren't the *slug* everyone has claimed you were over the years." I shake my head in disgust. "I thought you were better than that, Shep."

"I thought I was too."

"Then why did you do it?"

"I told you—I was jealous."

"Of what?"

He scrubs a hand over his face, and then does it again.

"Fuck!" he yells, and it echoes around us angrily. "Them, okay? I was so green over what they obviously had because it could have been us."

His hands slide through his hair, destroying the perfectly tousled look he had going on, just leaving it messy.

"That could have been you and me." He drops his head. "But I screwed that up, and Delia just sat there reminding me of all the girls I used to get you out of my head. The guilt crept in. Everything felt wrong and gross and I was just so fucking angry at her. I just sent it to a few guys on the team. We did that kind of shit all the time, passed photos around. It wasn't supposed to be anything serious. She wasn't supposed to know."

"I wish I could be mad at you and your jackass friends for passing nudes around, but that would be hypocritical. I've done that myself.

Usually, though, it's *unsolicited* dick pics from guys I *don't* know. You knew Delia. You knew her, and you *still* did that to her. That's wrong on so many levels, Shep."

"I know, but—"

I hold up my hand to stop him. "Furthermore, you cannot keep blaming your bad behavior on me and us and whatever we had. *You* fucked up. *You* did that, not anyone else."

His shoulders sag in defeat.

He's wrong, and he knows he's wrong, but that doesn't change anything, doesn't change what he did.

"I can forgive you for making a stupid shitty mistake, for being a complete tool for a moment in your life. We all make mistakes and I'd hate for all of mine to be held against me forever, but Delia's my friend, Shep, and you hurt her. Do you know how scared that makes me about wanting to take a chance on a future with you? What if I piss you off? What if something else makes you jealous? Will it be *my* picture you're sending out to people?"

"No!" he shouts. "No. I'd never do that to you." His teeth gnash together, jaw so coiled I can see the muscles jumping. He knows I've made a valid point. "That's not who I am…not who I want to be."

I can see the ways Shep's changed over the years. In college, he walked around like he was big man on campus, and he was in many ways. Now, though, he's humbler. He's settled into his fame…into himself. He's passionate about the charities he works with. He's not trying to be the cool guy anymore. He's just Shep.

Those parts of him I adore.

But the parts that don't own up to his mistakes? The Shep who continually blames everyone else for his actions? That's the same eighteen-year-old boy who shut me out because he was too afraid to admit he loved me because of *someone else's* failures.

Those parts of him I hate.

"Then prove it, because I want to believe you, Shep. I want to believe you so badly my bones ache with the desire to give in to you, to tell you it's all okay and sweep it under the rug—but I can't. This is about so much more than Delia. It's about what happened five years ago. It's about what happened last month."

"Denny…" He takes a step toward me and I retreat from his advances.

"No. Until you stop blaming everyone and everything else for your mistakes, I can't. I can't do this anymore." I wave a finger between us. "I can't do *us* anymore. It doesn't feel healthy or right. It feels toxic and wrong. It feels like unfinished business, and I want to be so much more than that."

He shakes his head, not wanting to hear what I'm telling him. "You are more than that—so much more."

"Tell that to all the people you've hurt and taken shots at because of your unresolved feelings for me."

We stand there in silence, letting the reality of what just unfolded hang between us.

I can't build a future with Shep when he's still hanging onto the past. We said clean slate, and none of this feels like a clean slate. It feels like we're just covering up old wounds.

"What can I do to change your mind?"

"Right now, I don't know. I need some time."

"Are we breaking up?"

"Yes. No. I really don't know, Shep. I wasn't aware we'd labeled this in the first place."

"Don't act like we had to. You know we didn't."

"Fine, but right now, I need space, okay? I need to think."

"Okay, okay. Fine, I get it." He holds his hands up in defeat. "But Den?"

"Yeah?"

Shep crosses the gazebo, and this time I don't run from him. His hands cup my face, and I worry he's going to kiss me—worry because I'm certain even now, I'd still kiss him back.

He's not a bad guy. I know that. He's made mistakes—too many to count—but deep down in his heart, I know he's not *bad*.

I read somewhere one time that good people sometimes do bad things, but that doesn't make them bad people.

That's so fitting for Shep, but it doesn't make me any less mad at him.

His fingers swipe over my cheeks and his hazel eyes bore into me. "For what it's worth, this was never unfinished business. It can't be, because I never stopped loving you."

He doesn't try to kiss me.

He just walks away.

And I'm left standing there feeling relieved, angry, and so goddamn confused.

Thirty-Two

SHEPARD

"I told you she should have heard it from you."

I sigh into the phone. "I know, AJ. I fucking know, okay? But I couldn't bring myself to say it out loud. It just felt...gross."

"That's because it was a gross thing to do. I didn't talk to you for months after that stunt, remember?"

"Yeah, I remember."

"She's not entirely wrong, though," he says. "You do make excuses for your actions."

"What the hell is this? Shit on Shep week?"

"No. This is Shep needs to get his shit together before he loses the love of his life week."

"Aren't you supposed to be on your honeymoon?" I growl at him.

"Yes—and, again, thank you for paying for it, you fucker."

"You're welcome."

"But," he says, continuing like I never spoke, "I couldn't leave my best man hanging. I had to check in on ya. You were kind of a wreck when we left.”

“You mean when Denver tore my heart out and then your wife slapped me?”

“You have to admit, that slap was pretty badass.”

“If it hadn’t hurt so bad, I might have even gotten a boner.”

“Shepard…”

I laugh dryly. “I’m kidding…kind of.”

“Have you talked to her at all this past week?”

“Not a word. It’s making me anxious as hell too.”

“Have you reached out to her?”

“Too fucking chickenshit,” I admit. “She’s scary when she’s mad.”

“She’s mad for a good reason.”

“I know. You keep reminding me. Makes me wish I had ignored your call.”

“For the tenth time this week? You wouldn’t dare.”

“Oh, AJ, it amazes me sometimes how little you know me.”

I can’t see him, but I’m certain he’s flipping me off right now.

“Look, man, you just need to buck up and talk to her. You’re not that guy anymore.”

“I told her that. She didn’t buy it.”

“Then *show* her.”

“How in the hell am I supposed to do that? Take out a fucking billboard that says how much I love her?”

“If that’s what it takes, do it.”

“Babe! I’m back from my massage! Let’s have sex!” Allie shouts in the background.

“Shit, man. I gotta go. Fix shit with Denver and don’t tell Allie I called you. She’ll say I’m betraying her again.” He pauses. “Wait, no, go ahead and tell her—the makeup sex was amazing last time. Bye.”

He ends the call.

I groan and toss my phone onto the counter, apparently a little too hard because the fucker bounces right off and smacks onto the tile floor of my kitchen. I cringe, because I just *know* my screen has cracked.

"Fucking hell," I mutter, covering my face with my hands. "This day blows!"

Steve lets out a bark, and I'm going to pretend that's his way of backing me up on this.

If I had just told Denny about what happened, maybe this wouldn't have—oh, who the hell am I kidding? She still would have been pissed, and rightfully so.

She's right, though, and so is AJ: I do hold on to the past. I use it to my advantage. It took Denny standing there pointing out all my fucked-up flaws to make me realize that.

She was wrong about one thing though.

I *have* changed.

Now I just have to find a way to prove it to her.

My palms are sweaty, knees weak, arms are heavy—but I most definitely do not have my mom's spaghetti vomit on my sweater, especially considering she's still pretty fucking pissed at me.

I rub my hands down my jeans for the millionth time. My nerves are absolutely shot right now, and I can't bring myself to do anything other than stand around like a moron.

The door in front of me swings open.

"How long are you going to stand out here? You're starting to creep out my neighbors. Janet called to tell me there's a 'strapping young man looking ready to faint' on my front porch. Since I'm not about to perform CPR on your ass and I'm too goddamn stubborn to call 911, why don't you just come in already?"

Zach stands before me, brows furrowed and jaw set with anger.

This is going to be fun.

He steps aside, waving me into his home for the first time in…well, way too fucking long for siblings who live in the same town half the year.

"Thanks, man," I say as I step over the threshold.

"Take your shoes off."

He leaves me standing in the foyer feeling unwelcome and awkward as hell.

See? It's already fun.

As I'm toeing off my shoes, an all-white pygmy goat wearing Ryan Gosling *Hey Girl* jammies and a diaper comes running up to me, butting his head against my shin in a way that almost hurts.

"Knock it off, you little shit."

"He's a really good judge of character."

I glance up to see Delia making her way down the hall. She has a small smile playing on her lips, but I know it's not for me.

My right cheek begins to tingle when I see her, and I know that's just the permanent reminder of the slap she gave me when Caleb dragged me to her apartment to "apologize". We both knew back then it wasn't much of an apology, but she let it slide anyway. I don't get how she let me off so easily because I deserved so much worse, and she deserved so much better than that half-assed apology I gave her.

Why am I just now realizing this?

"Yeah," I say. "I can see that."

"Leave him be, Marshy." She bends down and scoops up the goat then drops him off in a bed set up beside the stairs. "You can follow me."

I trail behind her as she leads us into the kitchen, where Zach is moving around the space like it's his domain.

"We're having personal pizzas for dinner. Hope you brought your own."

"Zachary!" Delia chides.

"Sorry, not sorry," my brother mumbles, pulling open the fridge and grabbing two bottles of water.

He hands one to Delia and pops open the other for himself, not offering me anything.

Yep. Fun, fun, fun.

"I'm guessing you're here because Denver found out about you fucking over my girl." Zach takes a swig of his water then pushes out one of those obnoxious exaggerated *aahs*. "Here to kiss some ass and show her you're not a total tool?"

I slide into a chair at their granite-topped island, take my cap off my head, and then scrub a hand through my hair.

"At first, yeah, I was only coming here for her, but then I saw Delia in the hallway and my cheek started tingling like it always does when she's around."

"Slapped ya that good, huh?"

"You did," I tell her. "And it reminded me of that shitty apology I gave you back then and how I never truly gave you a real one, the kind you deserved. If I were coming here for Denver, it would be the exact same thing again. So, no, I'm not here for her—or for me, for that matter. I'm here for you, Delia."

"For me, huh?"

I nod. "Yep. So, take a seat or keep standing or whatever it is you need to do, because I'm about to deliver the speech of a lifetime."

She and Zach exchange a look. He shrugs. "This is on you two. I'm going to keep making pizzas. I'm famished."

"You literally just ate an hour ago."

297

"You calling me fat, D?"

"Never." The grin she gives him says otherwise.

Delia makes her way around the island and takes the seat next to me. "You have my full attention, Shep."

She stares at me intently. I can't help but squirm around in my chair under her scrutiny.

"Well, fuck. Now I'm nervous."

She laughs. "Don't be. I promise not to slap you again...I think."

Zach coughs out a laugh but continues to act like he's invisible, working on flattening out the dough.

"Thanks. Super reassuring." I clear my throat. "So, I guess I never really explained to you why I did what I did."

"You said it was because I was pestering you about Zoe."

"Yes and no. Honestly, it was annoying as shit. I mean, it was college, Delia—that's what happens in college." I shrug. "People hook up and it doesn't work and that's that. I shouldn't have been grilled about it at Thanksgiving dinner."

"I was upset for my friend, but you're right. I mean, she did it to guys too, so there was no reason for me to jump on you about it. I'm—"

"Don't you dare," I interrupt.

"I'm with him," Zach throws our way.

Delia pretends to zip her lips closed and throw away the key.

"Anyway, yes, I was annoyed with you for putting all my business out there in front of my family, but it wasn't just that. I was jealous."

"Of what? My super sweet Ryan Gosling pajamas?"

"Totally." I laugh. "No, of you and Zach."

My brother pauses when I mention his name and I can feel his eyes on me, but just as quickly as he stopped, he's back to flitting around the kitchen.

"Why were you jealous of us?"

"You reminded me of what I could have had with Denver."

"How did that come about anyway?" Zach interjects.

"Eavesdrop much?" Delia teases.

"What? A guy can't have questions about a secret relationship his brother had in high school?"

"So nosy." She tsks.

"AJ wanted to propose to Allie in senior year and I thought it was a really stupid idea, so I reached out to Denver to ask her to help me convince our friends they were idiots and way too young to get married. One thing led to another and…yeah. We became friends, and then we became something more than that."

"Via texting?"

"Yep." I nod. "Which is another reason you two reminded me so much of us. You had what I was supposed to have: an unconventional beginning with a happily ever after. You pestering me about Zoe and all the other mistakes I've made over the years and my jealousy all rolled around in my head until I sent the photo."

"Why'd you take it to begin with?"

I wince. "Because I was a pig. I literally have no reason other than you were hot and I wanted it, so I took it. It was free porn."

"That's…thank you? I don't really know what to say to that."

"That 'free porn' really ended up costing you a lot, huh?" Zach grabs a container of cheese, plucking out a handful of fresh mozzarella and plopping it down onto another slab of dough. "Was it worth it?"

"Not even kind of. No offense, Delia."

"Trust me"—she holds her hand up—"none taken."

We fall into a silence, the only sounds in the kitchen coming from the giant knife Zach's now moving through the onions he's slicing.

Delia pushes her chair back and starts to stand. "Well, this has all been very inter—"

"I'm not done," I interrupt, and she falls back into the chair.

"You're not talking."

"You should hear the shit running through my head."

"Then spit it out."

She's so scary when she's serious, which isn't often.

"Fuck. Okay." I exhale heavily. "I didn't tell you all that to make it seem like I'm making excuses, because I'm not. I just wanted to explain what was going through my head at the time. The simple truth is, I did something stupid and wrong and dehumanizing. I shouldn't have done it."

I turn toward Delia for the first time. Looking into her eyes is painful, but it's a pain I deserve.

"Delia, I'm sorry. From the very bottom of my heart, I apologize. I'm not asking for your forgiveness. I mean, I totally want it, but I'm not asking for it. I just need you to know and understand that I regret that moment in my life so, so much."

I swivel toward my brother. He notices the movement and sets the knife down, giving me his full attention.

"I owe you an apology too, Zach. I'm sorry I betrayed your trust. I'm sorry I hurt your girlfriend, and I'm sorry I let you down."

Neither of them say anything for a long time, so long I almost feel as if I need to leave and walk away, let the pieces fall wherever they fall.

Delia's hand lands on my arm and I swing my attention her way, surprised.

Her lips part and I hold my breath, waiting for her words.

"First, I have to say this…" She grins. "*That* was the shit rolling around in your head?"

My lungs burn from the lack of oxygen and I finally take a breath, laughing heartily.

"Sorry, I'm not that good with words—probably why I always lash out with actions."

"Hmm, makes sense." She squeezes my arm. "Listen, I know you didn't ask for it, but I'm giving it to you anyway. I forgive you, Shep, but not for you—for myself. It's my way of letting all this go. I forgive you, but I won't forget. I'll always remember the betrayal and the hurt. I'm not saying things are always going to be shit between us, but don't expect me to run up and hug you when I see you any time soon."

"Thank you," I say quietly. "I don't deserve that, but thank you."

She gives me a small smile and pulls her hand away.

"What kind?" Zach asks abruptly, moving toward the fridge.

"Huh?"

"What kind?" He drags a third slab of dough from the fridge. "Toppings—which ones do you want?"

I grin.

Pizza is Zach's peace offering.

In that moment, I know everything with these two is going to be just fine.

If only I was so sure about things with Denny…

Thirty-Three

DENVER

"I miss Steve."

"You mean Shep?"

Yes. "No, I totally meant Steve."

It feels so wrong to miss Shep when he did something so horrible, but I can't help it. I've tried not to miss him. I've tried not to miss him with ice cream and chips and all the Oreos I could stomach, but none of it works. Not even binge-watching my favorite teenagers who use words that are way too advanced for their vocabulary to be realistic worked.

I still miss him.

It's that it feels so right, which means it can't be wrong...I think.

Monty crinkles her nose at me. "Steve's the pug, right?"

"The cutest pug in the whole freakin' world, yes."

"She totally means Shep," Zoe says, squeezing back between me and Monty on the couch. "Doesn't she, Delia?"

"She does!" Delia calls from the kitchen.

We're having a girls' night, sans Allie, who is *still* on her honeymoon. How that lucky bitch can afford two weeks away on her salary is beyond me.

"It doesn't make you a bad person, Denny," Delia says, popping into the living room from around the corner. "It makes you human. You're allowed to miss him."

"And you're okay with that?"

She sits cross-legged on the floor, a bowl of cereal balanced precariously on her lap. "If you're harboring feelings of hatred toward Shep because of me then you're harboring those feelings for the wrong reasons. I don't hate Shep. I hate what he did, but I don't hate him. We had a long talk over the weekend and we're in a better place now."

I sit forward. "You talked to him?"

"He came over for personal pizzas and finally gave me a real apology. It was…actually kind of nice. He was nice. Letting go of that hurt was nice. I mean, I'll never forget what he did, but I can be adult enough to move on from it."

She shovels a few bites of cereal into her mouth and shrugs.

"He…apologized?"

"Vwep," she answers, milk dribbling out of her full mouth.

"In case you were wondering, that's Delia speak for *yes*." Zoe pinches her arm. "You pig."

Looking embarrassed, Delia swallows and uses her t-shirt to wipe her chin off. "Sorry, I mean, yes, he did. He made sure to tell me he wasn't doing it for you or himself, but for me."

"Did he mean it?"

"You know, back when he first apologized, it was the most awkward thing of my life. It was completely half-assed and he wouldn't even make eye contact with me." She sets her bowl aside and pulls her knees up to her chest. "But when he was sitting in our kitchen, he faced me straight on, and it wasn't like the first time at all. It wasn't rehearsed or forced. It was genuine."

I consider her words, rolling them around in my head.

She rests her hand on my leg. "It's okay to forgive him. I do."

"You do?"

"Yes. I can't hold on to all that anger forever. It's not me. He made a mistake. He apologized. He's my boyfriend's brother. I can't freeze him out forever."

"You totally could," Zoe interjects.

"But that's not who I am, Zoe, and you know that. Hell, you should know that better than anyone. I mean, I did totally give you permission to date my ex-boyfriend."

"And I love you for that, I really do. Caleb is…" She fans herself. "Gah, I can't."

"He is pretty cute," Monty chimes in.

"I know! And that baseball cap." Zoe practically swoons. "Okay, okay, I'm done."

"Are you? Need a few minutes alone in Denny's bathroom?"

"You are *not* doing that in my apartment!"

Zoe shrugs. "I'll just wait until everyone's asleep."

"You're all a bunch of horndogs," I grumble, sinking lower onto the couch.

"You're just jealous because we all have hot wieners at home waiting for us and you don't."

"Oh my god, way to rub it in my face, Montana!"

"Can I just say Robbie was right? You saying wiener is the funniest fucking thing I've heard in my entire life." Zoe taps around on her phone and shoves it into Monty's face. "Say it again. I want to record this shit."

Monty's face flames red. "N-No!" She shoves the phone away. "You are like the female Robbie. It's so creepy."

"Creepy or cute?" Zoe argues. "Say wiener!"

"No, you creep! Go away!"

Monty flies off the couch, darting down the hall with Zoe hot on her heels, teasing her the entire way.

Delia laughs and pulls herself up on the couch, making herself comfortable next to me.

"You know, I used to believe in love and fate and the universe. I thought they were pushing me toward Shep, but now...now I'm not so sure. I don't know how any of that is possible knowing what he did."

"Wanna know my theory?" she says after a few moments of silence.

"Shoot."

"I think maybe the universe is pushing you toward Shep, and I think that's because you make him a better person."

"But do I, Delia? I mean, look what he did to you because of me. That doesn't scream *good person* to me."

"I'm not going to be mad at you for loving Shep. It's okay. You shouldn't be basing your decision to be with him off me anyway. Even if he never apologized, I still wouldn't judge you if you were with him."

"Love?" I choke out. "Who said anything about love?"

She bumps her shoulder against mine. "You can't fool me. I know what it's like to love a Hastings/Clark family member. It's exhausting and thrilling and that all-consuming kind of love. Even when you don't want to love them, you do."

I nod.

"It's okay to be mad at him and still love him, to want to wring his neck and kiss him all at once. No one is perfect. Sure, what Shep did was exceptionally wrong, but that doesn't make him a bad person entirely. He actually spent a good portion of Sunday telling us about the children's diabetes charity he's part of."

My lips involuntarily curl into a smile as I think of how excited Shep gets when he hears how much money has been raised for the charity at each gala we attend.

"He's so proud of it. The only time I've ever seen him so passionate about something and interested is when he's talking about baseball."

"And you," she adds. "He's like that when he's talking about you too."

"Moooooonty!" Zoe bangs against the bedroom door. "Just say wiener!"

"Go away!"

Delia and I fall into a fit of laughter.

I don't know what the future holds for me and Shep, but I do know I feel better knowing he stepped up and did the right thing by Delia and Zach. It doesn't erase all the worries I have about our future, but it's a start.

And a start is better than nothing.

"So what's going to happen with your article? Did you finish it?"

"Almost, but now I'm not sure I'll be able to submit it. I didn't quite finish out the agreement I had with Shep, so I don't know how ethical it would be to run something."

"I don't think Shep will, like, go after you or anything," Delia says, trying to reassure me.

"Did you think he would send a naked photo of you out to the entire baseball team?"

She opens her mouth then slams it closed again, shaking her head. "Touché."

"He wasn't always a total jerk, you know."

"I don't think he was ever a jerk. I just don't believe he thinks things through very well and acts on feelings rather than rationale. He just needs to…grow up a bit."

"How can you be so chill about all this?" I ask her. "So forgiving?"

"I learned a long time ago that I could harbor bad emotions for people and let them eat away at me, or I could face those emotions head-on and be happy." She smiles. "I choose happy."

"Choose happy, huh? Even if you're scared?"

"Oh god, *especially* if you're scared. That's usually the best kind of happy."

"I like you, Delia. I think I might keep you around for a while."

"I got that on video for Allie! Don't you *dare* try to replace me, Delia!"

Delia whips a pillow Zoe's way, smacking her phone out of her hand. "Monty's right, you *are* a creep."

"Ha! Take that, you wiener!"

"NO!" Zoe whines, scrambling for her phone and rushing back down the hall. "Say it again! I wasn't recording!"

"Do they make you want to nap too?" Delia says.

"All the time."

"Have you read the paper today?"

"Um, Allie, I *work* at the paper."

"Yes, I know, but you work in the sports department. Have you read the *rest* of the paper?"

"No. Why?"

She sighs. "Look in the personals."

"Allie, if this is another attempt to get me interested in someone else to get over Shep, it's not going to work."

"It's not," she promises. "Just go look. I'll stay on the line."

"Ugh," I groan. "Let me go grab a copy."

"I can't believe you don't read your own paper."

"Hush, Allie."

She doesn't hush. She keeps yapping away in my ear as I pull myself out of my chair and find a paper stuffed into my box in the mail room.

"—and then he asked me to lick him...*there*!"

"Oh my god, are you talking rim jobs right now?" I lean against one of the tables, balancing the phone between my ear and shoulder so I can use two hands to open the paper.

"Have you not been listening to me? My husband is a *freak*! It's like he saved all this weird shit for marriage and I cannot handle it."

"Can you not tell me about how you licked your husband's butthole?"

Susan, one of our interns, glances over at me with wide eyes.

"Hi, Susan, sorry. My friend is insane. I'm not the butthole licker, that's her."

I laugh at the alarmed look on her face and Allie yelling my name in my ear.

"I cannot believe you right now! I am so embarrassed."

"No you're not."

"Fine. I'm not. Did you grab a paper?"

"I got it."

"Good, now flip to the personals."

I search until I find the section she's talking about and scan the page, but nothing sticks out to me.

"I don't see anything."

"Look again. Closely."

"I don't—"

Holy shit.

Right there in the center of the page, there's a huge box that's clearly written by Shep.

Captain America Apologizes: Part One

Bucky,

I'm sorry for bailing on dibs.

I'm sorry for blaming everyone else's failures for my own.

I'm sorry I didn't give us a chance.

I'm sorry I treated you like you were nothing to me, especially when you were everything.

Most of all, I'm sorry for not believing in us like I should have.

Text me baby, one more time.

910-555-1027

"What the hell?" I mutter out loud.

"That's for you, right? I'm not wrong, am I?"

"No, that's definitely for me."

"I don't get why he's calling you Bucky or himself Captain America, but everything else made sense that it would be Shep. Plus, that is *definitely* his phone number. Is he an idiot or something? Does he not know how many creeps he's going to get blowing up his phone?"

"He's stupid, that's for sure." I smile. Bucky and Cap has *always* been our thing. Just us. Not even Allie and AJ know. "Why were you reading the personals?"

"Because I'm curious, duh. I always like to see those missed connection write-ups. Anyway, I hope he gets a gross dick pic, like one covered in warts or something real gnarly like that."

I laugh. "That is disgusting, but it would also be well deserved."

"So…are you going to text him?"

309

"I'm…I'm not sure, Allie. I don't know if I'm ready."

"I think you should make him sweat." She cackles. "It would be hysterical."

"You're kind of evil today."

"Am I? Oops." Only she doesn't sound sorry at all. "I shouldn't be like that to him, though. I mean, he *did* just pay for our honeymoon and all."

The phone nearly slips out of my hand.

"W-What?"

"I didn't tell you? Shep is the only reason we were able to *have* a honeymoon. He paid for the entire thing and surprised us with plane tickets the week before the wedding. All we had to do was get the days off work. Luckily, our bosses were insanely understanding."

I had *no* idea Shep did that for them.

"He didn't mention it at all in the weeks leading up to the big day?"

"Not a peep. I'm kind of…"

"Shocked? Yeah, I was too. I mean, Shep has always been good to me and AJ, but I never expected this. He went all out, too. The only thing we paid for was souvenirs. He thought of everything, even in-flight drinks."

Allie clears her throat, and I know I'm about to get an earful.

"Listen, I *do* think you should make him sweat it out. I think you should make him grovel, but…I also think you should give him a second chance. What he did to Delia was wrong and horrible and I want to kick him square in the nuts for it, but I've also known Shep for a lot of years now and I have never seen him be anything but kind. A little egotistical and a bit of a horndog, yes, but never mean for the sake of being mean. He's a good guy. He's just a dumbass sometimes."

I sigh. "I know that. I really do. I just…I want to be sure, you know?"

"You can't be unless you give him a chance, unless you take that leap."

"I know," I say again.

"I gotta run. Lunch break is over, but call me later, yeah? Let's grab dinner some night this week. I'm still pissed I missed out on your girls' night where you confessed your love for Delia and tried to replace me."

"I would never."

"Uh huh. Say that to the video evidence I have. Love you, Denny."

"Love you too, Mrs. Sutton."

We end the call and I pick the paper back up, reading Shep's apology again.

Then again. And again.

By the fourth time, I feel it. That block of ice that formed around my heart two weeks ago at the wedding…it begins to thaw.

For the first time in what feels like too long, I have hope.

Thirty-Four

CAP

Captain America Apologizes: Part Two

Bucky,

I'm sorry for that one time at the paper when I told everyone you
wrote like a kindergartener. Clearly you were first-grade level.
Or those times when I bragged loudly about my weekend escapades.
And for stealing that one article on repainting the parking lot from
you. It was a stupid article, but you deserved it a lot more than I did.
But I'm *not* sorry for joining the paper because it meant I got to be
closer to you. I'm not sorry for staring at you across the room, for
making you stay late because I was pushing my deadline until the
absolute max. Those stolen moments, the ones where it was just us (I
mean, that one weirdo kid with the glasses was there too, but he was
practically invisible) made it possible for me to breathe through all
the chaos in my life.

Even though you hated me through it all, I need to thank you for
that.

So. Yeah. Thank you.

Text me.
910-555-1027

Captain America Apologizes: Part Three

Bucky,

I'm sorry for all those times you had to see me walking across
campus holding the hand of another girl.

Mostly, though, I'm sorry that girl wasn't you.

Text me.
910-555-1027

Captain America Apologizes: Part Four

Bucky,

There's a huge part of me that doesn't want to apologize for
punching that guy over the way he was talking about you, but you
were right—I used that as an excuse for really bad behavior. I'm a
grown adult. I know better than to swing at someone like that.

That's not who I want to be.

I want to be better than that.

I want to be *worthy* of you.

(Btw, I'm not sorry for wanting that either.)

Text me, one more time.

910-555-1027

Captain America Apologizes: Part Five

Bucky,

I'm sorry for not saying sorry before I did.

I'm sorry for not being the man you thought I was.

I swear, he's still in here.

If you give me the chance, I can prove it to you.

Text me.

910-555-1027

Captain America Apologizes: Part Six

Bucky,

They won't let me buy any more ad space. (You really need to talk to them about this.) So I only have one more shot at this.

I've apologized for many things over the last few days, but there's one thing I can't and never will be sorry for.

Loving you.

I love you, Buck. More than you can ever imagine. I know I've sucked at showing it over and over again, but that doesn't change how I feel.

I love you. I never stopped loving you. I always will.

End of the line, Bucky. End of the line.

Text me, Bucky. Please. Just one more time.

910-555-1027

P.S. Steve misses you.

Thirty-Five

Denver: Okay. You have my attention.

Shepard: Thank fuck.

Shepard: It was Steve, wasn't it?

Denver: Duh.

Shepard: Do you know how many dick pics
I got? So. Many. I never want to look
at another penis again.

Denver: Do you do that a lot? Look at
penises?

Shepard: Well hell, I walked right into that one, didn't I?

Shepard: I meant, like, my own. I don't even want to look at my own penis.

Denver: Your poor, poor three inches.

Shepard: I miss you.

Denver: I know you do.

Shepard: This is when you say, "I miss you too, Shep."

Denver: Oh, it is?

Denver: Fine. I miss you too, Shep. A lot.

Shepard: Are you still pissed at me?

Denver: Yes.

Denver: But I don't think that's going to go away soon. I think I'm going to be mad for some time, and that's okay. It doesn't mean I can push all the other feelings I have toward you away too.

Shepard: I meant every word I said in the paper.

Denver: I believe you.

Denver: How did you know I'd even see it?

Shepard: Um, because you WORK at the paper. Duh.

Denver: You do know I don't read the entire thing, right?

Shepard: You don't?

Denver: No. Blew Allie's mind too.

Shepard: Is she how you found out about it then?

Denver: Yes. She reads it for the missed connections crap. She has me addicted to them now too.

Shepard: I could kiss Allie right now.

Denver: Can you please stop trying to make out with my best friend?

Shepard: I would if I had someone else to make out with…*wink*

Denver: The winking was redundant. I totally got that you were talking about yourself.

Shepard: Oh.

Shepard: DOWNLOAD ATTACHMENT

Denver: I didn't think it was possible, but he got cuter.

Shepard: Thank you. I get that a lot.

Denver: I obviously meant Steve.

Denver: But I appreciate you trying to include yourself in that picture.

Shepard: Just wanted you to see what you're missing.

Denver: Yes, an adorable pug. I can see that.

Shepard: I even miss your sass. Is that wrong?

Shepard: Wait, don't answer that. I don't care.

Shepard: Seriously, though, Den—when can I see you? The last two galas weren't any fun without you. Penny is a pitiful date. She doesn't tell a single person about my small dick. It's so not embarrassing and it's weird.

Denver: I don't know, Shep…

Shepard: Can I take you on a date?

Shepard: Not to the movies. Clearly we can't be trusted there. Or in any dark spaces, for that matter.

Denver: I…yeah. I think I'd like that.

Shepard: Okay. Be ready in twenty.

Denver: Twenty minutes?! You're crazy!

Shepard: Only about you.

Denver: It is nearly 11PM. I am NOT going on a date at 11PM.

Shepard: You are too.

Denver: SHEP!

Shepard: I'm not joking. I'm putting my shoes on right now.

Shepard: Be ready.

Denver: And if I'm not?

Shepard: You will be.

Thirty-Six

DENVER

I've never been so nervous to hear knocking on my door before, not even during college when Allie and I threw a crazy party and the cops were called.

That's nothing compared to Shep knocking on my door right now.

I pull it open and am met with the most unexpected sight.

"Steve!"

I grab the puppy from Shep's outstretched hands and snuggle him close. The pug licks happily at my face, and it's the cheeriest I've felt in weeks.

"Someone missed me," I say to Steve.

"Yes, someone did," Shep replies.

My eyes meet his for the first time in weeks, and it nearly knocks me backward.

There's stubble lining his chin, like he hasn't shaved in a couple days, and I have to say, it really works for him.

I don't notice that I've reached for him until my fingers collide with the rough stubble.

I pull away quickly, trying to compose myself.

"I, uh, I like that. It suits you."

"Yeah?" He runs a hand over the shadow. "Good. I was thinking of keeping it."

"You should."

He nods, smiling. "Then I will."

"God, this is awkward."

"It is, but I wouldn't have it any other way." He rakes his eyes over me, taking in my outfit, which is eerily similar to the one I was wearing that night in the grocery store, only this time I'm actually wearing a bra. "You, uh, ready for our date?"

"If you're about to hate on my outfit, I will strangle you."

"Ah, there's my asphyxiation-loving girl."

"Shepard..." I warn.

"What? I'm not saying a thing." He presses his lips together. "Come on, we're working on a tight schedule here."

"A tight schedule for our impromptu date at 11PM."

"Technically," he says, pulling his phone out of his pocket and glancing at the screen, "it's only 10:45."

"You are so annoying."

"You love it. Let's go."

Grumbling, I follow him out the door, not bothering to grab my purse because he is *so* paying for this entire date.

We make our way out of my building and I follow him down to his truck.

He pauses outside my door and turns to me. "I know it's kind of cliché, but it's all I could find this late at night."

"Okay..." I say, stretching the word out.

He pulls open the door and sitting on the seat is not one, not two…not even three, but *five* dozen red roses.

"What in the ever-loving fuck, Shep? That's a lot of money."

He shrugs. "I had to get you a dozen for every year I wasted."

"I… Hell, I have no idea what to say."

"Then don't say a thing." He slides Steve from my arms and opens the back door, where he then deposits the pup onto the bed that's sitting back there. "You know what they mean, right?"

I look up at him. "Yes, Shep, I do."

He nods once. "Good. Now get in. Time crunch."

I gather up the flowers and pull them to my nose, loving the way they smell, then haul myself into the cab. It's difficult maneuvering around with all the flowers in the way, but it's worth it.

Red roses mean true love.

Cliché, but still absolutely breathtaking.

The car ride is silent, and for the first time in a really long time with Shep, it's a comfortable silence, the kind of comfortable I've always craved when it came to him.

It's sad that it's taken us so long to get to this point.

"What are we doing here? They close in like ten minutes," I say as we pull into the lot at Smart Shoppe.

"Told you we were on a time crunch." He turns the truck into a parking spot but doesn't shut the ignition off. "Stay here. Last time we came here, I had to carry your ass all the way across the parking lot, and I am not doing that again."

"So rude, but I'll wait here—only because it's annoying to have to get out of the car with all these flowers, *and* someone needs to watch Steve."

"See? I'm so smart. Be right back."

He takes off jogging into the store, and I occupy myself with trying to arrange the flowers better so I'm not so cramped.

He returns with two full bags of stuff, and the store lights dim as he approaches the car.

"Boom. Made it." Shep tosses his bags into the back then climbs back behind the wheel.

"What'd you get?"

"Ice cream."

"What kind of ice cream?"

"Our favorite."

Our.

Even though he's just talking about ice cream, the word makes my heart skip a beat.

I like the way it sounds. I like the way Shep and I sound together.

I wasn't lying when I told him I was still mad at him, but Delia was right: I can be mad at him and want to be with him all in the same breath, and that's okay.

Shep pulls out of the parking lot and takes a left then another left two stops up.

I laugh when he pulls into a fast food joint, because I know just what he's up to.

He steers the truck to the drive-thru and rolls his window down.

Pointing at me, he says, "Don't you dare try to order any of that fancy stuff. Dollar menu only for you."

"I want two orders of spicy chicken nuggets, a large fry, *and* a vanilla milkshake."

"I already got us ice cream."

"Oh, the milkshake is for you. It's cute that you think I'm sharing that ice cream."

Smirking, he shakes his head and places my order for me, adding on a double cheeseburger and large fry for himself.

When we get through the line, Shep parks in the lot and motions for me to get out.

I grab Steve and his bed from the back then make my way to the bed of the truck, where Shep is already laying out a blanket for us to sit on.

We climb on up, our feet dangling comfortably off the back just like after the first gala we attended, and we dig into our food.

There's no conversation as we eat, because we don't need it. We're content.

After we finish nearly all the greasy goodness, Shep busts out the pints of ice cream, lining up all our favorite flavors.

"They only had one spoon," he says, holding it out to me.

I narrow my eyes at him. "Uh huh. How convenient."

"Guess we're just gonna have to...share."

"If I didn't have your cooties already, I'd complain." I snatch the lone utensil from his hand and scoop out a bite of mint chocolate chip. "But I guess since you bought me all this deliciousness, I'm gonna let it slide."

"*You?* Don't you mean *us?*"

There it is again, that skip.

"I like that thought...us," I admit quietly before shoving the spoon in my mouth to stop myself from saying anything else.

"I do too." Shep sighs heavily. "I meant everything I said in those ads, Den."

"You already said that."

"I know, but I really need you to know I meant everything. You have no idea how sorry I am. You were right—I do hold on to the past. I don't think, I just react, and I make excuses for that. I shouldn't do that. It's not fair."

"It's really not," I tell him. "Especially when you hurt so many people in the process."

"I don't want to be that person anymore."

"Then don't be."

"Is it really that easy?"

"Yes," I say emphatically. "You know, Delia told me she thinks I make you a better person."

"You do."

"I don't agree," I argue. "I think you're always a good person. You're just afraid to let people see that side of you, because you're scared they'll like you…and then leave you. So, you push them away before they *can* like you, because you're scared of heartbreak."

"Aren't we all?" he questions.

"Sure, but some of us are ballsy enough to face it anyway."

He chuckles. "Always gotta bring my balls into it, huh?"

"Well, if you'd actually use 'em once in a while…"

He shakes his head, trying hard not to laugh, because he knows I'm right.

He hops down from the truck bed and moves toward me, pushing himself between my legs. Cupping my face, he draws all my attention to him.

"Look, Den," he says, his soft hazel eyes holding my own. There's such sincerity in them that I can't imagine ever looking away. "I'm sorry. I should have told you about what I did to Delia. That wasn't cool of me to hide it. I should have been straightforward with you and honest about the mistakes of my past."

"Anything else hiding in that closet of yours?"

"No. That was it. Clean slate from here on out."

"Here on out, huh? You say that like we have a future."

For the first time ever, Shep looks sheepish, and a blush creeps up his cheeks.

I lied before.

This is my favorite version of Shep—humble, *vulnerable*.

"I'd like us to, Den." He whispers the words, so quietly I can barely him, but I do.

326

My heart skips another beat, or that final thin layer of protection around it shatters—I can't tell which.

All I know is I'm ready.

To say yes. For a future. For us.

"I'd like us to, too."

His face lights up. "Yeah?"

"Yes."

He closes his eyes, resting his forehead on mine and letting out a relieved sigh. "I'm going to do so much better this time. I'm going to be worthy of you."

"You already are worthy of me, Shep." I put my hands on his face, holding him to me. "You already are."

"I'm not, Den." He shakes his head. "You know I'm not, but I'm going to change that. I love you."

My lips curl into a smile at his words.

"Say that again."

"I love you."

"Are you sure?"

His lips capture mine in the softest kiss he's ever given me.

I feel hopeful. I feel good. I feel like we're going to make it this time.

He pulls away and I look up at him. He's smiling down at me with a mischievous glint in his eyes, and I know whatever he's about to say, it's going to make me love him even more.

"Yes, Bucky, about 9% sure."

Laughing, I say, "I'll take those odds with you."

"You know you're stuck with me now, right?"

"I know, but I'm only in it for the pugs."

"Until the end of the line?"

"The very end."

Let's Get Textual

A wrong number is supposed to be just that—a wrong number.

Delete. *Done.*

Do not continue to text. Do not flirt.

A wrong number shouldn't be the first person on your mind in the morning, or the last at night…and you're *definitely* not supposed to talk them into buying a baby goat.

Because that would be weird.

When Zach Hastings and I get into a wrong-number mix-up, we don't follow the rules. We keep texting and flirting, because he's wicked funny and perfectly nerdy and a wonderful distraction.

I'm not looking for love, and Zach definitely had the wrong number.

But maybe…

Maybe he's the right guy.

AVAILABLE NOW

I Wanna Text You Up

When I put up a *ROOMMATE WANTED* poster, he was the last person on earth I thought would respond.

He was also the last person on earth I'd agree to let live with me…on purpose.

But, here we are—roommates. I'm certain we can coexist without it being awkward, and I'm determined to make it work. There will be no sexual tension building with each accidental touch, no flutters when he wears that stupid backward baseball cap, and *definitely* no flirting when we text back and forth.

Caleb Mills can't be the guy for me. He's my best friend's ex-boyfriend.

And that would be wrong…*right?*

AVAILABLE NOW

Can't Text This

TEAGAN HUNTER

"Hi Monty. Wanna see my python?"

That's how I ended up in the bathroom of some dive bar with a stranger.

Me, Monty Andrews, the quintessential virgin girl next door.

I was *so* out of my element, but there was no denying our explosive attraction, even via text.

Commence Operation Bang Each Other Out of Our Systems, because that was all it was--unfinished business.

I had no intention of falling back into the sheets with the tattooed, muscly, dirty-in-the-best-kind-of-way single dad over and over again...but I did.

Everything was going great--until we discovered I was his son's teacher.

AVAILABLE NOW

ACKNOWLEDGEMENTS

For those who don't know, I never set out for *Let's Get Textual* to turn into anything other than a standalone romantic comedy for my newsletter. But once I started writing Zach and Delia, I couldn't stop...and I *had* to share them with just more than my newsletter readers. I was scared, nervous as hell because although I enjoyed writing books with a little more heart to them, I always wanted to write romcoms because I love to laugh. I wanted to be that author who made readers laugh. But I never felt like I could. I didn't think you would "get" my sense of humor. That I wouldn't be funny or good enough for you.

But you...you proved me wrong.

Not only did you devour and recommend and make *Let's Get Textual* into something I *never* thought It would be, you wanted more. More from these characters and their friends. You embraced them. Every single one—flaws and all. *You* did this. *You* made this series what it is. And *you* let me become the author I always wanted to be.

I can never, ever repay you for that.

So, thank you. Thank for taking a chance on Zach and Delia and Marshy. For allowing me to bring you into this new and kind of crazy world with this funky cast of characters.

Thank you for allowing me to make my dream a reality.

With love and unwavering gratitude,
Teagan

Other Titles by Teagan Hunter:
We Are the Stars
If You Say So

Let's Get Textual
I Wanna Text You Up
Can't Text This

Here's to Tomorrow
Here's to Yesterday
Here's to Forever: A Novella
Here's to Now

Want to be part of a fun reader group, gain access to exclusive content and giveaways, and get to know me a little more?
Join Teagan's Tidbits on Facebook!

Want to stay on top of my new releases?
Sign up for New Release Alerts!

TEAGAN HUNTER is a freelance cover designer by day. By every other free moment, a writer. She's a Missouri raised gal, but currently resides in North Carolina with her US Marine husband where she spends her days begging him for a cat. She survives off coffee, pizza, and sarcasm. When she's not writing, you can find her binge-watching various TV shows, especially *Supernatural* and *One Tree Hill.* She likes cold weather, buys more paperbacks than she'll ever read, and never says no to brownies.

You can find Teagan on Facebook:
https://www.facebook.com/teaganhunterwrites

Instagram:
https://www.instagram.com/teaganhunterwrites

Twitter:
https://twitter.com/THunterWrites

Her website:
http://teaganhunterwrites.com

Or contact her via email:
teaganhunterwrites@gmail.com